TO DIE IN JUNE

Alan Parks

TO DIE IN JUNE

Europa
editions

Europa Editions
27 Union Square West, Suite 302
New York NY 10003
www.europaeditions.com
info@europaeditions.com

Library of Congress Cataloging in Publication Data is available
ISBN 979-8-88966-036-1

Parks, Alan
To Die in June

Cover design by Ginevra Rapisardi

Cover photo: collage of unsplash images

Prepress by Grafica Punto Print – Rome

Printed in Canada

CONTENTS

WEDNESDAY 28TH MAY 1975 - 17

WEDNESDAY 11TH JUNE 1975
TWO WEEKS LATER - 27

THURSDAY 12TH JUNE 1975 - 39

FRIDAY 13TH JUNE 1975 - 81

SATURDAY 14TH JUNE 1975 - 105

SUNDAY 15TH JUNE 1975 - 123

MONDAY 16TH JUNE 1975 - 145

TUESDAY 17TH JUNE 1975 - 177

WEDNESDAY 18TH JUNE 1975 - 201

THURSDAY 19TH JUNE 1975 - 237

FRIDAY 20TH JUNE 1975 - 261

SATURDAY 21ST JUNE 1975 - 283

WEDNESDAY 25TH JUNE 1975 - 297

SATURDAY 28TH JUNE 1975 - 309

A WEEK LATER - 321

ACKNOWLEDGEMENTS - 327

ABOUT THE AUTHOR - 329

TO DIE IN JUNE

In memory of Agnes Leonard

"And where do we go from here?
Which is a way that's clear?"
—DAVID ESSEX, "Rock On"

"Wisdom comes through suffering."
—AESCHYLUS

He rolled over, yawned, got his cigarettes and matches off the night table and lit up. Lay back on the pillow and blew the smoke up into the air, traced the familiar cracks on the ceiling with his finger. Someone was up already; he could hear them in the kitchen, whistle of a boiled kettle quickly cut short. Between the other residents and the rumble of the underground trains in the tunnel below the building it was hard to sleep late. He'd been there for a couple of months. A bedsit in Govan. Five other lonely souls in five other bedrooms. A shared kitchen and toilet. Home. For now, anyway.

He looked at his watch, was getting on for half six. Time to get up. Today was the big day, after all. His freshly pressed uniform was hanging from the handle of the wardrobe. Could see himself in the mirror on the front of it. Twenty-two years old. Handsome as they come. Muscles in his shoulders moved as he sat up; the training was working.

He was supposed to be there at eight. Couldn't be late on his first day, needed to make a good impression. Swung his legs over the side of the bed. The plan was going fine so far. Phase two, as he liked to call it, began today. He stubbed the cigarette out in the McEwan's Pale Ale ashtray. Looked down at his hands, imagined what they would be doing soon if it all worked out. Something wicked this way comes.

WEDNESDAY

28TH MAY 1975

McCoy was leaving the station for the night. He was trying to carry two boxes of stuff he thought he might need at the new place and an Agnew's carrier bag with four cans and a bottle of whisky in it. He'd successfully made it to the front office without dropping anything when the desk sergeant put the phone down and held out a chit.

"My hands are full, Ross. What does it say?"

"A request to attend a crime scene from Detective Watson. It's on your way home," he said. "Sort of."

McCoy sighed, put the boxes down on the desk and read the chit. Was nowhere near his way home. "I live in Partick, Ross, not the bloody Calton."

Ross shrugged, went back to his paper.

"Is there no one else here?"

No response.

McCoy cursed, picked up the boxes and headed for his car.

It was one of those perfect summer nights that don't happen very often in Glasgow. Still some warmth in the air, sky just starting to go pink. Streets full of sunburnt kids and couples hand in hand making their way home. Even the drinkers outside the back of Buchanan Street Bus Station looked happy. Down to vests, faces red from lying in the park all day, passing a bottle back and forth.

"You just got me. I was almost clocked off," said McCoy, stepping out of the car. "Five more minutes and I would have been gone."

"Glad I caught you, then," said Wattie. "Thought you might be interested in this one."

"Just wanted the company, more like," said McCoy. "You no got enough people here already?"

He nodded over at the crowd on the other side of the road. Four or five uniforms unspooling a rope to seal off the site, two ambulancemen unfolding a stretcher, the police photographer under a black cloak winding a new film through his camera. All of them gathered around something lying on the ground. Something McCoy knew was going to be a body.

They were on a muddy square of dumped rubbish, crumbling masonry and broken bottles. The space between two buildings waiting to be demolished. Even though it was only five minutes from the bustle of Argyle Street, you would never know it; the area around the waste ground was deserted, a backwater in the heart of the city. A place for people who didn't want to be seen.

"I'm trying to get it all done before it gets dark," said Wattie. "Save us bringing in the lights and all that stuff."

McCoy looked up at the sky. Sun was already low, buildings casting long shadows. "Better hurry up, then. Now you've dragged me here, are you going to tell me what's going on?"

"Even better," said Wattie. "I'll show you."

They started walking towards the other side of the waste ground.

Wattie pointed up ahead. "Two boys taking a shortcut across here spotted what they thought was a pile of clothes. When they got closer, it turned out it was a man's body. They ran to that phone box over there and called it in."

"That's amazing," said McCoy.

"I know," said Wattie. "Wee buggers like that normally just scarper."

"Not that. That a phone box in Glasgow was actually working. That's a first. Make sure you put that in your report."

"Finished, Detective Inspector Smartarse?"

McCoy nodded. "So what's happened to him?"

"Looks like a natural death at the minute, no sign of anything else. By the look of him, he's been sleeping rough."

They got a bit closer, and Wattie told the uniforms to stand aside for a minute. McCoy steeled himself and walked over to the body, told himself there wasn't going to be any blood, that he was going to be okay.

The boys had been right: it did look more like a pile of clothes than anything else. But it wasn't. It was a small man bundled up in a filthy blue suit, white shirt missing most of its buttons, vest underneath, one black slip-on shoe lying on the ground, the other on his sockless foot. His head was arched back, eyes wide open to the sky, greenish bile drying around his mouth. He looked sixty-odd, face lined, scar across his forehead. Could have been ten years younger, was hard to tell. Living on the streets took its toll.

"You know him?" asked Wattie.

"You think I know every bloody down-and-out in Glasgow?"

"No. I just thought—"

"It's Jamie MacLeod, Govan Jamie," said McCoy. "Been on the streets as long as I can remember. Hangs about with my dad sometimes. Hard drinker, been arrested a few times for drunk and disorderly. Arrested him myself once when I was on the beat."

Stopped. There was a big smile on Wattie's face.

"What you smiling for?"

"No reason," said Wattie.

McCoy pointed at a patch of stamped-down ashes a couple of yards away. "Where's his pals? There would have been three or four of them, would have clubbed together for a bottle. Built a wee fire."

"Haven't seen anyone. Must have taken off when he died."

McCoy took out his cigarettes and lit up. Looked round the

site. "You know what? One day I'm going to get called to a place like this and it's going to be my dad lying there instead of him."

"That's a cheery thought," said Wattie. "You seen him lately?"

McCoy shook his head. "Saw him from the car a couple of months ago, Templeton Street. Had a bottle of wine in his hand, ranting and raving at somebody who wasn't there. Looked like he'd broken his nose."

"I wouldn't worry too much. Your dad's like a bloody cockroach; it'd take a nuclear war to get rid of that bugger. He'll outlive us both."

"Probably. Where's Phyllis?" asked McCoy. "What's she saying to it?"

"Not much. She's in Amsterdam visiting her sister. Back tomorrow." Wattie pointed to a young guy in a tweed suit with blond hair standing by the ambulance. "That's the locum. Colin Nichol."

He must have heard his name being spoken, walked over, hand out to shake. "Colin," he said. "I'm the temporary medical examiner."

"McCoy," said McCoy, shaking it. "Detective Inspector."

"And that," said Wattie, pointing over at the body, "is Govan Jamie."

"What?" said Nichol, turning to McCoy. "You know him? I can't believe it." He dug in his pocket and handed Wattie a fiver.

Suddenly dawned on McCoy. "Wattie? Are you telling me you got me out here just to win a bloody fiver?"

"No," said Wattie. "Would I do something like that? I just thought you'd want to see what was going on on our patch, that's all."

"Aye, right," said McCoy. "So, what's happened to him?"

"Provisionally?" said Nichol.

McCoy sighed. Every medical examiner's favourite word. "Just what you know so far; we won't hold you to it."

"Okay. He's elderly as you can see—I'm estimating early six-ties. Likely a heavy drinker, both his legs and feet are swollen. Yellowish tinge to his skin and the fact he's retaining fluid in his abdomen make it pretty certain. As to his death, I don't want to sound unprofessional, but it could be a number of things: liver failure, heart failure, a stroke—take your pick. Essentially, his time ran out. Drinking that heavily and living on the streets? At his age, that's just waiting for death to happen."

"But natural causes?" said McCoy.

"Certainly looks like it. I imagine you must have seen similar situations before?"

Too many times to count.

"Poor bastard," said Wattie. "Dying in a place like this. Any next of kin?"

McCoy shrugged. "I think he came over from Donegal years ago, fell out with his family. Used to work in the yards at Govan before the drink caught up with him. Liam might know. He knows most of these guys."

"Do we know where Liam is these days?" asked Wattie.

"If he's not drinking, he'll be around town, or he might be up at Blairgowrie, picking raspberries. If he's drinking, then who knows."

"I'll do the death certificate tonight," said Nichol. "Get it out the way."

"Cause of death?" said McCoy.

"Myocardial infarction," said Nichol. "Whatever caused it, he died because his heart stopped. It's what we usually put in cases like these."

He said goodnight and walked back towards the body.

"He any good?" said McCoy, watching him go.

"No idea," said Wattie. "Nice enough though. Going to Aberdeen for three months tomorrow."

"Lucky him," said McCoy. "All seems pretty straightforward here. You should be done in half an hour or so."

"Hope so," said Wattie.

"You all set for tomorrow?" said McCoy.

Wattie nodded. Recited: "If anyone asks why we're here, we've been temporarily relocated to the Possil station because of the restructuring due to the changeover from Glasgow City Police to Strathclyde Police."

"Good man. Stick to it."

"Possil, of all bloody places. Why there? It's the shithole's shithole."

"You'll love it. I used to do the beat there when I first started. Made me what I am today."

"Great, so now I'm going to turn into a moaning-faced bastard too. When was that anyway? Just after the war?"

"Very funny," said McCoy. Thought. "Must have been nineteen sixty-eight, round about then."

The streetlights flickered and came on, wasteland suddenly flooded with orangey light. If anything, it made the scene look even sadder. No forgiving sunset, just the harsh burn of sodium illuminating the dead man on the ground.

The ambulancemen were lifting the body onto a stretcher.

McCoy dropped his cigarette and stood on it. "A cardboard coffin and an unmarked grave. There but for the grace of God."

"Don't get all maudlin on me," said Wattie. "They know we're coming, do they? Possil?"

"Don't think so. Be a nice surprise for them."

"You ever going to tell me why we're really going?"

McCoy sighed. "You really want to know? I'm no supposed to tell anyone."

Wattie nodded.

"Give us that fiver and I'll tell you."

Wattie dug in his pocket and handed it over.

McCoy started to recite. "We're going because we've been temporarily relocated to the Possil station because of the restructuring due to the changeover from Glasgow City Police to Strathclyde Police."

"You really are a dick, McCoy. You know that?"

"Yep," said McCoy. "See you tomorrow. Possil, here we come."

WEDNESDAY

11TH JUNE 1975
TWO WEEKS LATER

Two

McCoy didn't notice the commotion at first. He was facing the other way, trying to reassure Margo that she wasn't too stoned to present the award, that all she had to do was take a couple of deep breaths and a few sips of water and she would be fine. Didn't seem the time to remind her that he'd said she shouldn't smoke the second joint. It wasn't until Billy nudged him that he looked round.

"I hate to tell you this," said Billy. "But I think those two are looking for you."

"What?" said McCoy.

Billy indicated the door. "One's pointing at you."

McCoy looked over the room full of tables and groaned. Billy was right. Liam Donaldson was waving at him from the doors to the function suite. Far as he could see, Liam had smartened himself up, was dressed in his Sunday best. Unfortunately, boots, old jeans and a ripped jumper were no dinner suit. To the attendees of the Scottish Variety Club Awards sitting round the tables, dressed to the nines, wine and champagne in front of them, he looked more like a tramp who should never have made it past the front door.

There was a boy who seemed to be with Liam. At least he was wearing a black suit, even if it was two sizes too big for him, as was the white shirt his skinny neck was poking out of. Whoever Liam and his wee pal were, they were definitely not invited guests of the Scottish Variety Club on their big night out.

Liam shouted over. "Harry!"

McCoy waved.

Liam managed to push aside the doormen trying to hold him back and started winding his way through the tables heading for McCoy, his suited pal trailing behind. Some of the guests looked on open-mouthed, others discreetly ignored the fuss and carried on eating their Chicken Balmoral.

"Friend of yours?" asked Margo, peering over the compact mirror she was using to apply a fresh layer of bright red lipstick.

"Yep," said McCoy. "Liam Donaldson."

And he was. Liam had helped him out a good few times. He knew the people who lived on the streets or the hostels; they trusted him, would talk to McCoy if Liam was there or had vouched for him. But this was the last place in the world he expected to see him. Not that you could miss him. Liam was a big guy, well over six foot and built like a farmer. The big scar on his ruddy face still visible through his greying stubble. Couldn't have been more out of place amongst the cocktail dresses and dinner suits if he'd tried.

Billy had found a bottle of red wine amongst the dead soldiers on the table, poured half of it into a beer mug and handed it to McCoy.

"Think you're going to need this," he said. "By the way, is he going to kick your head in? Because if he is, don't look at me. I'm too good-looking to be punched." He looked around for another glass, couldn't find one. Muttered "fuck it" under his breath, turned away from the tables and took a swig from the wine bottle.

Liam and pal squeezed past a table that included a surprised-looking Lulu and stood in front of them. One of the doormen caught up, grabbed at Liam's arm. Liam turned to him, looked like he was about to lamp him, when Margo cleared her throat.

"These are our guests," she said, addressing the doorman

with all the hauteur of her upper-class upbringing. "Please re-
frain from treating them as anything less."

The doorman looked like a ticked-off schoolboy, wandered
off muttering to himself.

"Mr. McCoy!" said Liam. "Did you no hear me shouting?
Wattie told me you were here."

"Did he?" McCoy making a mental note to pay Wattie back
somehow.

He looked at Liam, breathed a sigh of relief when he realised
he was sober. Eyes were clear, hands weren't shaking, no smell
of old beer and stale sweat.

"Aren't you going to ask your friends to sit down?" asked
Margo.

"Eh?" said McCoy, was the last thing he was planning to do.

Margo extended her hand to shake. "As Harry is being too
rude to introduce us, I'm Margo Lindsay. Pleased to meet you."

Liam wiped his hand on his jeans, shook hers. Looked
suitably starstruck. Well, it wasn't every day you met one of
Scotland's most famous actresses.

"I'm Liam and this is Gerry," he said. "Pleased to meet you."

"Sit down." She turned. "Billy, could you be a dear and
budge up?"

Billy, all pointy beard, patched denim suit and big platforms,
picked up his wine bottle, shuffled into the empty seat beside
him, and Liam sat down. Gerry found a spare chair on the other
side of the table, sat down, and started eating the remains of a
bread roll he'd found on a side plate.

"Billy, Liam. Liam, Billy," said McCoy.

Billy nodded hello. "Glad there's someone else no wearing
a dickie bow," he said, gesturing at his suit. "Want some wine,
pal?"

"What are you doing here, Liam?" said McCoy.

"I went to Stewart Street a few times, left messages for you.
Did you no get them?"

"I'm not there any more, Liam. I'm up at Possil now. Did they not tell you?"

"Aye, eventually."

McCoy wasn't surprised. Ross at Central was useless at the best of times.

Liam took the wine bottle off Billy, started to pour most of it into a beer glass. Just as McCoy was about to tell him to take it easy, the house lights went down, the music started up and a spotlight hit the podium on the stage.

"Oh, hell," said Margo. "You sure I'm not too stoned, Harry?"

"You're fine. Knock 'em dead," said McCoy, slowly realising he was having one of the strangest evenings of his life. All he could do was sit back and hope things didn't get any worse.

Michael Aspel, the presenter for the night, got up on stage, took the applause and spoke into the mic. "Ladies and gentlemen! Please welcome to the stage Scotland's Oscar-nominated actress, the one and only Margo Lindsay!"

The clapping started, a spotlight hit Margo, and she stood up and started to weave between the tables towards the stage. All eyes followed her, the long dress covered in thousands of tiny white sequins shimmering in the light.

"So it's true. You're really going out with her?" said Liam, watching Margo climb the steps, take Michael Aspel's hand and kiss his cheek. "How the fuck did that happen?"

"Met her on a case last year."

"Wasn't her brother that nutter with his own private army?"

McCoy nodded. "A few weeks ago there was the shipyard workers' thing in George Square. The demonstration. Managed to stop some wanker in a uniform trying to arrest her, so she took me out to dinner."

Billy turned away from the crowd and took another swig of the wine from the bottle. Grimaced. "Talk about punching above your weight," he said.

Margo approached the microphone. McCoy had lied—she did look a bit stoned—but he didn't think anyone else would notice.

"Thank you. It's my great pleasure to be asked to announce the winner of the Scottish Comedian of the Year Award." She smiled, opened the golden envelope. Looked out at the audience. "And the winner is Stanley Baxter!"

McCoy turned to Billy. "Were you not supposed to win that?"

Billy shrugged. "I've got my street cred to look after. Too soon to be one of the chicken-in-a-basket crowd."

As Margo embraced a delighted-looking Stanley Baxter on stage, McCoy saw his chance of escape.

"They'll be talking to the press for a while," he said, turning to Liam and Billy. "What do you say to us fine gentlemen retiring to the bar for a real drink?"

The hotel bar was empty, just a couple of refugees from the ceremony gathered around one of the tables and a small crowd of hairy folkies at the far end. Some in dinner suits, some not. McCoy got himself, Liam and Billy a double whisky and Gerry a Coke. Was only when they were walking towards a table at the back of the bar that McCoy noticed one of the wine bottles from the table poking out of Liam's pocket. He was just about to tell him to put it back when they heard a shout of "Billy!" They turned. Hamish Imlach, bow tie already gone and shirt half undone, was with the folkies standing along the bar, waving him over.

"I'll see you back at the table, eh?" said Billy, smiling. "The boss calls."

McCoy, Liam and Gerry, half-eaten roll still in hand, sat down at the table. McCoy undid his bow tie, finally allowing himself to breathe.

"Okay, Liam, what's the big emergency?" he said, taking a sip of his whisky. "This is supposed to be my night off."

Liam nodded over at Gerry. "Gerry there came to me a couple of days ago. I didn't believe him at first, but I think he's right. That's why we had to come here tonight before anything else happens."

"Right about what?" said McCoy, puzzled.

"Two dead bodies," said Liam. "And nobody gives a fuck."

THREE

The folkies and Billy were getting loud at the end of the bar, laughing, telling jokes, ignoring the tuts of some of the Rotary Club types who had sat down at a nearby table. McCoy had to lean forward to make sure he was heard.

"Liam, what are you on about?"

Liam nodded over at Gerry, who was digging in the pocket of his suit. He came out with some bits of butcher's paper that had been folded and folded. "Gerry's going to tell you. He gets a bit flustered if he has to talk for long, so he wanted to write it down for you."

Gerry held out the paper to McCoy. McCoy took it and looked at him properly for the first time. The boy's hair was like fur, was that thick. Cut short into his head. He had a lop-sided smile, bright blue eyes. Looked like some kind of wood-land creature. McCoy couldn't work out what age he was, could be anything from thirteen to seventeen, fuzz of bum fluff on his chin. His suit was something else. Looked like the person who'd died in it was still in there with him. It poked out at all angles; one leg seemed to be longer than the other. His black shoes were polished, but the sole was coming away from the leather on both of them. Didn't seem to have any socks on.

McCoy unfolded the paper. He could kill Liam. And Wattie.

But Liam wasn't a fool; he wouldn't have come to get him if he didn't think something was really wrong. The paper was covered in neat writing, all in blue ballpoint pen. He sighed, started to read.

When Titch died I was sad. He started screaming and crying and he stood up and staggered about and he almost fell into the fire and burned. We got him to the Royal but he didn't come back out again. He had died. I had been praying with both hands holding my St. Jude medal but it did not work. He is in Cadder cemetery now in a big hole with other men. His coffin was made of cardboard. I asked Joe what he had drunk but he didn't know all he knew was it was in an irn bru bottle but it wasn't irn bru because it was brown, not orange.

Liam and Gerry were staring at him, waiting. McCoy could see Margo across the room with Stanley Baxter and whatever his name was, Hudson from *Upstairs, Downstairs*. She waved over and he waved back, tried to look apologetic. Started to read again.

I'm not sure what happened after that. All I know was I was in a place but I did not know if it was a hospital or a prison but after a few weeks I was back out and that's when I heard Govan Jamie had died. He was Govan Jamie because the other Jamie was Highland Jamie. I asked what happened to him and Mary with the red coat told me he started screaming and crying and he said to her Christ Mary help me I can't see and then foam came out his mouth and he died. Because of these two things I am here. Liam said he knew a policeman who would try to help called Harry McCoy and I should talk to him. I am worried and I am scared the same thing will happen to another man or woman I know. Will you please find out what happened to Titch and Govan Jamie? Please. I will help you. I have written this down because sometimes when I talk the words come out wrong. I thank you again and may the Lord Baby Jesus and St. Jude watch over you.

McCoy sat back in the chair and folded the paper up again. Gerry was still staring at him with wide eyes, fingers on the St. Jude medal around his neck. He sighed, tried to think of a reason to send him on his way, but he couldn't.

"You had your dinner?" he asked.

Embarrassed, Gerry shook his head.

"Stay there. I'll get you some sandwiches."

McCoy walked over to the bar. Could hear the cheer for the big turn of the night coming on through the wall. The Three Degrees. Sounded like their first number was "Everyone's Gone to the Moon." Not really his kind of thing but they sounded pretty good. He ordered two rounds of cheese sandwiches and another Coke, added on a beer and a whisky for himself. Billy was standing on a chair now, telling some story with all the actions, looked like he was pretending to be Jesus on the cross. Unsurprisingly, the Rotary Club chaps had moved away. The drinks and sandwiches came, and he swallowed back the whisky, felt a tap on his back. He turned round and Margo was standing there.

"You still hungry?" she said, kissing his cheek.

"Not for me. For the boy over there. Don't think he's eaten anything for a while."

"You're a soft touch, Harry McCoy."

"'Fraid so."

She kissed him again. "And that's why I like you. Who is he anyway?"

"Some boy called Gerry, and I can't tell if he's barking mad or he's just discovered two murders."

THURSDAY
12TH JUNE 1975

Four

Even though Possil Station was new, less than a year old, it hadn't taken long for the interview rooms to become like all the others in the stations across the city. A bare room, a metal table, four chairs bolted to the floor and two striplights in a wire cage on the ceiling. Smell of stale cigarette smoke and stale sweat.

Judith West was sitting across from McCoy and Wattie, in her orange chair, an untouched mug of tea in a smiley mug in front of her. She'd put the Bible she'd been carrying down on the table beside the legend CUMBIE RULE YA BASS scrawled in black felt pen. She looked forty-odd, blonde hair pulled back, no make-up. Her hands were shaking, eyes darting between the two men. She'd arrived at the station five minutes ago, crying, shouting that her boy had gone.

"I went into his room to wake him at seven and he wasn't there."

McCoy looked at the clock on the wall. Twenty-five to eight, they'd lost time already.

"What's your address, Mrs. West?" asked Wattie.

"Hillend Street, number fifty." Her eyes fixed on him. "Maybe he woke up and went for a walk? Maybe that's it? Got lost?"

Wattie nodded. "It'll be something like that, you know what kids are like."

McCoy stood up, opened the door and stepped into the corridor. Sammy Rossi was standing there waiting for instructions.

Gravity of the case meant his usual snotty attitude had disappeared for once.

"Nine-year-old boy, Michael West. Been gone at least half an hour, possibly overnight. Get the beat boys and anyone else in the station up to Hillend Street, start looking. Sheds. Doocots. Coal bunkers."

Rossi nodded, hurried off down the corridor, and McCoy stepped back into the interview room and sat down.

"You think he's gone in somewhere like that and fallen asleep?" said Judith West.

McCoy nodded. No point in telling her that it wasn't what he meant at all. He meant they were really looking for a body that had been dumped quick, probably somewhere in the back courts or gardens around the house.

"Mrs. West, can you just talk me through exactly what's happened? Did you put him to bed last night? Check in on him?"

Judith West's eyes kept flitting about the room, trying to work out how she'd ended up in a place like this, in a situation like this. Her face suddenly crumpled again. "Sorry," she said. "I'm sorry."

"No need to be," said Wattie, handing her a folded white hanky from his suit pocket. "I've got a wee boy myself; I can only imagine what you're feeling. You're right to be worried, but we'll find him, I promise."

She took the hanky, balled it in her fist and nodded. "I put him to bed just after eight, checked in on him when I went down, that must have been around eleven, eleven thirty."

"And everything was fine?" asked Wattie.

Another nod, another twist of the hanky.

"Your son's full name?" said McCoy.

"Jeremiah Michael West," she said, turning to him. "Jeremiah is a family name; he gets called Michael."

"Date of birth?" said McCoy.

"Twenty-second of June nineteen sixty-six."

"We're going to need a photo of Michael," said McCoy. "Do you have one on you?"

Judith West shook her head.

"Okay," said McCoy. "We'll get one from the house."

"We don't have any."

"No photographs?" said Wattie. "You must have some, surely." "We don't approve of photography," she said. "We should be remembered by the lives we lead, the good we have done, rather than by a physical likeness."

"What?" said McCoy. "I'm sorry I don't—"

"I should have said earlier," said Judith. "My husband is the pastor of the Church of Christ's Suffering." She tried to smile. "We don't adhere to many of the ways of modern life."

"Maybe the school took one? A class photo?" suggested Wattie.

Another shake of the head. "Michael doesn't go to school. We teach him at home."

McCoy raised his eyebrows. "And the council's okay with that?"

"As my husband says, we answer to the Lord Jehovah and nobody else. We have a right to teach our children our beliefs and not have them taught someone else's. How can that be wrong?"

McCoy sat back in his chair. There was a look in her eyes when she talked about her religion: shining eyes and a conviction that the Lord was on her side and no one else's. It was the same look he'd seen in every Christian Brother and priest that had battered the shit out him when he was a wee boy.

"So this morning?" said McCoy.

"I got up at six thirty. I prayed for ten minutes or so in my room and got dressed."

"Your husband?"

"Asleep," said Judith West. "He sleeps badly, so I let him stay in bed. I went into the bathroom, got washed, and then I went to wake Michael up."

"You said this was at seven?" said McCoy.

"Yes. I pushed the door open. His bed was empty, so I went downstairs. The front door was ajar, but I didn't think anything of it. My husband's mother often comes round and makes breakfast. She's eighty-four now and is getting a bit absent-minded—I thought she'd just forgotten to close the door behind her. I went into the kitchen, but his grandmother wasn't there and neither was Michael. And that's when I started to panic."

Her face crumpled again, and she wiped her eyes with the hanky. Tried to pull herself together. She pushed the hanky up her cardigan sleeve. McCoy caught a quick glimpse of a long thick scar on the inside of her wrist before her sleeve covered it up again.

"Then I ran out the door and into the street and I couldn't see him, so I went round to the back courts and tried to find him, but he wasn't there either. I was shouting for him, and I was starting to be scared, so I ran down here to the station." She stopped. "Should we go and search for him? Should we do that?"

"We've got people doing that now," said McCoy. "Was the front door forced?"

"I don't think so," she said. "I don't know." Her head went down, hand reached for the Bible. "My beautiful boy. What are we going to do?"

Wattie reached his hand across the table and held hers. "Don't worry, we'll find Michael. We can—"

Judith's head suddenly snapped back, her hand pulled away from Wattie's and she let out a scream. Her eyes rolled back in her head, she started clawing at her face, nails going in deep, drawing blood. McCoy jumped up, ran around the table and grabbed her, trapped her arms behind her back, tried to stop her from doing any more damage to herself. She was screaming and crying now, neck taut, blood running down her face, eyes rolling. She surged forward; McCoy could hardly hold her.

"Is it not enough, Lord?" she shouted. "Have I not suffered enough?"

And then she went limp, fell back into McCoy. He stumbled, tried to hold her upright, managed to lower her back into the chair. Her head slumped forward, and she was quiet.

"Fuck sake," said Wattie. "I think she's fainted."

He ran out the room to get the medic, and McCoy just sat there, tried to calm down. Across the table Judith West stayed silent, chin resting on her chest, tears dripping off her chin. McCoy turned away, didn't want to look at the blood that was running down her cheeks, landing on her white blouse, forming bright red circles as it seeped into the cloth.

FIVE

Hillend Street wasn't far. Only took them a few minutes to get there from the station. Foot on the gas, siren blaring.

Wattie pulled over and McCoy got out of the car. Four or five panda cars were parked there, gardens already full of uniforms.

"Looks like Rossi got them out quick," he said.

"Be the first time that bastard's done anything quick," said Wattie, shutting the car door.

They walked up the path to number 50, a large, double-fronted sandstone house, and rang the bell.

"I still can't believe that," said Wattie. "Was like *The Exorcist*, like she was possessed or something."

"What did the doctor say?" said McCoy.

"Said she's going to dress the cuts on her face, then give her a sedative. She's hoping she won't need stitches. You'd have to be in some state to do that to yourself."

"If it was Wee Duggie, if it was him that was missing, you'd be in as bad a state as she was."

"True," said Wattie. "Probably even worse."

Another panda car pulled over, cops getting out fast.

"Did you get the word out to the other stations?" said McCoy. "This search'll take more than our lads."

Wattie nodded. "Eastern and Townhead." He peered down the road at the car's number plate. "That's a Townhead car here already, I think."

McCoy stepped up and rang the bell again.

"Maybe he's out looking," said Wattie. "I would be."

McCoy was just about to remind Wattie to get the family officer up to the house when the door opened. A tall middle-aged man was standing there, sandy hair swept back, shirt and tie. He had a bowl of cornflakes in one hand and a spoon in the other. Looked surprised to see them.

"Can I help you?" he said, smiling.

For a moment McCoy thought they must have got the wrong house. "Reverend West?"

"That's me. And you are?"

McCoy dug in his pocket and pulled out his warrant card. "Detective Inspector McCoy and Detective Watson. Your wife told us—"

West's face fell. "Is she okay? I thought she'd just gone for a walk."

"What?" said McCoy, feeling completely wrongfooted. "You do know your son is missing? Your wife is very distressed."

West looked at them both. "You'd better come in," he said.

He led them through a long dim hall to a living room at the back of the house. The décor looked like it hadn't changed much since Victorian times: heavy patterned wallpaper, country scenes in frames, a studded leather couch. Big window looking out to the back garden. There were cardboard boxes piled up against the far wall, Bible tracts spilling out of one that had burst open. A silhouette of Christ on the cross on the front and "We must suffer to heal' written beneath in black capital letters.

McCoy and Wattie were directed to the couch; West sat on an armchair opposite them.

"I don't have a son," he said.

"What?" said McCoy. "Your wife said Michael was—"

"We were never blessed with children. We tried, but it wasn't in God's plan. It's something my wife has found very difficult to endure, almost impossible."

McCoy looked down at his notebook, trying to work out what was going on. "She said you had a son called Michael, that he was nine, that he had disappeared from the house this morning."

West thought for a minute, seemed to be counting in his head. "Sadly, my wife had a miscarriage nine years ago. She often imagines what the boy would have been like if he had lived. She had one of these episodes before, four or five years ago; she went to the local primary and tried to enrol a child to start school. Said we had a son called Michael who was five. Can I ask where she is now?"

"She's still at the station," said McCoy. "She got herself in quite a state, and we had to call the doctor."

West nodded. Looked away into the garden. When he looked back his eyes were glassy, full of tears. He wiped them with the back of his hand.

"I hoped she was doing better. She hasn't mentioned Michael for a couple of years. Maybe she's been bottling it up inside. I hope she hasn't caused you any trouble."

McCoy suddenly thought. "Do you mind if we use your phone?"

"Of course, it's in the hall."

"Wattie, away and call the station. Call the search off."

Wattie nodded, got up and left.

"I'm sorry, Inspector," said West. "It seems your men have been sent out for nothing."

"Better to be able to call them off than to lose time if a child was really missing. Has your wife been seeing a doctor, someone like that?"

"If you mean a psychiatrist, then no. It's not a practice our church believes in. We believe in God and we believe in prayer. God will see us through this trouble as he does all trouble. Are you a believer, Mr. McCoy?"

McCoy shook his head.

"That's a pity. Maybe you will come into the fold one day."

"Maybe," said McCoy. "Stranger things have happened. Not many though."

West smiled politely. "When can I collect her? My wife."

"Anytime," said McCoy, standing up. "She's down at the Possil—"

He stopped talking. Through the window, he could see a uniform in the back garden poking about in the bushes. "Sorry. Word won't have reached them all yet."

The uniform turned round, saw McCoy, saluted and moved off towards the monkey puzzle tree at the back of the garden.

McCoy turned from the window and found West was holding out a couple of the tracts. "Your wife mentioned your mother, that she sometimes comes round in the mornings?"

"My mother lives in Canterbury," said West, "in an old folks' home. Hasn't left it for years."

McCoy realised West was still holding out the tracts.

"Have a look, if you have a moment. Christ is always ready to welcome his errant children home. Services are at six P.M. on a Sunday. The Church of Christ's Suffering."

McCoy took the tracts, said thank you, and put them in his pocket. Knew fine well the Church of Christ's Suffering was the last place on earth he'd be on Sunday morning.

Six

McCoy and Wattie had just walked back into the station, sat down at their desks, when Long, the station head, opened his office door. Saw McCoy. Pointed. "My office. Now!"

McCoy swore under his breath as he walked towards the glass-walled office in the corner. Everyone on the floor watching the bad boy going to get a row from the headmaster. Sammy Rossi looked delighted, was sitting at his desk with a big grin on his face. A grin McCoy would have dearly liked to punch down his throat.

Long shut the door behind him and sat down at his desk. No offer for McCoy to sit in the seat opposite. Same as usual, had hardly spoken to him since he had arrived at the station. Long's office looked barely occupied. No pictures of his family on the desk, no untidy piles of paper, just a pen and a notepad sitting there in front of him. Long was a thin man, tall. The nervy type: bitten fingernails, too much energy and nowhere for it to go. He'd his shirt-sleeves rolled up, tie loose. Looked up at him.

"What the fuck did you think you were playing at, McCoy?"

"The woman reported a missing child so—"

"So you scrambled half the Northside police force to descend on Hillend Street to look for a boy who didn't even bloody exist!"

"She seemed genuine," said McCoy, trying to keep calm. "I had no reason not to believe her."

Long looked incredulous. "She came in here with a Bible

the size of a telephone directory, then started clawing at her face and screaming blue murder. Did it not occur to you she was fucking mental?"

After that, keeping calm wasn't an option any more.

"What did you want me to do? Wait until the duty social worker turned up and asked her a few questions? Prepare a report on her mental health? And while she's doing that her son is fuck knows where, with fuck knows who, doing fuck knows what to him?"

Long's face started to go red.

"Don't you lecture me," he said. "Don't you fucking dare. You remember who you are and where you are. This isn't Central, and you're not Murray's golden boy here. You're one of mine and you sent everyone off on a wild fucking goose chase this morning."

It had been a long time since a superior officer had talked to McCoy like that, and he wasn't having it. He was a detective inspector, not a bloody beat cop who'd fucked up his first arrest.

"The real problem isn't to do with me, is it?" said McCoy. "It's about you having to explain to the higher-ups that it was a false alarm. It's not about what I should or shouldn't have done. This is about you worrying that you'll look like a prick to Pitt Street. Well, tell them it was me. I've no problem explaining what happened. I stand by what I did. The fact there was maybe a missing boy was the important thing, not my bloody reputation."

Long looked like he was about to get up from behind the desk and go for him. Voice went low. "Get out my office, McCoy, and if you ever speak to me like that again, a formal warning is going on your record. Do you understand me?"

McCoy could barely say it, managed to get it out. "Yes, sir."

When he came out, the office was quiet, heads down, not wanting to catch his eye. All apart from Sammy Rossi, that was. He was still sitting there, grin on his face.

McCoy walked over, put his palms down on the desk and leaned into his face. "You got something you want to say to me?"

Rossi shrugged and held out his open hands. "Not a thing. Why would you say that, McCoy?"

McCoy could feel his hands bunching into fists. "Don't push it, Rossi. Don't fucking push it."

Rossi went back to his typing and McCoy walked back to his desk feeling like he'd just fucked the whole Possil operation up. There was no way Long or Rossi were going to be his pals now. It was halfway to all-out war. Plan was that he and Wattie were going to be everyone's chum, get close to everyone. Even before this morning's shitshow, they were about as far away from that as you could get. Murray was convinced that a recent spate of post office robberies were happening on the Possil Station patch for a reason. Someone on the force was helping them out. He wanted McCoy to get in with the local force, find out who was involved. Wanted to leave Wattie out of it, was scared that if he knew why they were really there, he would give it away. McCoy had argued with him, told him Wattie wasn't that daft, but Murray was adamant. Only McCoy was to know.

McCoy sat down at his desk, lit up. Tried to calm down.

They'd been there for two weeks, and everyone was still treating them like the shite on the bottom of their shoe. Forgetting to tell them about meetings, forgetting to include them in briefings, forgetting to tell them everyone was heading down the pub after work. McCoy was constantly fighting back the urge to tell them all to get to fuck but he knew he couldn't. He was here for a reason, and Murray wasn't going to be happy if he'd messed it all up before he even got started.

He was so deep in thought he didn't notice Wattie until he was standing in front of his desk pulling his jacket on.

"We need to go," he said. "Body's been discovered."

SEVEN

McCoy leant back on the fence opposite the flats in Keppochhill Road, felt the sun on his face, watched the buses on Saracen Street go by and took a slug of Irn-Bru from the bottle. He counted down from ten, tried to stop the dizziness. Didn't work. He swilled the drink around his mouth, spat it out on the pavement. Smell of the blood seemed to have got right into his throat, couldn't get rid of it.

The door of the close across the street swung open, and Sammy Rossi and Wattie stepped out into the sunshine. Couldn't have looked more different if they'd tried. Wattie, tall, broad and fair while Sammy Rossi was slight, olive complexion and receding black hair. He'd a brown suit on, brown shirt and a brown spotty tie about as wide as a tea plate.

"Thought you were coming back in?" said Wattie, walking towards him. "Get lost, did you?"

"Something like that," said McCoy.

He had absolutely no intention of going back into the flat. Once was more than enough. Had no desire to see the old man lying on the kitchen floor again. His blood covered all the lino on the floor, had even splashed up onto the fridge and cupboards. Still, if someone batters your face to a pulp with a half-brick that's bound to happen. A brick that they had left buried in his face just to ram the point home.

"I heard you weren't keen on blood and guts," said Rossi. "Make you feel a bit queasy, did it?"

Then he grinned. Luckily McCoy's desire to punch him in the face had simmered down to a low resentment.

"You know him, do you?" said McCoy.

Rossi nodded. "Malky McCormack. Small-timer. Did a bit of this, a bit of that. Sold on stolen goods, petty theft. Normally in the Saracen or the bookies next door."

"So why's he all over his kitchen floor?" said McCoy.

"Not only all over the floor," said Wattie. "They had a right go at him before. Fingers on his left hand are bent right back."

"Nasty." McCoy was glad he hadn't noticed that particular detail. "So why didn't he just tell them what they wanted to know?"

"No idea," said Rossi. "But it's not like Malky. He was a tout as well. Hung about on the edge of the big boys, kept his ears open for what information he could sell on. Wasn't averse to dropping someone in it for a couple of quid."

"Maybe he just didn't know what they thought he did," said Wattie. "No one would go through all that and keep their mouth shut. Pain would be too bad. They wouldn't be able to."

"What's the neighbour saying?" said McCoy.

"You can ask her yourself," said Rossi. "Said she wanted to talk to whoever was in charge. She's coming out to speak to you."

"Shite. Thanks for that."

"You're welcome," said Rossi. Grinning.

"Is that him?"

They turned to see a middle-aged woman in a housecoat and slippers marching down the path towards them.

McCoy straightened up. "I'm Detective Inspector McCoy. And you are?"

"Meg Malone," said the woman. "Should you no be in there looking for clues or something?"

"My colleagues are covering that," said McCoy, nodding to Wattie and Rossi. "Do you want to tell me what happened?"

She looked exasperated. "What? Have they no told you?"

"If I could hear it directly from you?"

Meg Malone shook her head. Started. "It's my turn to do the close," she said. "So I figured I'd get it done before I go in for my work. So I gets the bucket and the mop and the bleach and I open my front door. First of all, I think it's muddy footprints outside my door. Wasnae happy, I can tell you. So I starts with the mop and scrub away at them and then the mop comes away all red and then I'm thinking, is this paint?"

"And this was when?"

She thought. "About quarter to nine. Normally leave at half past. I work in the bakers up by the Ashfield. Lunchtime's always busy, need to get everything ready beforehand."

"What happened then?" said McCoy.

"What happens is I follow the footsteps up the stairs, and they lead to Malky's house, and I chap on his door to give him a piece of my mind and it swings open and then I'm thinking the stupid bugger's come home drunk and forgot to close it, and then I see all the bloody footprints on the carpet."

She stopped for a minute, voice started to wobble.

"Then I see Malky lying there all battered and I get a real fright. Get back to mine and call the polis."

She got a hanky out her housecoat pocket, blew her nose and wiped the tears from her cheeks.

"Were you and Malky friendly?"

"No really," she said. "Used to find him asleep outside my door some Friday nights when he was too pissed to make it up the stairs. Never out the bloody pub, Malky."

"Can you think of any reason why anyone would want to hurt him?"

She thought for a minute. "No really. He wasn't worth bothering with, to be honest. Wasn't much of anything. Don't know why anyone would care about him enough either way to batter him. Certainly wouldn't be a lovers' tiff, I'll tell you that for nothing. He was honking most of the time, filthy—nae woman in her right mind would go near him. Still, he was one of God's creatures, didn't deserve what happened to him."

She looked around and spotted a uniform starting to rope off the garden. "I don't want to go back in there, not with all that blood up the stairs. Will somebody clean it up?"

McCoy pointed over at the young guy in uniform. "He can help clean things up. You don't have to see it again."

She nodded, started walking over to him.

McCoy watched her go. Didn't blame her; he didn't want to look at all that blood again either.

"So somebody hit him a few times, hard enough that he was bleeding at the close entrance then marched him upstairs to his flat?" said Wattie. "That what we're thinking?"

"Looks like it," said McCoy. "Rossi?"

Rossi nodded. "Old guy like him, pissed, wouldn't be hard. Poor bastard must have been terrified. Probably knew what was going to happen to him when he got upstairs."

McCoy imagined the walk up the stairs. The fear and the knowledge of what was to come. Whoever or whatever Malky was, nobody deserved to die like that.

EIGHT

McCoy sighed, sat back in his chair and looked round the office. He could hardly believe it, but he was actually missing Central in all its run-down glory.

Wattie was pulling a Matchbox toy car out his pocket. He shook his head. "The wee bugger thinks it's funny. Hides them on me." He put it on the desk. "Always finding the bloody things."

"What happened with Judith West?" said McCoy. "Did you hear?"

"Medic cleaned her up, scratches weren't as bad as they looked. Refused the sedative apparently. Was against her religion."

"Christ," said McCoy. "Remind me never to join the Church of Christ's Suffering, right miserable bunch they are."

Reminded him. Took the tracts out his pocket and dropped them in the bin. Silhouette of the crucified Christ looking up at him. *We Suffer to Heal.*

Dropped a copy of yesterday's *Daily Record* on top of them.

"Need to get on with Malky," he said. "Can you do the next of kin, death certificate, background checks, see if Malky's had a run-in with anyone lately?"

Wattie nodded. Picked up the phone.

McCoy called over.

"Rossi?"

Rossi stopped typing, looked up, couldn't have looked less interested if he'd tried.

"You started the initial report?"

Rossi nodded down at his typewriter. "What? You think I'm sitting here doing my knitting?"

McCoy gritted his teeth. Tried to sound pleasant. "Great. When you've finished, away round to the Saracen and see if he had a fight or left with anyone last night. Check the bookies as well—if he had a big win, that might have been a reason to kill him."

"Okay," said Rossi.

"Then better go back to the flat as well, have a proper dig around. The body should be gone by now, should be clear."

"You not want to do that?" Rossi asked, all innocent.

"Nope. Find out from Phyllis when the autopsy is. Not sure it's going to tell us anything we don't know already, but you never know."

McCoy stood up, got the jacket off the back of his chair.

"Where you off to?" said Wattie, putting his hand over the mouthpiece of the phone.

"A walk. That all right with you, is it?"

"Get us a packet of crisps, will you?" said Wattie. "And a Mars bar. I'm starving."

McCoy saluted, walked across the office floor, heading for the door. The lights started flickering and went out just as he reached it, and moans went up from everyone in the room. Electrics on the blink again.

Wasn't sure where he was going. Just knew he wanted away from Rossi and Long and to get some air. Possil Station was winding him up. Any more shite and his ulcer would start playing up, and that was the last thing he needed. He turned into Saracen Street and looked up and down. Couldn't face the Lido. Might be someone from the station in there. Decided to head up to the cafe next to the Vogue cinema, get a cup of tea and a smoke, try and have a proper think about Malky and what had happened to him.

He was just walking past the Balmore bar when the pub

door banged open and a young guy—long hair, tight T-shirt and jeans—ran out the pub, straight across the road and up Bardowie Street. He had his hands up to his face as he ran, blood pouring through his fingers. Was halfway up Bardowie Street before McCoy had realised what had happened.

He pulled the pub door open and stepped into the gloom. Took his eyes a few seconds to adjust, and when they did, he couldn't believe it. Stevie Cooper and Jumbo were sitting at one of the tables, Cooper with a big grin on his face and Jumbo putting something into the Gola sports bag at his feet. Cooper was dressed in a short-sleeved blue shirt, dark jeans, blond hair in a quiff. Blackhill's very own Jimmy Dean. Jumbo, all six foot four of him, had his usual jeans, shirt and sandshoes. Cooper's shadow. There in case muscle was ever needed.

The pub was quiet; punters, heads down, were filling in bookie lines with wee pencils or staring into their drinks. Anything but looking at Stevie and Jumbo.

"McCoy!" said Cooper. "Fancy seeing you here. Come and sit down."

McCoy ignored him, walked over to the barman, got his warrant card out his pocket and held it out. "Did someone just get slashed in here? Young guy. Long hair."

The barman stopped rubbing a dirty cloth round the inside of a pint glass. Tried to look as puzzled as possible. "In here, pal? You must be joking. Been dead quiet all afternoon."

McCoy turned to the rest of the punters. "Anyone just see a guy running out here, blood pouring out his face?"

A few shaken heads, a few murmurs of no, a lot of looking at the floor, no one wanting to catch his eye.

"What are you blabbering on about, McCoy?" said Cooper. "Sit down and have a drink. Barman, get him a pint."

McCoy knew when he was defeated. Sat down at the table, Cooper still grinning away. Pint turned up and he took a drink. Put it down on the table.

"What you doing in here, Stevie? Long way out your way."

"Was up at Sighthill Cemetery. Mrs. Crawley, old next-door neighbour. Saying my last farewells. Thought I'd drop in for a wee drink on the way home."

"So who was he?"

"Who was who?" said Cooper, all innocent.

"The guy that just ran past me with half his face falling through his fingers. The one you just slashed."

"No idea what you're talking about, McCoy."

"That right? Well, call me Sherlock bloody Holmes, but there's a spray of blood on your shirt, and I'm guessing if I go rooting around in Jumbo's bag there, I'll find the razor that did it."

Cooper ignored him. "She was a good woman, Mrs. Crawley. Used to feed me when there was nothing in the house."

"Cooper, for fuck sake I saw him!"

Cooper put his pint down, leant into McCoy's face. "There was no slashing. There's no razor in Jumbo's bag. Got me?"

McCoy sat back in his chair, knew it was pointless. If Cooper wasn't going to talk about what had happened, then he was scuppered. No chance any of the punters would spill the beans. They were more scared of Stevie Cooper than the police. Probably rightly.

"If it hadn't been for Mrs. Crawley and her home-made soup," said Cooper, "I'd have wasted away."

"I like soup," said Jumbo, then smiled.

"You got one of your comics, Jumbo?" said Cooper. Jumbo nodded, got a *Commando* comic out his bag.

"Well, away and sit at that table over there and read it. I need to talk to Mr. McCoy."

Jumbo got up and moved to another table, the old man he sat down beside looking at him with fear in his eyes.

"C'mon. Who was he?" said McCoy.

"No idea," said Cooper. "Some cunt who works for Archie Andrews who asked me what I was doing in one of his pubs."

"And you opened his face for that?"

Cooper shrugged. "Message sent."

McCoy took another drink of his pint. He'd known Cooper since they were wee boys, when they were both in and out of children's homes and Cooper had been his protector—as much as he could be—and he knew this mood. *Don't press me.* Changed the subject.

"What else you doing today?"

"Fuck knows. Might go and see my boxers at the gym. Sparring day today."

McCoy smiled. "I told you being rich and successful wouldn't suit you."

"Paul's running the pubs and protection in Royston—last thing he wants is his dad looking over his shoulder. Big John and Mack are looking after Springburn. All I seem to do is have meetings with accountants and lawyers."

"Well, it's hard work making your ill-gotten gains disappear before the taxman gets them."

"You're telling me."

"You need something to do."

Cooper grinned. "Funny you should say that. Been having a think."

"About what?"

"Here."

"Possil? Why?"

"Archie Andrews is getting on. No obvious successor. Might be time for me to do what I do best."

"Start a war?"

"Not yet. Start with a few skirmishes first, test the water. Hence the boy with the opened face. He'll be running right back to Andrews now. I've got Royston. Possil is the logical next step."

"Christ, Cooper. You know I'm stationed here just now?"

"How could I not? You've been moaning about it for the

past two weeks. Where do you think I got the idea? You being here could come in handy."

"Stevie, I don't want to get—"

Cooper put his finger up to his lips, made a *shh* sound. "Not up to you, pal. You owe me, McCoy."

He was right: he did owe him, owed him a lot. Without Stevie Cooper one of the most evil men McCoy had ever dealt with would still be walking the streets.

"You okay with that?" said Cooper.

He knew what he was being asked. *You with me or against me?* That's the way it went with Cooper. McCoy nodded. Couldn't really do anything else.

"Good man. And now I need to get going." Cooper stood up and Jumbo was up too, falling in beside his boss. "Tell you what, Harry, why don't you come and see me tonight at the baths? We'll have a proper wee chat. About the shitehole that is Possil and what we are going to do about it."

McCoy watched Cooper and Jumbo leave the pub. Drained the last of his pint and wondered what on earth Cooper had in store for him.

NINE

Coming on for Midsummer's Day, and Possil Station was still dark and gloomy. There were windows everywhere, but the light didn't penetrate far into the vast open-plan office. At least the lights were back on again. McCoy was back at his desk, trying not to think about what Cooper had said and what he was expecting him to do. Last thing he needed was more trouble.

"How did it go this morning?" Long was standing by his desk, some young guy in a brand-new uniform hovering behind him.

No "hello." No "how you doing?" He was still talking to McCoy like he was a junior officer. Time to grit his teeth again.

"Fine, sir, just getting the train rolling now. Wattie's just making some calls. Once I've spoken to him I'll get you a preliminary report."

"This is young Hood." Long nodded to the uniform. "He's just started. First placement."

Hood was tall, even for a polis, built like a wrestler. The perfect beat cop. McCoy recognised him—he was the uniform who had been outside the close at Malky's murder scene.

"How'd you get on with Miss Malone?"

"I helped her mop up the close. Spent the whole time standing over me telling me I was doing it wrong."

His accent was half Glaswegian, half something else. Aberdeen?

McCoy smiled. "You'll soon find out police work's not all

bank robbers and shoot-outs. It's people like Miss Malone ex-pecting you to do her bloody chores for her."

McCoy watched Long escorting Hood on his tour of the of-fice and started making a list of things to think about for the Malky McCormack case. Ten minutes later he'd managed to write "Friends?" in his jotter. Mind wasn't really on it. Not to-day.

"My ear's bloody burning," Wattie said as he put down the phone. "Been on this thing for hours. All for a load of shite that doesn't get us anywhere. What's that?" He was pointing at the dinner suit in the drycleaner's bag that was hanging behind McCoy's desk.

"It's a dinner suit," said McCoy.

Wattie let out a low whistle. "How much did that skin you?"

McCoy sighed. Wasn't going to get out of it. "Nothing. It was Margo's dad's. Just dropping it off at the dry cleaner's."

Wattie grinned, couldn't help himself. "Still going on, is it? You and the lefty film star?"

McCoy nodded. "Anything to say about it?"

"Nope," said Wattie pleasantly. "There's a surprise. You hungry? I'm starving."

"How can you be starving?" said McCoy. "You've just had an entire bloody Mars bar and a bag of crisps."

Wattie shrugged. "Could stay here and have a chat about your new girlfriend or we can go to the Lido and I'll tell you where my sore ear got me. Up to you . . . "

An easy choice.

The Lido cafe was halfway down Saracen Street. As usual, it was mobbed; they had to wait for an old couple to finish their teas before they got their table.

"All yours, boys," said the old man as they stood up. "Off to Arnott's so she can look at stuff and not buy anything."

The old woman pretended to cuff him and they toddled off towards the door. Wattie and McCoy sat down and ordered.

Didn't take long for the food to turn up. Worked like an oiled machine, the Lido cafe. Punters in and out all day.

"So where did your hot ear get you?" said McCoy as he took a bite of his roll and sausage. Just about burnt his mouth off, took a quick swig of Coke.

Wattie flicked his black notebook open. Started reading. "One Malcolm James McCormack born in nineteen ten in Rottenrow Hospital. Dad was a riveter, mum worked as a cleaner. Worked as a barman most of his life until the drink took over. Never married. No kids. Two arrests, both for drunk and disorderly." Flicked through a couple of pages. "Edith Watson is the next of kin. No relation to my good self. She's his cousin, lives in Falkirk. I called and told her Malcolm had passed away and she asked me if I thought it was going to rain this afternoon and where her good umbrella was. Away with the fairies."

"You speak to Rossi?" said McCoy as a gaggle of schoolkids came in and gathered round the front counter, asking for the penny tray.

Wattie nodded. Took a bite of his toastie and wiped some melted cheese from his chin.

"Rossi is a fucking arse like the rest of them but he's no a bad copper. Does his job. Seems Malky was in the pub last night as he was every night. Ran out of money so started wandering around asking the other punters to buy him a drink. Landlord had warned him about it before, bought him a pint and said after that he was on his way. No big win at the bookies—most he ever bet was ten pence."

"Last of the big spenders."

"No one went home with him. He finished his pint, said goodnight to the landlord and off he went."

McCoy pushed his roll away and lit up. "So why on earth would someone want to torture and kill a nobody like Malky McCormack? I don't get it."

Wattie shrugged. "Kids, maybe? Doing it for kicks? Doesn't seem likely though. You no want that?"

McCoy shook his head and Wattie pulled the plate with the half-eaten roll towards him.

"Maybe he owed money?" said Wattie, chewing away.

McCoy shook his head.

"He didn't have enough to borrow big. No car, no jewellery, nothing like that. Most a moneylender would have lent him would be a couple of quid and nobody's going to murder someone for that."

Wattie grinned. "You sure? This is Possil, don't forget. Up here they eat their young."

"The door and the lock were intact?" Wattie nodded.

"So he let them march him up the stairs, whoever they were, then let them in. Maybe he knew them?"

"Or maybe he was just too scared to say no."

"True." Struck him. "He still had his coat on, didn't he?"

"As you would remember if you hadn't scarpered away from the crime scene as soon as you could. Thought you were supposed to be getting better with blood?"

McCoy ignored him.

"Means they were waiting for him, watched him go up to his close. Which means it was definitely him they were after—that's not just kids wanting to batter some old bugger for cheap thrills."

"Malky's still waters must run deep," said Wattie.

McCoy sat back in the booth. Tried to think. Watched the kids picking out sweeties.

Wattie held his napkin over his mouth. Burped softly. "What are you thinking?"

"What I'm thinking is it doesn't really matter if Malky knew anything or not. The people that killed him thought he did."

"So?"

"So what could a nobody like Malky McCormack know that was worth battering him to death over?"

Ten

McCoy and Wattie had finished for the day, were standing outside the station, trying to decide whether to go home or head to the pub. Sun was just starting to go down, end of another perfect summer's day. McCoy was just about to suggest going up to the Viking for a change when he heard a shout.

"No way! That you, McCoy?"

He knew who it was before he turned round, same wheezy voice as always. He turned and, sure enough, it was Cuthbert Moss. He strolled towards them, the usual fag in the corner of his mouth no doubt responsible for the wheezing. He was a tiny man, Cuthbert, five foot if he was lucky. Despite the weather, he was dressed in a bunnet and zipped-up anorak, milk-bottle specs perched on his bulbous red nose.

"How you doing, Cuthbert?" said McCoy.

"Me? Brand new. What you doing up this way?"

McCoy pointed in the vague direction of the station. "Working up here for a while."

"Just like old times, eh?"

When McCoy had been a beat cop up here for a couple of years Cuthbert had taken a shine to him, steered him right a good few times, told him about the local characters, where the shebeens were, who was running them, what villain was out of Barlinnie, who was headed back in. Even sold him information for the price of a couple of pints. All useful stuff for a green polis trying to get ahead.

Cuthbert looked at him. Waiting.

McCoy sighed, nodded at the Saracen up the street. "Fancy a pint?"

Cuthbert smiled, revealing missing front teeth and black gums. "Well, if you insist, I won't argue."

Wattie pulled McCoy aside. "You're on your own, Harry. No way am I going for a drink with that wee weirdo. I can smell him from here. I'll catch you tomorrow."

Hurried off towards his car before McCoy could stop him. He didn't blame him; Cuthbert was what was known as an acquired taste. Still, he owed him a pint at least.

They walked along the road towards the pub, Cuthbert moving slower than he used to. McCoy had to wait for him to catch up a few times. Old age had begun to creep up on Cuthbert. Sleeves of his anorak were frayed, suit trousers shiny, hands shaking as he went to light another cigarette. He'd seemed old back when McCoy had started. God knows what age he must be now. Coming on for eighty, maybe.

The Saracen was the kind of place where a battered face or blood down someone's shirt didn't attract much comment, even if it was the bouncer at the door that was sporting both. He nodded hello as they went in, wiped the dripping blood off his chin with his shirt sleeve.

"Sean McKenna's nephew," said Cuthbert. "No a bad lad. Bit wild though."

Cuthbert shuffled to a table at the back of the pub and lowered himself down with a grunt. McCoy went to the bar and got two pints from the barmaid and brought them over. Cuthbert took a gulp of his, swilled it around his mouth like a fine Château Latour, swallowed it over and lit up another fag.

"You heard about Malky McCormack, I trust?"

McCoy nodded. "It's my case."

"Is it now?"

"You know something about it?"

Cuthbert shrugged. "Might do."

McCoy stuck his hand in his pocket. "How much?"

"For an old pal like you? A fiver. And another pint."

McCoy handed over the money and headed back to the bar. It was way over the odds for any information Cuthbert might have, but he didn't grudge giving him the money. Cuthbert had been good to him, and God knows he looked like he needed the cash.

The barmaid was now a barman. A fat bloke with an eye-patch and a dirty "Sail the Caribbean" T-shirt on. McCoy decided he'd probably heard every pirate joke going already and just asked for another pint. Barman went to pour it, but the stream of lager from the tap spluttered and stopped.

"Shite," he said. "I'll need to change the barrel, no be long."

McCoy nodded, turned and looked round the pub. Most of the clientele seemed to be like Cuthbert or Malky McCormack: old men wearing too many clothes for the weather, staring into space or counting piles of small change on the tables, desperately hoping they had enough for another drink.

Cuthbert was gazing up at the TV on the wall. Horse racing through the snow of static. Being in here, Malky's local, was making it seem even stranger that he'd been murdered the way he had. Malky was a man who'd spent his days in places like this, measuring out the afternoon in slowly sipped pints and growing panic as he ran out of money—what secret could a man like that have that was worth killing for? McCoy had no expectations that Cuthbert would really know anything. It was just less embarrassing for both of them for him to sell a tall tale than to ask outright for some money.

Long John Silver was back. As was the lager. McCoy paid him for the pint and walked back to Cuthbert and sat down.

"Spit it out, Cuthbert," he said. "What have I got for my big investment?"

Cuthbert settled back into his chair, prepared for his big

moment. "Well, who should I see hanging about across the road from Malky's flat when I was going home last night?"

McCoy sighed. "I don't know. Who did you see? Miss World? Sean Connery?"

"Stop being a smartarse. None other than Joseph Monaghan."

McCoy sat back; he wasn't expecting that. "You saying he killed Malky?"

Cuthbert shrugged. "What else would a bastard like him be doing up here? This is way out of his patch."

McCoy thought. "It's a bit below his level, is it not? Battering some old alky to death. Monaghan would get someone further down the food chain to do something like that. Besides, I thought he was retired from all that now. He's got a couple of pubs in Govan, hasn't he?"

Cuthbert sat there, beatific smile on his face.

"Ah, what else do you know, Cuthbert? Spit it out."

Cuthbert looked back and forth, checked nobody was listening, and leant towards McCoy, milking it to the last drop. "Monaghan is retired—you're not wrong there—happily pulling pints for the good people of Govan. But lately a certain someone has brought him out of retirement to deal with a few pressing matters, shall we say."

He sat back, triumph on his face.

Loath as he was to feed Cuthbert more ammunition for his big moment, McCoy couldn't help himself. "Okay, I know you're dying to tell me. So who are we talking about?"

Cuthbert tapped the side of his nose. "Come on, Harry. You always were a clever boy. Work it out. Chain of command."

McCoy sat back, thought. Then it dawned and he grinned. "Your arse, Cuthbert. Don't tell me you're talking about Duncan Kent?"

Cuthbert's face fell. His bombshell hadn't had the desired effect.

"There's no way Duncan Kent has got anything to do with

this," said McCoy. "He's been covering the tracks and severing the ties for years and years. The wife runs about twenty charities, always in the bloody paper. There is no way he's going to get involved with someone like Monaghan again." He smiled. "You've called that one wrong."

Cuthbert harrumphed. "I'm no the one saying Duncan Kent. You are. All I did was say I saw Monaghan." He downed his pint, banged the empty glass on the table.

McCoy had forgotten how much of a pain in the arse Cuthbert could be. "C'mon, Cuthbert, don't get all huffy on me. Just think about it for a minute. Sure, Monaghan is an evil enough bastard to do something like that, but why Malky McCormack? He's a nobody. Two convictions for drunk and disorderly, that's it. He's no Al Capone. Why would Monaghan risk coming out of retirement to spread him across his kitchen floor?"

Cuthbert jammed his bunnet on his head, stood up and headed for the door. McCoy was tempted to let the grumpy bastard go, but even if he was wrong about Monaghan, he still knew more about Malky McCormack than anyone else he was likely to talk to.

He called after him, "C'mon, Cuthbert, don't be like that!"

Cuthbert kept walking.

"I'll get you another pint!"

Cuthbert slowed down. Time to bring out the big guns.

"And a whisky!"

Cuthbert stopped and turned around. "A double?"

"Christ! Okay, a double. Now, will you come back and stop being a big wean?"

He did, and they sat for an hour or so, going over old times, people they'd known, Cuthbert getting more and more vague as the drink went down. Was telling McCoy some long rambling story about his pal stealing a car, then finding out it was Jock Stein's and being so ashamed that they'd parked it back outside his house in the middle of the night. McCoy was nodding along, getting ready to make his exit, when Cuthbert suddenly refocused.

"Did you talk to the sister?"

McCoy was confused. "Jock Stein's sister?"

Cuthbert scowled. "Don't be so bloody stupid. Malky's sister. What's she saying to it?"

Now he was really confused. "Malky doesn't have a sister. Next of kin is some old cousin in Falkirk who's away with the fairies."

"Well, when I say it's his sister, it's not actually his sister. It's his stepsister, ex-stepsister, whatever you call it. Norma McGregor. I saw her the other day."

Cuthbert went to raise his pint to his mouth when McCoy took his arm and stopped him.

"What are you doing, you clown!" said Cuthbert.

McCoy spoke very slowly and very clearly. "You need to tell me about the sister, Cuthbert. The sister."

"Buy us another pint."

"I will," said McCoy. "Just as soon as you tell me about the sister." Cuthbert nodded. "Fair dues, fair dues. Malky always called her his sister, though they weren't related. She's the daughter of one of the women his dad was with before Malky was born. What a cunt *he* was. Used to work up at the Saracen Foundry, a welder. Big lump of a man. He'd go from woman to woman, living in their homes, not paying rent, eating food that should have gone to their weans; didnae marry any of them until he knocked up Malky's mother. Ended up in the jail for battering—"

"Cuthbert! I'll batter *you* in a minute. The bloody sister!"

Cuthbert held his hands up in surrender. "Sorry, son, I'm rambling. She looked after him for a while when he was a wee boy. When the dad was in the jail. They stayed close."

"And?"

"And I saw her the other day. She was up here at his flat. All dolled up, she was, two bags of Marks and Spencer's food with her, in a black cab as well, and she kept it waiting while she went in and delivered it. So where's she getting the bloody money for that? She's a cleaner, has been all her puff, hasnae got two pennies to rub together."

"Good man!" said McCoy, clapping him on the back. "Now we're talking! I'll get you another pint."

Cuthbert started laughing, laughter that soon turned into a coughing fit. McCoy clapped his back again and headed for the bar. When he got back, Cuthbert had calmed down, calmed down so much so that he was leaning against the wall half asleep.

McCoy shook him. "Here's your pint. You okay to get up the road?"

"Aye, son, fine," he said, waving McCoy away, eyes still closed.

McCoy shook him. Hard.

Eyes opened. "What do you bloody want now?"

"The sister. Where do I find her?"

Cuthbert yawned. "Saturday Vigil Mass at St. Teresa's. Don't know where she lives, but she's there every week come hell or high water. Come find me and I'll introduce you."

McCoy waited a bit, slipped another couple of quid into the snoring Cuthbert's anorak pocket and walked up to the bar. Long John Silver was reading the *Evening Times* now, finger tracing every word.

"Do me a favour?" said McCoy. "See that he gets up the road, eh?"

No response.

One of the old boys at the bar spoke up. "Don't ask that bugger," he said. "He wouldnae gie you the steam off his pish. I'm on his landing, I'll see he gets home."

McCoy bought the old boy a drink and headed for the door, walked past Sean McKenna's nephew and his bloody shirt and out into the evening sunshine. Glasgow looked cheery for once. But in amongst the kids with shorts on, the full-up buses and empty taxis, and the queue for the ice-cream van, there was someone who knew what had really happened to Malky McCormack and why. All he had to do was find them. Looked like a trip to St. Teresa's to find Norma McGregor might be a good place to start.

ELEVEN

I t had become the easiest place to find him. Every evening Cooper went swimming at the private baths on Arlington Street. Whatever the clientele of elderly professionals and lecturers from the university had thought about him at first, he was one of them now. A regular. An Arlington man.

McCoy pulled the door of the baths open and stepped into the warm mist of chlorine-smelling air. He nodded at the man on the desk and went through into the main pool area. It was a long room with wooden arches in the ceiling, a pristine pool, wicker chairs sitting along the walls. Cooper was the only one in the water, powering up and down, Jumbo sitting on a wicker recliner by the side, keeping watch as always.

"How many to go?" asked McCoy.

Jumbo counted on his fingers. "Five."

Jumbo had two interests in life, gardening and *Commando* comics. He'd asked Cooper if he could go and work for the Parks Department, and Cooper had doubled his money and said no, the garden at his house was big enough for any man to work on. So Jumbo was back on bodyguard duty wearing new denims, new sandshoes and a new jumper. You tended to do what your boss wanted if he'd already cut off one of your fingers when he wasn't happy with you.

McCoy sat down and watched Cooper finishing his lengths. He yawned, yawned again. Warm air in the baths and the day he'd had were making him sleepy. Seemed like a week ago he'd thought Michael West was missing, not this morning. Then there'd been poor Malky, and now he had to deal with Cooper. Was more than enough for any day. He wondered how Judith West was now. Far as he was concerned, what she needed was a few tranquillisers and a good night's sleep, not more praying and waiting for God to make it all better.

Wasn't long until Cooper emerged from the water, grabbed a towel from Jumbo and started to dry himself off. McCoy looked him up and down. No new scars, no new bruises: made a change.

"Five minutes," Cooper said, and headed for the changing rooms.

McCoy got out his cigarettes, then thought better of it. Didn't seem right in a place where people came to get healthy. He wasn't looking forward to his chat with Cooper. Thought of helping Cooper do his dirty work was making his heart sink. If Murray found out, he was a dead man. Murray had made it plain more than once that Cooper was supposed to be off limits.

When Cooper appeared, wet hair combed into a quiff, he looked like he'd invested in some new togs too. Still wearing jeans and a short-sleeved shirt, but they looked brand new, better quality. New watch as well, a big shiny thing it was, a red and blue metal band around the face. Cooper was a rich man now, was starting to look it.

"So," he said, sitting down, "what have you got on Archie Andrews?"

"Us? Nothing. You probably know as much about him as we do."

"Fucking polis, bloody useless. I know he's got four pubs, moneylending business all through Possil, a shebeen in Stonyhurst Street and another one in Allander Street, three or four girls in each. Anything to add?"

McCoy thought for a minute. "There was talk of him having a garage in Fruin Street. Stealing high-end cars, Rovers, Jags, respraying them, putting new plates on, then flogging them down south. Don't know if it ever came to much."

"That right?" said Cooper. "Maybe you're not entirely useless then. Anything else?"

McCoy shook his head.

"What I really need," said Cooper, "is something on his number two."

"Rab Jamieson?" asked McCoy.

Cooper nodded. "He's the only one that has a chance of power once Andrews is gone, so I need him taken care of."

"I'll have an ask about," said McCoy. "See if there's anything worth knowing."

"Good man. And I'll find out about the garage." Cooper sat back in his chair and lit up. No qualms for him. "Did I tell you? I phoned my dad in Belfast, told him about Mrs. Crawley. Thought he might want to come over for the funeral." He smiled. "He couldn't even remember who she was."

"Sounds like your dad, all right. You remember the state of his old flat?"

"Hard to forget," said Cooper. "Don't think I've ever seen a place so filthy before or since. Wasn't much interested in keeping house, my old da, was he?"

"Nope. I remember turning up there once when I'd run away from . . . Where was it now?" said McCoy, trying to remember.

"Barnardo's," said Cooper.

"Barnardo's," said McCoy. "Soon as I saw the state of your dad's flat I wanted to go back."

Cooper laughed. "Mrs. Crawley used to grab me sometimes in the close, drag me into their flat, wash me in the sink, make me sit there in a towel until she washed my clothes and dried them. I must have been five or six. Mrs. Crawley looked after me the best she could. I stayed at hers more often than I stayed at my dad's. It was warm down there and you got fed. She was a good woman."

Cooper stood up. Nodded at Jumbo.

"You off?" asked McCoy.

"Got a date."

"Oh aye," said McCoy. "Anyone I know?"

"Might do. She's on the back of the lager cans. Gail. Ex-Miss Scotland."

McCoy let out a low whistle. "The one with the long blonde hair?"

"And the rest. Not just you that can punch above their weight."

"Why does everyone keep saying that to me?"

"Because you look like a bloody tramp," said Cooper, heading for the door. "That's why. Remember about Jamieson." Stopped. Looked back at McCoy. "And by the way, Gail wants to meet your film-star girlfriend. Need to sort something out."

McCoy nodded, hoped Cooper and Gail would forget that idea. Looked down at his suit. Cooper might well have a point.

The hill leading up to his flat at the top of Gardner Street always seemed steeper when you were carrying something. Never mind the stairs after that. By the time McCoy put the Indian carry-out bag and the Agnew's bag full of cans down outside the door and fumbled in his pocket for his keys, he was sweating, could feel his shirt sticking to his back. Cooper was right. Couldn't remember the last time he'd bought a new suit. Or shoes. Or some shirts.

He sat at the table eating his lamb dhansak, flicking through the paper and watching the TV. More Common Market stuff, was all that was on these days. Wondered what Cooper and his Tennent's Lager Lovely were eating. Definitely not a takeaway curry, that was for sure. He turned his can around and peered at the back. Shona. Red hair and a swimsuit. He got the other cans out the bag and found one with Gail on it. She was looking at the camera, hair all tousled, hot pants halfway up her arse and a tiny bikini top. Didn't look like the type whose idea of a night out was a lamb dhansak at the kitchen table. Hoped Cooper had remembered his wallet.

He opened up Gail's can and went back to his paper. Turned the page, and there was a big advert for Jackson the Tailor's summer sale. An omen. Maybe he should smarten himself up, make an effort for Margo, if no one else. Could go to the shops on Saturday. Give him something to do before the Vigil Mass with Cuthbert.

He woke up at half four, birds singing away, light coming through the living-room curtains, cans and remains of the curry in front of him on the table. He'd been so tired he'd fallen asleep at the table.

He yawned, stretched his back, and made for the bedroom. Cooper was right: he needed to smarten himself up. Didn't just look like a tramp, was starting to act like one. Another couple of years like this and he'd be another one sitting in the Saracen asking around for money for a last pint.

FRIDAY

13TH JUNE 1975

Soon as McCoy opened the car door he could smell it. Burnt wood and a sort of chemical smell like nail varnish remover. He got out of the Viva, saw Wattie sitting on the back step of the station, sunglasses on, bacon roll in one hand, pint of milk in the other. He was chewing away, reading the back page of the *Daily Record*.

"What's that bloody smell?" said McCoy.

"*Garffrrm*," said Wattie. Swallowed his mouthful of roll and tried again. "Garage up the road caught fire in the middle of the night. Lots of paint in there, apparently, hence the stink."

Couldn't be, not so soon. "What garage?"

Wattie kept his eyes on the news of Celtic's midfield problem and shrugged. "Forgotten the name of it. It's in Fruin Street, about halfway along."

Had to be Cooper. Never thought he'd move so fast; he'd only told him about the garage last night. He must be serious about trying to take over. The war was about to begin, right enough.

Wattie balled up the paper bag his roll had come in and threw it in one of the big bins lined up in the yard.

"Want to go and see?" he asked. "Fuck all happening in there. No bugger'll even look at us, never mind talk to us."

They went the back way, walking through the streets of industrial units and storage places, smell of burnt paint getting stronger as they went. Passed a couple of caravans selling rolls and teas to the guys from the units.

"Do you think I look like a tramp?" said McCoy as they turned into Fruin Street.

Wattie stopped. "What?"

"You heard. Be honest."

Wattie looked him up and down. Grimaced. "Maybe not quite a tramp . . . "

"Thanks," said McCoy. "Thanks for that. Thanks for your vote of confidence."

"What? You asked me. What's brought this on?"

"Nothing. Just think I might need some new clothes, that's all," said McCoy.

"Might be an idea, but for fuck sake don't go to John Collier's or bloody Jackson the Tailor's. Go to Forsyth's."

"That's not cheap," said McCoy.

"No, but you've got the money and it's quality stuff." Grinned. "Wouldn't want to make a show of yourself when you're hanging about with Margo Lindsay's smart set."

"Wish I'd never asked," said McCoy.

"Want me to come with you? Give you some tips?"

"No, I bloody don't."

Wattie shrugged. "Just asking. It's nice to be nice."

McCoy walked on. He was never going to hear the end of it now.

McCoy had been expecting a normal garage with petrol pumps and a forecourt, but it was just a warehouse like all the other ones in the street. Well, it had been, wasn't much of anything now. Most of the walls had gone, just concrete pillars holding what was left of the roof up. Some of the piles of wood around the garage were still smouldering, sending wisps of smoke into the sunny sky. There were a few burnt-out cars inside. Windows, paint and tyres gone, just metal shells distorted out of shape and stained black with the heat. Dust of grey ashes covering everything.

McCoy held his arm over his mouth and tried to block out the chemical smell. Wasn't doing much good.

"It's an insurance job, apparently," said Wattie. "Bloke who owns it wasn't making money off it any more, decided to cash in."

"Who told you that?" said McCoy, trying not to cough.

"Rossi," said Wattie.

"How did he know?"

Wattie shrugged. "According to him, it's Archie Andrews that owns it. Name's nowhere near it though—be some sucker's name on the deeds."

"Fountain of knowledge, our Rossi," said McCoy.

"It's his patch, has been for years. He's a dick, but he seems to know what's going on around here."

Or he's been told what to say, thought McCoy. Made Andrews look better if the word got out that he'd done it himself for the insurance money. Andrews would know though, know somebody was after him. Was just a matter of time before Cooper let him know it was him. Might well have guessed already, sending one of his boys on his way with an open face had to be a clue. Maybe Rossi was more than just a message boy for Archie Andrews after all.

A section of the roof cracked and fell down onto the cars. More dust blew up, swirled round them. McCoy put his hands over his face, but he wasn't quick enough. Throat and nose full of the stuff. He coughed a few times, sneezed, tapped Wattie on the shoulder.

"This smell's giving me the boak," he said. "Let's go."

"Malky's post-mortem is today," said Wattie as they crossed at the lights. "We should go and see what it says."

"I'll take a wild guess: cause of death half a brick battered repeatedly into his face."

"Might be something else. You never know."

"Might be, but it won't." McCoy leant over and spat in the gutter. "I can still taste that bloody garage. I need a drink, a Coke or something."

They turned right into Balmore Road, heading for the cafe

in the row of shops by the Vogue cinema, and stopped. A police van was stopped halfway up the hill in the middle of the road, traffic starting to queue up behind it. A panda car was parked alongside, a traffic cop trying to wave the cars and buses past.

"Must have broken down," said Wattie. "Bad place to do it."

A uniform walked towards them as they reached the van, was about to shoo them off until they took out their cards.

"What's going on?" said Wattie.

"Someone's chucked themselves off the bloody bridge onto the train tracks," he said. "It's grim."

THIRTEEN

The bridge on Balmore Road crossed over the tracks of a disused railway running about fifty feet below. It was a deep cutting that was partly overgrown, rusty tracks starting to disappear in the undergrowth. The remnants of the old Lanarkshire and Dunbartonshire line, long gone.

McCoy walked around the police van, heading for the bridge, dreading getting there, knew he had to look. He edged along one step at a time. Steeled himself and peered over the wall. Down below, a woman was lying on the tracks. Her head was at an angle it shouldn't be, not if your neck wasn't broken. She was surrounded by an ever-increasing pool of dark blood. He stepped back quickly, head already spinning.

"What did you do that for?" said Wattie.

"I don't know," said McCoy. "I wish I hadn't."

"I'll go down there and see if they've identified anyone. You stay here."

"Don't worry, I will." McCoy was already retreating up the hill.

He watched Wattie duck between the police cars and pull himself over the wall, jump down onto the grassy verge and start making his way down the slope towards the three officers standing by the body. Wasn't much for him to do but wait, so he wandered over to the other side of the road, making sure he didn't catch another glimpse, then stood outside the paint shop in the old railway station and lit up. After seeing Malky yesterday the last thing he needed was more blood and guts.

A crowd was starting to gather: shoppers stopped getting into town, people who'd got off the buses. A female officer was trying to shoo away a group of kids trying to peer over the side of the bridge. People lined up at windows on the top deck of a bus that was slowly easing round the van. He heard a siren and watched an ambulance come up the hill and pull in beside the police van.

He'd just finished his cigarette when Wattie, white-faced, climbed over the wall and walked back to him. Must be bad if it had affected Wattie; normally he was fine with the kind of stuff McCoy couldn't cope with.

"That was brutal," he said. "It's like your worst nightmare. Her neck must have broken on impact, her head hit right on the track and—"

"Okay! Okay!" said McCoy. "Spare me the details. Do we know who it was?"

Wattie nodded. "They got the ID from her handbag. You're not going to believe it."

"Who is it?"

"It's her from yesterday," said Wattie. "Judith West, the one that was in the station."

"Christ," said McCoy.

Wattie held out a well-worn Bible. "Left it on the wall when she jumped."

McCoy opened it at the front page. There was a bookplate, little blue flowers and praying hands surrounding a name.

Judith West.

"She wasn't messing about," said Wattie. "According to the witnesses, she just put the Bible and her handbag down on the wall, climbed up on it and jumped. Head first. Must have had enough of everything—the idea of the wee boy, all that."

McCoy thought back to her in the interview room, clawing at her face, screaming. They should have known she might try something like this, should have paid more attention. Should have cared more.

McCoy heard a shout, looked up the street and swore under his breath.

"What? What is it?" Wattie turned to see. "Shite!"

Reverend West was running down the hill towards them.

FOURTEEN

W attie set off at a pace, ran up the hill towards the pastor and managed to get in front of him. West suddenly realised he was being blocked and twisted out of Wattie's grip, started running again. Wattie swore and set off after him, caught up and rugby-tackled him, both of them going down. West struggled to get away, but Wattie had his arms around him, holding him tight.

McCoy ran towards them. "You can't go over there, Reverend. Please, it's for your own good."

"Is it her?" West said. "Is it Judith?"

McCoy nodded. "We think so."

And with that, all the fight went out of him. His body slumped, he stopped struggling, just lay there on the ground. McCoy nodded at Wattie, and he let go of him, got up and helped West do the same.

"The shop," McCoy. "Take him in there."

Wattie put his arm around West's shoulders and walked him towards the paint shop. His head was down, tears rolling down his face. McCoy pulled the door open and they went in. The punters in the shop stood there open-mouthed, tins of paint and rolls of wallpaper in their hands, no idea what was going on.

"Give us a minute, eh?" said Wattie. "Step outside, please."

He held up his police badge, and the punters shuffled towards the door in silence, staring at the weeping man. West slumped down onto the floor of the shop, wiped the snot and the tears from his face with his shirt sleeve. Wattie went over to the owner behind the counter, explained what had happened, asked him for a glass of water.

McCoy sat on the floor next to West and held out the Bible. "Is this hers?"

West nodded. Started to cry again. His shirt was torn, tie askew, looked like he'd been in a fight more than anything else. Wattie got the glass of water from the shopkeeper and handed it to him. He took a couple of sips, seemed to calm down a bit.

"Sorry," he said. "I'm sorry. She said she felt better, said it was out of her system, that she was going to go for a walk, get some fresh air. I wanted to go with her, but she said she needed some time to herself, to talk to God. I told her that . . ." He looked at them. Something had dawned on him. "Did she suffer?"

"Absolutely not," said Wattie. "Was over in a second."

West's face crumpled again. "I should have been more careful. Shouldn't have let her go."

McCoy remembered the scar he'd seen on Judith West's wrist as she pushed the hanky into her cardigan sleeve in the interview room. "Had she tried it before?"

"Years ago. I found her in the bathroom. She'd taken a razor blade to her wrists. I tried to . . ."

West started sobbing again, and McCoy put his arm around his shoulders and let him cry. Told Wattie to go and arrange for a uniform to drive him home.

"Is there someone who can sit with you? Someone we can call?"

West wiped his eyes. "James. James Booth. One of our congregation. He was my best man. He works in the garage in Chryston."

"Okay, you can pick him up on the way home."

Wattie appeared at the door. "Car's outside. You ready to go, Mr. West?"

West didn't look like he was ready to do anything, slumped on the floor, eyes red from crying. He nodded.

"I'll help you," said McCoy. "Come on."

McCoy pulled West up, walked him out the shop and helped him into the back of the waiting car. Tried to get him in before he had a chance to look at the ambulance and the mortuary van parked on the bridge. Didn't have to worry—West just sat there in the back seat, head down, seemed to be praying.

The car drove off slowly, weaving its way through the crowd and the panda cars and down the hill towards town. McCoy watched it go. The image of West's face when he found out his wife was dead stuck in his mind. Thought of saying a prayer himself.

He went back into the shop to say thanks to the owner and saw the Bible still on the floor. West had forgotten it. He picked it up, started flicking through it. Judith West had done lots of underlining, had written notes beside certain passages. Different pens, different ink. Looked like she'd been doing it for a long time. Edges of the cover starting to fray. He stopped at one passage that had been scored out. *NO* written beside it in big black letters. From the surrounding passages McCoy worked out it had been 1 Peter 4:1. He held the page up to the light, could just about make out what was written under the felt pen.

Therefore, since Christ suffered in his body, arm yourselves also with the same attitude, because whoever suffers in the body is done with sin.

He closed the Bible. Who knew what had been going on in Judith West's mind? Maybe the poor woman had suffered enough, maybe she was better off now. That's what people told themselves, wasn't it? Made them feel better. He stepped out of the shop and into the sunlight, made his way round the ambulance and the panda cars and the crowd of kids and started walking back down the hill to the station. Wasn't sure it was making him feel any better at all.

FIFTEEN

M cCoy sat down and put the bottle of Irn-Bru and the cheese salad roll he'd bought on the way on the desk. His stomach hadn't been that bad for a while. Still the occasional bout of agony from his ulcer if he ate what he shouldn't or drank too much, but he thought he could get away with the cheese roll.

He took an experimental bite and chewed it over. No immediate alarm bells. Lights in the ceiling started to flicker. A groan from the office. Electrics again. McCoy waited to see if they would go out or recover. Stopped flickering after a few seconds, looked like they were okay. He glanced round his desk for something to read, couldn't see anything, tried the bin at his feet for yesterday's paper but that had been emptied. All that was left was Judith West's Bible. He sighed. Opened it.

He flicked through, read a few chapters of Deuteronomy. Grim stuff. Was just about to shut it when he noticed an envelope tucked into the back. He pulled it out. The envelope was good quality, newish. He held the cheese roll between his teeth, opened the envelope up and took out a photograph.

It was a picture of a boy, very pale, about seven or eight years old. He was standing in a garden, smiling at the camera, toy truck in his hand. McCoy was just about to put it away when he noticed something. Peered closer. On the right-hand side of the photo, the branch of a monkey puzzle tree was just coming into frame.

He opened his Irn-Bru and took a drink. Studied the photo again. A wee boy about the same age as the one Judith West had claimed had gone missing standing in her back garden. The boy Reverend West said didn't exist. Could be anyone, he supposed, a nephew, a next-door neighbour's kid. Still.

He stood up and walked towards the back of the office where a young woman was sitting at a desk in the corner. Long hair, round wire specs and Laura Ashley dress making her look like she'd just stepped out of an Edwardian portrait. They'd been introduced when he'd been given the tour of the station on his first day, but he couldn't remember her name for the life of him now. What he did remember was that she did liaison with families. Acted as a bridge between them and the police.

She looked up as he approached. Seemed friendly enough.

"Hi there," said McCoy. "Wonder if you could help me out with something."

She smiled. "You can't remember my name, can you?"

"Sorry. Not good with names."

"Helen." She sounded resigned. McCoy obviously wasn't the first to forget her name. "What is it?"

"Need to check with the doctors round here, see if a boy called Jeremiah Michael West is registered anywhere. Also, the schools, see if he's enrolled in any of them. Check the birth certificates, maybe."

"You got an address?"

"Fifty Hillend Street."

She was scribbling on the notepad in front of her. "Date of birth?" He checked his notes from Judith's interview. "Twenty-second of June, nineteen sixty-six."

She looked up at him. "That it?"

"'Fraid so."

"Birth certificates are a nightmare—unless you're certain he was born in Glasgow?"

"I'm not," said McCoy.

"Great." She pushed the notepad away from her. "And why exactly can't you do all this yourself?"

"Eh, I thought this was your area of expertise."

"Couldn't be arsed, more like. Give me a couple of days. I know someone at the Registrar." Put her head down, started typing.

That was him told. McCoy walked back to his desk. He started writing his preliminary report on Malky's murder to give to Long. An hour or so later he was finished. Put it in a buff folder, sat back in his chair and lit up.

The new boy, Hood, emerged from the kitchen, mug of coffee in his hand, wandered over.

"How'd you get on with the witnesses from the bridge?"

"Fine, I think," said Hood. "I gathered the statements up and gave them to Mr. Watson. Their accounts all seemed much the same. The woman just climbed up on the wall and jumped. No hesitation."

McCoy still couldn't quite place his accent. "Where you from, Hood?"

"Born here but spent a long time in Elgin."

That explained it. Half Teuchter. "And what made you want to be a cop?"

Hood thought for a minute. "Because it's a good thing to do. Stand between the good and the bad in this world."

"Fair enough," said McCoy.

"The man who doesn't value himself, can't value anything else. We have a duty to do what we believe in to maintain order."

"That right?"

He nodded.

McCoy held out the buff folder. "Do me a favour—put this on Long's desk?"

Hood nodded, took it, and wandered off again. McCoy watched him go. Strange one, right enough. He looked at his watch. Swore. He was running late already.

SIXTEEN

Wattie was waiting outside the mortuary when he got there. Jacket off already, sleeves rolled up. Reading something scribbled on a bit of paper. He looked up as McCoy got out of the taxi.

"What's that?" asked McCoy.

"List of things I've got to get for the wee man's party." He folded it up, put it in his pocket. "Can't believe you're coming here voluntarily. I thought this place gave you the heebie-jeebies."

"It does, and I'm not," said McCoy. "Away in and get Phyllis, tell her I'll meet her at the steps."

McCoy sat down and lit up. The Saltmarket was busy as always, lawyers in suits with files under their arms going back and forth from the courts, punters in and out the shops, kids heading for the swings on Glasgow Green. Wasn't long before Wattie emerged from the mortuary with Phyllis Gilroy, the medical examiner. She sat down next to McCoy on the High Court steps and took her sunglasses off.

"I didn't perform the autopsy on Malcolm McCormack myself. Dr. Lawson did it." She held out a folder. "But he is very thorough."

"Want to just give us the highlights?" asked McCoy.

She sighed, opened it up, skimmed down the page. "As expected, cause of death was massive trauma to the frontal area of the brain. The half-brick." Kept skimming, eyes going back and forth.

"He was not in great shape, even for a man of his age: lungs destroyed by heavy smoking, liver enlarged . . ." More skimming, then she closed the file. "That's about it, bar the grisly details. Was that what you were expecting?"

"Pretty much," said McCoy. "How did you get on with the other stuff?"

"Oh aye, what other stuff is this then?" said Wattie, suddenly interested.

McCoy ignored him, and Phyllis dug into her bag and brought out another couple of files, sat them on her lap.

"What are they?" asked Wattie.

"People," said McCoy.

Wattie muttered something under his breath about someone being an arse.

"In answer to your original question, it's not common practice," said Phyllis. "Elderly alcoholics who die on the street are not routinely autopsied, unless there are suspicious circumstances and in the case of"—she flicked through the two files on her knee—"Jamie MacLeod or Charles Moody, there weren't any."

"So what happened to them?" asked McCoy.

"Charles Moody died in the hospital. The Royal. His death certificate was issued there by"—she peered at the file again—"Dr. Ahmed Ali. The cause of death was organ failure brought on by acute alcohol use. Standard stuff."

"Jamie MacLeod?" asked McCoy.

Phyllis closed the file. "That was the one the locum did a few weeks ago, the one you were at?"

McCoy nodded. "Govan Jamie."

"I have to agree with what Nichol has put here. Old age and life on the streets, drinking every day, I'm amazed he lived that long. His skin and the whites of his eyes were yellow. He had oedema—"

"Eh?" asked Wattie.

"Swollen feet and ankles. Caused by the beginnings of liver failure. In cases like that, it doesn't much matter what goes on the certificate. At some point, his heart would have stopped no matter what: we normally put heart failure."

"No autopsy?" asked McCoy.

Phyllis shook her head. "No call for it. Now, are you going to tell me why I've been digging out these reports?"

"It's a strange one," said McCoy. "There's a kid, Gerry, got Charles Moody to the Royal when he was dying, and he got to hear about how Govan Jamie died in the same way—both of them taken bad right after drinking some hooch: lots of pain, foaming at the mouth. He's convinced the two of them were poisoned, killed deliberately. But Gerry's about as flaky as they come. Think he's a bit touched, to be honest."

Wattie snorted. "You mean that wee guy with the giant suit that was with Liam the other day?"

"What happened to the bodies?" asked McCoy, ignoring Wattie.

"Buried at the Corporation site. Unmarked graves, card-board coffins. You know what happens in cases like this."

McCoy nodded. He did. All too well. "Will you do me a favour? If any more guys on the street die of alcohol poisoning, can you let me know and do an autopsy?"

Phyllis sighed. "Only for you, McCoy. Only for you." Put her sunglasses back on. "How's life with the film star?" she asked, grinning. "You should have seen Murray's face when I told him."

"It's good. She's away to the country for a couple of days."

"You must bring her round for dinner. I think I went to school with her cousin."

McCoy said he would.

"Now," said Wattie, once Phyllis had gone back into the mortuary, "are you going to tell me what we're really doing here? And please tell me that big-suited nutter Gerry has got some evidence."

McCoy dug in his pocket, pulled out Gerry's letter. Lit up as Wattie started to read.

"Who's Titch?" he asked, halfway through reading.

"That's Charles Moody," he explained.

Wattie frowned and kept reading. Half an Embassy Regal later, he sighed, folded the letter and handed it back.

"This isn't evidence. This is a hiding to nothing. And it's not what we're supposed to be doing. We should be concentrating on Malky McCormack's killing."

Wattie stood up. Yawned and stretched. "Gerry's a nutter, all right, but he couldn't have designed it better, could he? It's got your name written all over it."

"What's that supposed to mean?"

"People nobody cares about being murdered. All according to some guy who may or may not be touched. McCoy to the rescue. And just to add to the attraction, it's not the case Long wants us to be working on."

McCoy couldn't help himself. Smiled. "Think you're pretty damn smart, don't you, Mr. Watson?"

"Not smart, just someone who's had the misfortune to work for you for a few years." He pointed across the street to the ice-cream van parked outside the gates to the green. "C'mon, you can buy me a cone and tell me how we're going to catch the great Glasgow poisoner of nineteen seventy-five before I go off and buy a load of bloody balloons."

McCoy stood up, caught sight of someone across the road, standing in the doorway of the Whistlin' Kirk pub. Gerry. Black suit and black shoes, hair like fur, staring over at them. McCoy turned to tell Wattie to wait a minute, turned back, but Gerry was gone.

SEVENTEEN

McCoy walked out the station and lit up. Sun was starting to go down. Sky turning a vibrant orange. Was trying to decide whether to go to the Co-op and buy something for his tea or just get a cab to the Shish Mahal. Was a fairly good bet he'd end up there with his paper, a pint and a curry in front of him. Was just about to move off when he felt a tap on his shoulder. He turned and Rossi was standing there.

"Want something?" he asked through gritted teeth.

Rossi smiled, looked about as sincere as a used-car salesman. "How's about you and I go for a drink?"

Was the last thing McCoy expected. "What?"

"Think we got off on the wrong foot. So, by way of trying to make amends, let me buy you a drink. It's Friday night, been a long week. You don't have anything on, do you?"

He hadn't. Margo had gone up to the family pile for a few days, had a meeting with the estate manager for the property she'd inherited after her brother died. Had to decide what to do with it. Such were the problems of being an heiress.

Fuck it. The curry would have to wait. This was what he was here to do, get in with the Possil polis. "Okay. Let's go."

McCoy sat in the passenger seat, listened to Rossi chatting away about shifts. Something had to be up. Rossi must have an ulterior motive for his invitation; he'd find out what it was soon enough. His thoughts drifted back to the wee boy in the photo he'd found in Judith West's Bible. Maybe Helen whatshername would turn something up. Just have to wait and see. None of it made sense though. If there was a son, why would Reverend West be hiding it?

McCoy looked out the window and saw they were coming onto Great Western Road. "Where we going? Wintersgills?"

Rossi shook his head. "Mayfield Hotel. Got a nice wee lounge. I like it."

That was a surprise. The Mayfield Hotel may have had a nice wee lounge, but as far as McCoy could remember, it also had rooms that rented by the hour rather than the day. Rossi pulled the car over in West Princes Street. It was a funny part of town. The hotel was opposite Queen's Crescent, a quiet street that curved around a fenced-off garden, housed a weird assortment of Air Force clubs, the Burma Star Association headquarters, things like that. The Mayfield looked much the same as any other small hotel: sign in the window saying *Vacancies*, another one advertising a residents' TV room. A man hurried down the front stairs as they approached, head down, walking fast.

"You come here often?" asked McCoy as they walked up the steps.

Rossi nodded, pushed the door open. "A good few years."

The hallway of the hotel was warm, with deep pile carpet, a reception desk with no one behind it, the faint smell of air freshener. Piped music, sounded like Cliff Richard and the Shadows.

"This way," said Rossi.

McCoy followed him down the corridor past the TV room—nobody in it, silent TV showing the news—and into the lounge. Seemed to have a nautical theme for no real reason. Pictures of boats on the walls, miniature ships' steering wheels and toy yachts on the front of the bar in the corner. There were four or five round tables and a net on the ceiling, plastic fish caught in it.

Rossi rang the bell on the bar, and a man appeared a few seconds later. He was tall, broad, hair in a Brylcreem side shed. Couldn't have looked more like an ex-cop if he'd tried.

"All right, Sammy," he said amiably.

"All good, Tom," said Rossi. "This is McCoy, the new boy at the station. Thought I'd introduce him to the pleasures of the Driftwood."

Tom leant across the bar, hand out to shake. McCoy took it. Wasn't surprised when Tom's thumb slid across his fingers. No luck there, pal.

"Nice to meet you," said Tom. "What can I get you?"

McCoy couldn't see any pumps, so he asked for a whisky. Rossi got a gin and tonic, and they sat down.

"Tom used to be CID," said Rossi. "He's a good guy. Keeps the bar open if we're going at it."

"Good to know," said McCoy.

Rossi looked around as if he was surveying his kingdom, took a sip of his drink. "So how are you enjoying life at Possil?"

"Not much."

Rossi grinned. "Things'll get better, you'll see. Takes us a wee while to warm up."

"That garage up the road. Wattie said you knew something about it?"

Rossi nodded, pleased with himself. The man in the know. "It's one of Archie Andrews' places. Wasnae making enough money, so he torched it for the insurance."

"Smart," said McCoy.

"Don't get to be where Archie Andrews is by being a dunce." McCoy was just about to ask how Rossi knew about the garage when he heard laughter in the hallway. Long and another couple of senior detectives appeared. All suits and loosened ties and pushing and shoving. Hyped up. McCoy's stomach turned over; this must be the real reason Rossi had invited him for a drink. Good chance he wasn't going to get out of the Driftwood without a kicking.

Long and his pals seemed to be regulars. Barman knew their orders without asking and brought them over to the table as they sat down. One of the detectives whose name he couldn't remember held up his glass.

"Another week done," he said, and they all clinked glasses.

McCoy took a sip and realised they were all looking at him. Maybe this was it. A nice wee chat and then a kicking round the back of the hotel.

"You're not on the square, are you, McCoy?" said Long.

"'Fraid not," said McCoy. "They're not too keen on my sort."

One of the detectives laughed, said something about Papes not being good enough to get in.

Long lit up a Dunhill, blew the smoke in McCoy's face. "Even so, you've got a good reputation, a good polis."

"You chatting me up, Long?" asked McCoy. "A wee dance before you fuck me over?"

Long smiled. Didn't say anything.

McCoy decided to just get on with it. If he was going to get a kicking, he'd rather get it over with quick. "Tell me this, Long. If I'm such a great guy, why have you and your cronies been treating me like shit?"

Could hear one of the detectives draw in his breath. Long didn't flinch. Just took another drag of his cigarette, blew the smoke up into the ceiling. "We're a suspicious bunch, like to get the measure of a man before we make our minds up as to whether or not he's one of us."

Tom the barman reappeared, stood behind the bar polishing a glass. Didn't want to be left out. He looked like the kind of ex-copper who missed kicking the shit out of people and getting away with it.

"I already told you, Long. I'm not a Mason and I'm never going to be."

"That's not what I'm talking about." Long leant forward and looked McCoy in the eye. McCoy could smell the gin on his breath. Trace of some sort of aftershave. Stink of his Dunhill cigarettes. "Can you be trusted? Really trusted, Harry boy?"

McCoy shrugged. Was getting a bit sick of Long's Big Man act. "I suppose you'll just have to find out."

They locked eyes. No way McCoy was breaking away first. He didn't have to.

A big grin spread across Long's face. "Christ, McCoy, don't look so bloody worried!" He reached into the inside pocket of his jacket and pulled out five envelopes. "Every Friday, me and the boys come here to have a drink, wind down after the week and we share out the Friday money."

"Which is?"

"Just some tokens of appreciation from men like Tom here. Tokens to make sure we don't enquire about what happens up-stairs. Grateful landlords who know their pubs aren't going to have any trouble, shebeens that we avoid raiding, adult shops allowed to stay open, that sort of thing. You get me?"

McCoy nodded.

"And once in a while, we fry some bigger fish. Get a bit more involved, if you get my meaning, and that makes the Friday money look like spare change. So what I'm really ask-ing you, Harry boy, is: are you okay with that? With helping out sometimes, making sure everything moves along nicely? Getting your hands dirty, if needs be?"

McCoy answered straight away, no hesitation. "You can count on me. You don't need to worry about that. Need some reward for this bloody job sometimes."

Long handed McCoy an envelope, held up his glass and turned to the rest of them.

"Gentlemen, a toast! To the newest member of the Friday Club!"

SATURDAY

14TH JUNE 1975

EIGHTEEN

H ow much was in the envelope?" asked Chief Inspector Murray, taking a sip of his tea.

"Forty quid," said McCoy.

"You didn't spend it, did you?"

"Too bloody right I did! I had to buy them drinks all night, pretend I was celebrating being a member of their stupid bloody club. No way was I spending my own money to do that."

They were sitting at the big table in Phyllis's kitchen, french windows open to the sunny back garden. At the end of the garden, a good twenty yards away, a table and chairs were set out beneath a tree. Phyllis was sitting there, cup of tea in hand, *Glasgow Herald* spread out in front of her. To complete the feeling of domestic bliss, Murray was dressed in his day-off clothes. Cords, brown brogues and an open-necked shirt. McCoy took a sip of his tea, feeling a bit rough after last night's drinking. Suddenly occurred to him.

"Phyllis?" he shouted.

She looked up.

"You need any help with the garden?"

She nodded immediately. "God, yes, it's too big for one person. I didn't know you were interested in gardening?"

"Me? Oh no, not me. Got a pal who'd love to help you out. Doesn't need paid, just loves working with plants. He's good at it too."

"That sounds ideal," said Phyllis. "But I'd need to pay him something. What's his name?"

"Jumbo."

Murray stared at him. "Cooper's bodyguard, you mean? Here? Are you bloody mad?"

"He's harmless. Like a wee boy. Doesn't know any of Cooper's business."

Murray didn't look too happy. "He better bloody not." He scratched at the reddish stubble on his chin. "It's hard to believe Long, of all people, is in on it. Always thought he was a good man. I thought it'd be one of the Glasgow boys there organising it."

"Oh, he's in on it, all right, up to his arse in it," said McCoy. "Having said that, it's not exactly the biggest case of corruption I've ever come across."

Murray harrumphed. Started packing his pipe. "Corruption is corruption. Always starts small. And a fish rots from the head down. If they're happy taking money from the small fry, then they'll end up doing worse."

"Think that's what he was trying to imply, that they go further than skimming protection money for the bad boys of Possil. And was I okay with that."

"Wouldn't surprise me."

"So what do I do now?"

"You keep tight to them. Make sure they trust you. Keep your eyes and ears open. We need to know who's behind these post office robberies. They've been getting more brutal each time. You know what happened at Balmore Road, don't you?"

McCoy nodded.

"Postmaster got shot and died in the hospital later. Nasty stuff."

"You still convinced someone in the station's helping them do it?"

Murray nodded. Lit up his pipe, momentarily disappeared in a cloud of tobacco smoke. Waved it away with his hand. "Happens the same way for every robbery: someone makes sure the police get there just too late and someone makes sure the car gets away."

"Long?"

"I would think so. He's the station boss. Who are the other candidates?"

McCoy shrugged. "Rossi's a follower. Wee slimy guy. Can't see him setting anything up. Other two just seemed along for the ride."

Phyllis's voice wafted over from the garden. "Hector . . ."

"Shite," muttered Murray, "she's got a nose like a bloody blood-hound." Shouted over, "Just putting it out now, darling." Took a deep drag from his pipe before he did. "And," he continued, "Long's got an ex-wife and two kids to pay for in Newcastle and a new wife here with a baby on the way. Forty quid a week isn't going to make much of a dent in those bills."

He stood up, walked over to the Aga and put the kettle on again.

"How are you getting on with the restructuring?" asked McCoy. "Are we all Strathclyde boys now?"

"Sadly, we are," said Murray. "Amount of bloody waste beggars belief. Anything with City of Glasgow Police on it, even if it's brand-new stuff, gets binned. No longer usable. Stationery bill to change everything to the new logo would make your eyes water."

"All for the greater good though," said McCoy.

"We'll see about that. Anyway, more importantly, Phyllis tells me it's still going strong with the esteemed Margo Lindsay. She's a good-looking woman, you know."

"I noticed."

"How did that happen? According to the paper, she's a real lefty, not the type to associate with an oppressor of the people like yourself."

"I met her last year, her brother's case. You remember?"

Murray nodded. "Hard to forget. Evil bastard that he was. What does she have to say about that?"

"Not much. She hadn't seen him for years. Had an argument with him about recruiting young guys for his private army, never really spoke to each other since."

"And you got together how?"

"I was walking through George Square the other week, and there she was, at some rally for the shipyard workers. I stopped some arse of a uniform arresting her. She took me out to dinner to say thanks, and that was that. Kismet."

"You're punching above your weight there."

McCoy sighed. "So everybody keeps telling me."

Murray put fresh mugs of tea on the table and sat down. "How's Watson getting on?"

"Fine. You need to stop worrying about him—he's turning into a good cop. We should tell him why we're really at Possil."

Murray looked doubtful. "Let's get you in with the bloody Friday Club first. Let's hope he's not picking up your bad habits."

"I don't have any."

"Yes, you bloody do, and waifs and strays is one of them. Which reminds me: Phyllis told me about your wild goose chase."

"Might not be," said McCoy. "Might be a couple of murders."

"No, they bloody aren't! Alkies living on the street don't have a long life expectancy. Not with the stuff they drink. Besides, who would want to murder some random tramp?"

McCoy shrugged. Wasn't going to get into this if he could help it. It would only make Murray angrier. And no way was he mentioning the mysterious Michael West and the photograph of the boy in the back garden.

"You hear me, McCoy?" growled Murray.

McCoy saluted. Stood up. "Loud and clear."

"You're there to keep an eye on what's going on at that station. That's your job, so no chasing after alkies."

McCoy nodded.

"Remember, Phyllis has got enough to do without doing favours for you."

"Yes, Herr Murray."

"Don't be so bloody cheeky. Just get in with Long, be pals. Find out what those bastards are really up to."

NINETEEN

In a fit of largesse McCoy had agreed to drive Cuthbert up to St. Teresa's for Vigil Mass. A fit he was regretting. The combination of the sun baking through the windows and Cuthbert's neglect of personal hygiene was a potent one. McCoy rolled down the window, tried to breathe through his mouth.

St. Teresa's sat on a large green space overlooking the bottom of Saracen Street. A twisting driveway led up the hill to the big brick church. McCoy pulled in beside a Ford Capri and got out the car as fast as he could. Lit up to try and smell something else, even if it was only cigarette smoke. Cuthbert had wandered over to the edge of the car park and seemed to be coughing up most of his lungs.

McCoy called over. "You okay?"

Cuthbert held a hand up, spat prodigiously and wandered back. "Too many bloody cars in this town now, exhaust gets into your lungs."

To say nothing of the forty Capstan a day, thought McCoy.

"You all right to go in?"

Cuthbert nodded. "Never better."

St. Teresa's had been built in the fifties when church attendances were still huge. Designed to accommodate a couple of hundred people, the church's imposing size made Saturday's little crowdscattered amongst the pews look even more pathetic. Cuthbert took two hymn sheets from the smiling woman at the door, handed one to McCoy, and they sat down in one of the pews at the back.

"Is she here?" said McCoy.

Cuthbert pointed to the front of the church. "Second row from the front, blue coat."

Norma McGregor was sitting alone, head bent in prayer. Just as McCoy got up to go and speak to her, the priest walked up to the altar and began the service. McCoy sat back down.

"Great," he hissed at Cuthbert. "Now we're going to have to sit through the whole bloody thing."

Cuthbert removed his bunnet and examined the hymn sheet. "I'm sure a little bit of atonement for your past sins won't do you any harm, Harry McCoy."

And with that, he stood up and launched, in a surprisingly loud and tuneful voice, into the first line of "All My Rivers Flow to Thee."

McCoy had sat through enough services in enough chapels to know exactly what he was in for. Three hymns, two readings, a sermon, communion and a prayer. Unless the priest was particularly slow, he had about forty minutes to kill staring at the back of Norma McGregor's head before he could talk to her about who would have wanted to kill Malky.

He started to drift away as the priest droned on. If Cuthbert was right and Norma had come into money, what did that have to do with her brother's murder? Whoever killed Malky certainly thought he knew something: what if they thought his sister did too?

A line was forming to take communion. Norma stayed put, didn't get up to join them.

Cuthbert nudged McCoy. "Guilty conscience. She normally takes communion. Must be something on her mind, something she hasn't confessed."

McCoy drifted off again, stared at the stained-glass window behind the altar, the low summer sun outside making the red and purple panes glow. Christ sitting on a throne surrounded by his disciples.

Felt a dig in his ribs. Cuthbert had a triumphant grin on his face. "See who just walked in?" he said. "Don't doubt me again, Harry Bloody McCoy."

McCoy turned.

Duncan Kent and his wife were easing their expensively dressed selves into a pew by the back door. Duncan Kent was wearing a dark suit, white shirt and sober navy-blue tie. His wife looked like she'd given his cheque book a severe battering. Beige tailored suit, beige high heels, hair and make-up immaculate. They looked more like they were on their way to Rogano's for dinner than a Vigil Mass in a shitty part of Glasgow. And now that McCoy thought about it, Kent was as Protestant as they came. A Rangers-supporting Mason. Had to be something important to get him to set foot in a Catholic church.

The service eventually drew to an end. The priest said the final prayer, blessed everyone, and then it was over. McCoy turned, but Kent and his wife were already walking out the door. The congregation stood up and started shuffling towards the exit. Norma hadn't moved. McCoy went to approach her, but Cuthbert held his arm.

"Maybe give her a minute. She's still praying. Her brother's just died, remember."

Being in a church seemed to be turning Cuthbert into the very model of consideration. They sat for five minutes or so waiting for her to finish, then Cuthbert stood up.

"C'mon, I need a fag."

Last thing McCoy expected to see when they stepped out of the church was Kent and his wife standing in the car park. "What are they waiting for?"

"Not what," said Cuthbert. "Who."

McCoy lit up and handed Cuthbert his fags. Then he realised Norma had already walked past them and was hurrying across the car park.

"Shite," said McCoy. "How did she get past us?" He started walking after her.

Duncan Kent suddenly stepped out from behind his car, hands held up. Norma stopped dead in her tracks, looked like she'd seen a ghost. Kent grabbed her arm, leant in and hissed something into her ear.

She tried to push him away, but Kent held on tight, kept talking. He went to grab her other arm and Norma took her chance, brought the heel of her stiletto down onto Kent's foot. Hard. His face contorted in agony and Norma wriggled free.

"Leave me alone! I'll tell them! I'll fucking tell them if you don't!"

She started to say something else, but no sound came out, just her lips moving. She stopped, looked wide-eyed, terrified, tried to walk away, but it was like her legs weren't working properly. She stumbled. Kent reached out to catch her, but it was too late. She fell headfirst onto the concrete with a sickening crack. Must have been wearing a wig that slipped off, and a dark patch started spreading out on the concrete beneath her.

For a few seconds nobody moved. McCoy felt a bump as the priest barged past him and ran over to where Norma was lying. He grabbed her hand, looked up. "Call an ambulance! Quick!"

McCoy ran towards his car, would be quicker to call it in on the radio. Had to jump out the way as Kent's Jaguar drove past him, out the gates and accelerated towards town. Kent looked grim, hands gripping the wheel. His wife was holding a hanky up to her shocked face, trying to wipe away the tears.

TWENTY

Wattie and McCoy watched the ambulancemen roll the wheeled stretcher carrying Norma McGregor towards the waiting ambulance and load her into the back.

Wattie turned away from the departing vehicle. Didn't look happy.

"You should have told me you were coming here with Cuthbert," he said. "It's work. I shouldn't have had to hear you on the bloody radio. You're supposed to keep me in the know about Malky's case."

"I know," said McCoy. "I'm too used to being a one-man band. Sorry."

Wattie didn't seem convinced. "Don't give us it. You haven't been a one-man band for years. You just tell me stuff when it suits you. Anything else you're hiding?"

McCoy thought of Murray, the Friday Club, the envelope Long had handed him. The fact he planned on going to Reverend West's church tomorrow.

"Nope," he said, lighting up. "Not a sausage."

"You think she'll be okay?" said Wattie.

McCoy shrugged. "Didn't look too good—was like she'd had a stroke or something."

"You said Kent was talking to her? What was he saying?"

"Don't know, I couldn't hear. Whatever he said to her, she was scared. She said if he didn't leave her alone, she'd tell everyone."

"Tell them what?" asked Wattie.

"God knows. Kent must have come just to see her—can't think of any other reason for a bluenose like him to be at Mass." He dropped his cigarette on the ground and stood on it. "Cuthbert seems to think he had something to do with Malky's death."

"Duncan Kent?" asked Wattie. "No way. Far as I know, he's well out the game, too busy building bloody shopping centres and getting his photo in the paper. And isn't the wife some kind of Lady Bountiful? *The elegantly dressed Kathy Kent opens yet another children's home.*"

McCoy nodded. "I can't really see him having anything to do with it either, but we can get him in on Monday, see if we can push him a bit. Wouldn't hold your breath though. Kent's been interviewed more times than you've had hot dinners—chances of him letting anything slip are zilch."

Wattie looked at his watch. "That's eight o'clock. Me off the clock. Saturday night, after all." He started walking down the hill to his car. "Come on. You can buy me a drink to make up for being a dick."

Twenty-One

They decided to head towards home and stop at a pub on the way—the Victoria, if McCoy had anything to do with it. That way he could get a bit pissed, get a fish supper and walk home after. They didn't make it that far. They were sitting at the traffic lights on Union Street, McCoy pretending to listen to Wattie telling him that Wee Duggie had bitten some other wee boy at nursery, when McCoy turned the police radio up.

"Unit in attendance at reported fatality at banks of Clyde at Carlton Place and the suspension bridge."

McCoy nodded down to the left. They were only minutes away. "Want to take a look?"

"Nope. I'm off work, and so are you."

They were. But curiosity got the better of McCoy. "Just a wee look?"

Wattie sighed, pushed the indicator down, and turned into Jamaica Street.

As they drove over the Wellington Bridge McCoy could see a couple of panda cars, lights spinning, parked in Carlton Place by the river. Mortuary van reversing into a space between the pandas.

"Probably some poor bugger who's chucked himself in," said Wattie.

"Probably," said McCoy. "Soon find out."

Carlton Place ran parallel to the river, a wrought-iron fence separating it from the tangled bushes of the bank and the sluggish brown water of the Clyde itself. It was all offices, law-yers and accountants, so it was quiet at night, offices shut. Not many people around. They pulled in by the mortuary van and got out.

Hood was standing by the suspension bridge, stopping peo-ple walking over to the cars to have a look, asking them to keep moving.

McCoy walked up, nodded hello. "What's going on?"

Hood stood up straighter and pointed over the fence at the riverbank. "There's a body down there. One of the Sally Army blokes called it in. A down-and-out, it looks like."

"That right?" said McCoy.

"Shite," said Wattie. "Now we're going to have to go and look. Why can't it have been some posh businessman? Then you wouldn't care, and we could go and get a pint."

"Come on, it'll take five minutes," said McCoy. "Just want to see if I know him."

Wattie swore under his breath, followed him through a gap in the fence and into the long grass and bushes. The closer you got to the river, the dirtier and oilier the undergrowth became. Halfway down, in the lee of some bushes, were the remains of a fire, discarded cans, flattened-out cardboard to sit on. Looked as much like a kids' den as anything else.

"This bugger better have been strangled or stabbed," said Wattie as he shuffled down the bank trying not to slip. "If he's been poisoned, I'm going to be really pissed off."

McCoy nodded to the two uniforms by the body, showed them his warrant card, and squatted down beside the man.

He hadn't been shot or stabbed. He was sprawled out on the grass, an anorak on, jeans, platform shoes. His head was back, mouth open, greenish bile drying on his chin. Looked like he'd had a fit. Both hands were closed tight, arms stretched out. He looked fifty-odd, reddish-brown hair and beard, pair of specs lying next to his head.

"You know him?" said Wattie.

"Nope." McCoy stood up.

"I do." A young guy in a grey Salvation Army uniform was making his way down the bank. Looked more like a rugby player than a man of God. Full beard, neat brown hair, broad shoulders. "That's Callum Munroe. He comes to our soup kitchen at the end of the week when the money's run out. Has a problem with the drink, that's where all his money goes." He held his hand out to shake. "Kenny Lowell."

McCoy shook it, introduced himself. "You find him, did you?"

Lowell nodded. "There's often a few of our customers down here. They like it. It's pretty well hidden, hard to see them from the bridge; they get left alone. I came down to tell them the soup kitchen was about to open, but there was no one around. Just Callum lying there. I thought he was asleep at first but . . ." He looked down at the man. "God rest his soul."

McCoy glanced around the scene. All the discarded cans were old and rusty, pictures of the Lager Lovelies fading away. Callum hadn't been drinking from them.

"There should be a bottle somewhere," he said. "What was he drinking?"

"I didn't see one," said Lowell. "Maybe he was with some others, and they took it?"

"Maybe," said McCoy.

He looked at Lowell again. There was something familiar about him. "Do I know you from somewhere?"

"I don't think so," said Lowell. "Obviously we have dealings with the police from time to time, but I don't think we've met."

"Your face is familiar," said McCoy.

"Ah." Lowell looked a bit sheepish. "I know what it might be. I'm on a recruiting poster. Think I was the only officer they could find that was under twenty-five. Trying to get younger people to join us. Maybe that's it."

"Must be."

Lowell turned his attention to the road. "If that's it, I should get back and help. The hall is in South Portland Street, just up there. There's quite a queue of people already. Lentil soup tonight. Word spreads—it's always popular."

"That's fine," said McCoy. "One of the uniformed officers will come and take your statement."

Lowell had just disappeared up onto the road when a female voice rang out. "I'm going to kill you, Harry McCoy."

Phyllis was walking down the bank towards them. Brown lab coat over a multi-coloured dress, white rainboots completing the look. "I was at a very nice dinner at my old neighbour's in Park Circus, just about to enjoy my beef Wellington when I got the call. I've left Murray there. Not happy having to chat with people he doesn't know, especially people who don't want to talk about policing. Told me to tell you he's going to kill you too."

"That makes three of us," said Wattie. "All I wanted was a bloody pint and now I'm standing here trying not to breathe in the smell of the bloody river."

Phyllis sniffed. Grimaced. "Yes, it does have a tang of sewage about it. The picturesque trout stream it once was is no more, sadly." She looked at McCoy. "But I made a promise, so here I am."

She crouched down by Callum Munroe's body, took a torch from her bag, and shone it in the dead man's face. Glassy eyes fixed on the sky. Took out a tongue depressor and used it to open his mouth further. Peered in.

She stood up, broke the tongue depressor in two and put it in a plastic waste bag. "Don't hold me to it—"

"Provisionally."

"Provisionally," she said, "I'm pretty certain he died of pulmonary asphyxiation."

"Which is?" asked McCoy.

"I think he choked on his own vomit. When the amount of alcohol in the blood is very high it suppresses the gag reflex. You throw up and it goes back down into the lungs."

"Lovely," said Wattie. "Now you've managed to put me off my pint."

"Will you be able to tell if he was deliberately poisoned?" asked McCoy.

"Possibly," said Phyllis. "It rather depends on what he was poisoned with—if he was, that is. I'll let you know as soon as I do."

"Thanks for this," said McCoy. "Might be important."

"It's a wild goose chase, if you ask Mr. Murray." She smiled and walked back up the bank to her car to help her assistant with the rest of the equipment.

"Callum Munroe must be the only down-and-out in Glasgow you don't know," said Wattie. "You're slipping. Now can we go for a bloody drink?"

McCoy nodded, but he wasn't really listening. He was thinking. This was the third dead down-and-out roughly the same age as his dad. If someone was deliberately poisoning men like that, he had to get a hold of his dad and quick. Warn him. Trouble was, he had no idea where to find him.

They walked up to the street and found Hood still standing there.

"You on for the night?" said Wattie.

Hood nodded. "All for some drunken waste of space."

McCoy bristled. "That waste of space is somebody's son, somebody's brother, somebody's father. Don't you forget it."

Walked away before he said anything else. Anything he'd regret.

"What's that about?" he heard Hood ask.

"Harry McCoy, that's what that's about," said Wattie. "You'll learn."

SUNDAY

15TH JUNE 1975

The Church of Christ's Suffering turned out to be a small wooden hall with a green metal roof at the wrong end of Auckland Street. McCoy's heart sank when he saw it. No way was he going to be able to get in and out without being seen. He was going to have to sit through another bloody church service. Checked his watch. Ten to six. Time for a fag beforehand.

The congregation, such as it was, arrived in dribs and drabs. A tiny wee woman with a stick and callipers on her legs. A couple clutching big Bibles. A family—man, woman, two little boys—all dressed in their Sunday best. Couldn't be more than twenty people. Suddenly occurred to him that—unshaven, in a checked shirt he hadn't bothered to iron, well-thumbed Bible in hand—he probably fitted right in. A hymn started up; he knew he couldn't avoid it any more. McCoy dropped his cigarette on the pavement, stamped on it and headed for the door.

Felt eyes on him when he walked in, a new worshipper. The hall was arranged like most churches, rows of pews facing a simple altar. It was also boiling hot. Sun had been baking down on it all day. Only two windows, looked like they hadn't been opened for years. Soon as McCoy sat down in the back row he started sweating. There was a painted banner hanging above the altar. Black words on red.

ALL MUST SUFFER FOR ALL TO HEAL.

Cheery stuff.

He was just undoing the top buttons of his shirt when West

appeared at the altar, black suit, hands clasped in prayer. He led them in a few hymns to start. Ones McCoy didn't know. Wasn't sure if that was because they were Protestant ones or because they were special ones for West's church. After that was done, West waited until everyone had quietened down, stared at each of the congregation in turn and started to speak.

"My friends, we have to understand that evil is not an abstract notion. It is here, living amongst us, in this church, even in my own home." He stopped, looked at them. "And that evil rose up two days ago and took hold of my beloved wife, Judith. It told her that she would be better to take her own life than to pray and ask forgiveness. It took her by the hand and led her out of our home and onto Balmore Road, where it whispered to her, forked tongue in her ear, and told her she should jump off a bridge and end her life."

McCoy saw that the wee woman with the callipers was crying at this point, then realised that most of the rest of the congregation were crying too. Whatever West was, he was an old-fashioned preacher, the type you used to find in seaside tents and revival meetings. The type that knows how to work a crowd. And he wasn't finished yet.

"It breaks my heart to say this, but we all know where Judith has gone." A moan from the couple with the Bibles, a cry of "No!" from the man with the family. "She has gone to the place without love, the place of eternal damnation that is hell. Make no mistake, God is very clear, very clear. Suicide is a sin. A venal sin. To place your will over God's is unforgivable."

West stopped again, and for a moment it seemed as if he was going to break down. Then he steeled himself, wiped his forehead with a hanky, and grasped the sides of the lectern with both hands.

He spoke quietly and deliberately. "My wife is in the place of no love because evil managed to find a way to entrap her. You all knew Judith, all loved Judith as I did. She was a kind and faithful servant of the Lord and of this church. Ask yourself this, my friends: if a woman like that can fall, be tricked by an evil spirit, could you?"

He looked round the congregation again. Some stared into his eyes; some, heads down, were too scared to meet his gaze. McCoy directed his eyes to the banner behind the altar. Hoped it would be over soon.

"And when I ask that, I know the answer: each one of us could. So what we must do is work harder to show God our commitment, our determination and our suffering. As Christ suffered on the cross, as he suffered from the lashes and the kicks of the Roman soldiers, the crown of thorns rammed on his head, the sword that penetrated his side, so too must we suffer so we can know his healing."

He wiped his brow with the hanky again; the heat in the hall was getting worse.

"Go home tonight, my friends. Start work anew. Suffer for us all to heal together. Only then can you know the true path of Christ, the true pain of the road to the cross, and only then will you feel the glory of his love."

He made his way to the altar, stumbled, just about fell. The white shirt under his suit was wet with sweat. He held up his hand.

"I ask you to forgive me, friends. I am very tired. Judith's passing has made me examine my faith anew. I have been heading down that difficult path in the past two days and will be for many more days to come. I am in a desert trying to find a way forward. I take on the burden of Judith's fate. Could I have done more? Could I have prayed more? Could I have saved her from the serpent whispering in her ear?" He shook his head. "My friends, I don't know. The only way forward is to ask for the comfort of Christ, for his love and forgiveness."

The church was silent, all eyes on West.

"I bid you goodnight and I ask you to go home with the

Lord and thoughts of poor Judith in your heart." A tired smile. "Maybe a shorter ceremony does us all good once in a while. Let's finish with a reading from the First Epistle of Peter . . ."

McCoy didn't stay for that. He walked out the hall and into the warm June evening. He sat down on the wall opposite, flapped his open shirt to try to cool off and watched the congregation leave. Some of them were still in tears, some had the light of renewed belief shining in their eyes. Five minutes later West appeared, locked the hall behind him. He saw McCoy and wandered over, heavy bag over his shoulder. He really did look worn out, like all his strength had gone.

"I thought I saw you there, Mr. McCoy. Did you enjoy the sermon? Did you get anything from it?"

"Sorry to disappoint you. I wasn't there for the good of my soul. I was there to return this." He held out Judith's Bible.

West's face crumpled when he saw it. "Thank you. It means a lot to me." He took the book and held it to his chest.

"This was in it." McCoy showed him the envelope and took out the photo.

West examined it closely.

"Recognise him, do you?"

West shook his head. "I'm afraid I don't."

"That's your back garden, isn't it? The monkey puzzle tree. Boy aged about eight. Why do you think Judith had this photograph?"

"I have no idea," said West. "It could be a neighbour's child, anyone. The extent of the disturbance of her mind was vast. As I said, she sometimes believed our unborn child had survived and grown up. Maybe this is just a manifestation of her despair."

"So it's not Michael?"

West sighed. "There is no Michael, Mr. McCoy," he said. "There never was."

"In that case, you won't mind if I keep the photo?" said McCoy.

"Not at all," said West. "Means nothing to me."

McCoy turned to go.

"Don't let yourself get dragged down by this, Mr. McCoy," said West. "Don't go looking for things that were never there. My wife was not well and met a fate I would not wish on anyone. And I am left here alone to grieve. Have some mercy on us. Pray for us if you can."

TWENTY-THREE

McCoy walked up Auckland Road, trying to work out what he really thought was going on. The easiest explanation was the obvious one: Judith West was mentally disturbed, mind broken by her miscarriage, so disturbed she couldn't take it any more and killed herself. It made sense, wrapped everything up neatly, so why was he still carrying the photo of the wee boy in the garden around with him?

He turned into Balmore Road, just at the Glen Douglas pub, and stopped. Gerry was standing by the door with a hat out, asking the punters for money when they went in or out. Didn't seem to be having much luck as far as McCoy could see. Most of the blokes just hurried past him, didn't give him a second glance. Gerry was chancing his arm; if the landlord found out he was there, he would chase him. Must be desperate.

"Gerry! What you doing up this way?"

Gerry pointed down the hill. "I picked some flowers from Springburn Park to lay down where the lady jumped."

"Did you know her?"

"Not really. Her church ran a soup kitchen sometimes, in the winter. I used to go. She was nice."

Gerry nodded. Looked down at the ground. "One sermon was enough for me. Too much about suffering, not enough about helping." He took the two or three coins out the bunnet, put it on his head. "Not doing very well here. Might try down at the Saracen."

They started down the hill towards Saracen Street and

the police station. Walked past the bridge where Judith West had jumped. Gerry wasn't the only one who had left flowers; there were a few bunches on the wall, all wilting in the heat. McCoy watched him stop, arrange his bunch; seemed to be mumbling some kind of prayer. Finished, he looked up at the sky.

"Done?" said McCoy.

Gerry nodded and they started walking again.

"There's another body," said McCoy. "Found him by the Clyde last night. Callum Munroe. You know him?"

"A wee bit. When I was drinking. I shouldn't say this about him now he's dead but I didn't like him much."

"Why not?"

"He was a bully. Used to pick on people, take money off them sometimes, take their bottle and not give it back."

"He pick on you?"

"Sometimes."

Gerry was having a hard time keeping up, and McCoy was anything but a fast walker. His gait was unsteady, like he had difficulty making his legs work. McCoy realised that was why one of his shoes was almost gone; one foot constantly dragged behind him.

"We're going to do an autopsy. See if he was poisoned," said McCoy.

"That's good."

McCoy stopped. "That it? I thought you'd be delighted."

Gerry tried to smile.

"You okay?"

Gerry looked anything but. Thinner than the last time McCoy had seen him, dark smudges under his eyes.

"I'll be okay," he said. "Sometimes things are just hard. I'm scared a lot of the time, tired all the time, scared that if I died no one would even notice."

"Where you staying tonight?"

"Not sure. It's a nice night. Back to Springburn Park, maybe."

McCoy dug in his pocket. Handed him a few notes. "Stay at the Great Northern tonight. You look like you need a good night's sleep, son."

Gerry took the money, put it in the pocket of his suit.

"Autopsy results will be a couple of days," McCoy said. "Come and see me at the station then, eh? I'll let you know what the story is."

Gerry seemed too tired to argue or to say thank you. McCoy watched him make his difficult way down to Saracen Street. How long would someone like Gerry survive when the winter came? He looked at his watch. Getting on for seven. Maybe it was Gerry, but he felt like company tonight, didn't want to be alone. Decided to go and see Cooper. Sit in his back garden, drink until he felt better or didn't care any more. Either one would do.

TWENTY-FOUR

That right?" said McCoy, taking a swig of the can Cooper had given him from the cupboard in the kitchen.

Jumbo nodded. "I took the cutting from one of the plants in the park. They're coming on well now."

McCoy looked over at a row of small plants at the edge of the flower bed in Cooper's garden. Cooper had gone in to make a phone call, and Jumbo had taken the opportunity to tell McCoy all about what he had been doing in the garden that week.

Jumbo was explaining how he'd maybe put too much fertiliser in round the roses and that he was a bit worried he'd over-watered the pampas grass. McCoy drifted away. Couldn't get the picture of Gerry walking down the road, head down, foot dragging, out of his head. Maybe he'd talk to Liam, see if he could keep an eye out for him. Gerry was right about West though: too much suffering. Seemed to be the whole point of his church: tell people that unless they suffered, they wouldn't be saved. Taking the message of Christianity too far, McCoy thought. Took another slug of his can. He wasn't going to think about it any more tonight; he was going to sit in the garden, enjoy the weather and get slowly pissed.

Iris appeared in the doorway, face tripping her as always. She seemed to be the only woman left in Glasgow who based her look on Joan Crawford in her heyday. Red lipstick, satin turban, eyebrows painted on. McCoy had known her for years, since she used to run one of Cooper's shebeens. Now she had become a kind of housekeeper in the big house. Hadn't made her any happier as far as he could see.

"Jumbo?" She held out a one-pound note. "Do me a favour and run over to the chemist, get me some Askit Powders, eh?"

"Got a headache?" asked McCoy.

"Aye. Started as soon as you turned up. Funny, that."

"Off you go, Jumbo. You can tell me about the other plants when you get back," said McCoy.

"The dahlias at the back—"

"Will you shut up about your bloody plants," said Iris. "McCoy's not interested. Take this money and go. My head's bursting."

Jumbo's face fell.

"That's where you're wrong, Iris. I am interested," said McCoy. "Way you've changed this garden is amazing, Jumbo. So amazing I've got you another gardening job."

"What?" asked Cooper, appearing out the back door and sitting down on a deckchair.

Jumbo was looking at McCoy as if he'd told him he'd won the pools, Cooper as if he'd like to strangle him.

"Working for a very nice lady who needs some help with her garden—it's too big a job for just her," said McCoy. "I told her you would be ideal."

"Who's that?" asked Cooper.

"Never you mind," said McCoy. "That's between me and Jumbo."

Jumbo grinned.

"Away and get Iris's medicine," said Cooper. "I need to speak to Mr. McCoy."

Jumbo took Iris's pound note, walked back into the house, big smile on his face.

"You trying to annoy me?" said Cooper.

"Nope," said McCoy. "It'll do him good. Give him a bit of independence."

"I'll tell you what will do him good: me not toeing his arse and—"

Cooper never got to finish his sentence. Jumbo appeared back in the doorway, panic on his face.

"Mr. Cooper! You have to come! Now!"

McCoy had never seen a car on fire before, but he had now. They stood back from the front window and watched it burn. The fire had totally engulfed Cooper's Jaguar, only the occasional glimpse of the bodywork visible through the guttering flames. The smell of burning rubber and petrol was everywhere, thick black smoke spiralling up into the darkening sky, already higher than the house.

"What happened?" asked Cooper.

"I was just going for Iris's messages, stopped to look at the lawn, was looking a bit dry—"

"Jumbo, for fuck sake!"

"Sorry. Then a car come along, very slow, stopped right there." Jumbo pointed at the road at the bottom of Cooper's driveway. "And a man got out the back, threw something and then the car just went boom! Flames everywhere."

"You see what kind of car it was?" asked McCoy.

Jumbo nodded. "A Cortina, blue."

"Great," said McCoy, "just like half the bloody cars in Glasgow. You see the man who threw it?"

"He had a scarf and an anorak with the hood up. I didn't see his face. I'm sorry."

"That's okay, Jumbo, not your fault."

The flames died down. Everything that could burn must have done, only the bare twisted metal left. Cooper led them outside, his hands balled into fists. A few of the neighbours had come out of their houses too, were standing in groups. A kid with a camera tried to get closer, the mum grabbed him by the collar and pulled him back.

The heat had been so strong it had blistered the paint on the front door of the house, the window frames too. The concrete driveway was black now, scorched. The metal of the car body was glowing red-hot, mangled into distorted shapes. McCoy told Jumbo to get the garden hose fixed up, get it spraying onto the remains of the car. Jumbo nodded, ran round the back of the house.

Cooper was staring at the burnt-out shell of the car, eyes far away.

"You okay?" said McCoy.

"Me? I'm brand new." He grinned. "Looks like the war has finally started."

TWENTY-FIVE

I t didn't take Cooper long to assemble the troops. Within an hour or two the house was full of young guys in denims drinking from cans, joking with each other, telling war stories. Someone had put on the new Bowie album; "Win" was playing over and over. There was no reason for McCoy to stay there, but he did. Something about the high spirits and the excitement was infectious, despite where it was going to lead.

He sat down at the kitchen table next to Paul Cooper. Only seventeen, and already he was almost as big and broad as his dad, same blond hair, same big smile. The heir apparent. He had three Stanley knives on the table in front of him, a pile of spare blades and a pile of matches. He took one of the matches and sliced it longways with the Stanley knife. Unscrewed the side of the knife and laid a spare blade on top of the one that was already there. Carefully inserted the half matchstick between the blades and screwed the knife shut again.

"What's all that for?" asked McCoy.

Paul grinned, held up the knife, the two blades separated now, a quarter of an inch between them. "You slash someone with this? Cut's too wide to stitch properly, makes a right mess of someone's face. Like tramlines."

"Ah," said McCoy, wishing he had never asked. "You no worried about something like that happening to you?"

"Nope," said Paul, grinning. "No fucker'll ever get close enough to do anything to this pretty face."

McCoy hoped he was right. No one needed to have their face

destroyed at seventeen. Jumbo was wandering round handing out cans of lager from a cardboard box. Some of the boys were nice to him, said hello, said thank you, some just treated him like a waiter, took a can without even looking at him.

"You do me a favour, son?" said McCoy.

"Sure."

"Watch out for Jumbo, eh?"

"I'll try," said Paul. "But he'll be with my dad, and you know what he's like. He's no going to be standing at the back watching what's going on."

Paul went back to customising another Stanley knife. McCoy lit up. Paul was right. Whatever Jumbo was, he was loyal. He would stick to Cooper like glue. Just had to hope he managed to stay out of trouble. He watched him do his rounds with the box, a wee boy trapped in a fighting man's body.

Eventually he reached them, and McCoy took a can and walked out to the garden where Cooper was talking to some guy he didn't know. Didn't want to know him either. He'd a long scar on his neck, hands like hams, leather jacket and jeans, look in his eye McCoy had seen before. Usually on people who'd been in Barlinnie jail for a long, long time.

The guy nodded. Told Cooper, "It's done," and wandered back into the house.

"Who was that?" McCoy said, watching him go.

"Better you don't know," said Cooper. "He was in Peterhead when I was there. For hire. Won't join up with anybody permanent. Says he likes the variety."

"Nice."

"That's the last thing he is. Was in there for using a fork to take someone's eye out."

McCoy looked back into the house. Twenty or so lads milling about, waiting on their instructions from Cooper. Whatever he was going to ask them to do, it wouldn't go well for some of them. A&E in the Royal would be busy tonight.

"You sure about all this, Stevie?"

"This?" said Cooper, taking McCoy's can from him and taking a slug. "This is just boys' stuff. My boys fighting Archie Andrews' boys. Won't get me anywhere, but I have to do it."

"Do you? Really? Some of these guys are bound to get hurt."

Cooper looked at him as if he was mad. "Say I didn't. My car gets set on fire outside my house and I do nothing. I may as well roll over and let Archie Andrews fuck me any way he wants. This is my reputation, you know that."

"Suppose so."

"Ever since we were wee boys you always did everything you could to avoid trouble. It's not in your nature, McCoy, and it never will be." He pointed into the house. "These guys are like me when I was that age. Could not wait to start scrapping. It's in their nature. Don't you worry about them."

"I punched Rab Thomas once," said McCoy. "When we were in Barnardo's."

"Aye, and who had to get you out of trouble with his big brother? It was me that had to batter Davey Thomas, not you."

"True."

"Besides, it's good for Paul. If he's going to take over one day, he should see this. Know how to organise it."

"I thought dads were supposed to teach their kids how to swim or ride a bike, not how to launch a bloody gang war."

"Aye, well, to each his own. What did your dad teach you? How to get pished?"

"That and how to rob an electric meter," said McCoy. "You seen him, by the way?"

Cooper shook his head. "Used to see him every so often outside the off-licence on Maryhill Road, asking folk for money, but not for a couple of months."

Someone inside the house had put *Beggars Banquet* on, turned up the record player. The boys were jumping around, singing along, arms round each other's shoulders.

"This is only the beginning," said Cooper. "The real fight's not started yet. Archie Andrews is old and vulnerable, and that makes him dangerous—probably knows this is his last hurrah. Going to take more than a few of his boys getting a doing to shift him."

"So how are you going to do it?"

"We," said Cooper.

"We." McCoy's stomach turned over.

"You're going to help me. Find out about that second of his, Rab Jamieson. Then find out something that will help me get Archie Andrews alone."

"Stevie, I'm not sure I—"

He stopped. He knew Cooper too well, and the expression on his face said, *I'm not asking.* It wasn't worth the protesting; nothing was going to change his mind. McCoy would have to do it whether he liked it or not.

"I'll get it done," he said.

"Good man."

Cooper handed him back the empty can and walked towards the house, arms held up in victory, singing along to "Street Fighting Man" at the top of his voice. Boys inside the house turned to him, took up the song until they were all singing it. Faces bright, ready for the fight, ready for anything Cooper asked of them. He walked into the house, and they surrounded him, cheering and singing.

McCoy watched them for a while. Cooper was right: he'd never had a taste for fighting. Saw Paul holding up a Stanley knife in one hand, an axe in the other, big roar from the boys. The leader in waiting.

Hoped Jumbo would be okay. That was all he could do. Hope.

TWENTY-SIX

McCoy was on his way home from Cooper's, walking down the hill to his close, when a car parked across the road flashed its lights. He walked over.

Long rolled down the window. "Get in," he said. "Time to start earning your money."

McCoy got in. Knew this was coming, just hadn't expected it to be this quick. A trial: *are you really one of us?* He lit up as Long did a U-turn and headed down the hill towards Dumbarton Road.

"Where we off to?" said McCoy.

"Anderston," said Long. "Going to help someone remember properly."

McCoy wasn't sure what he meant, but whatever it was it didn't sound good. Don't do anything illegal, Murray had said. Easy for him to say, not so easy for McCoy to do. He would just have to run with it, do as little as he could.

"Why me?"

"Why not?" said Long. "You're one of us now."

"Fair enough."

Ten minutes later they pulled up outside one of the few remaining closes in Houldsworth Street and got out. Wasn't much left of Anderston now, motorway had flattened it. Just a few empty streets and the noise of the cars on the Kingston Bridge overhead.

"Just follow my lead. Do what I say," said Long as they climbed the stairs.

McCoy nodded, bad feeling in the pit of his stomach.

Long knocked on a door. After a minute or so it was opened by an old man in a cardigan and slippers, hair all over the place.

"Can I help you boys? Just fell asleep in my chair there. Bloody TV's enough to send anyone to sleep. All repeats."

Long held out his warrant card. "Need to have a wee word, Mr. Shaw."

"No problem, son, come away in."

Shaw led them into a tiny living room with an armchair, a table and a set of drawers with a black-and-white TV on it. Flowery wallpaper and an oval mirror on the wall hanging from a chain. The room smelt stale, like sheets that hadn't been changed for months, clothes that hadn't been washed.

Shaw sat down on the armchair, smoothed his hair down.

"Need you to stand up a minute," said Long.

Shaw looked puzzled, but he got up, stood there in front of the electric fire, and Long punched him in the stomach. Hard. Shaw crumpled immediately, let out a cry. Long guided him back into the armchair.

"Just wanted to show you this isn't the usual kind of visit," he said. "This is different."

Long crouched down so his face was level with Shaw's. Shaw had tears rolling down his cheeks, looked absolutely terrified.

"You told the other polis you saw someone running out Woodlands Post Office with a gun in one hand and a brown mailbag in the other. Then you picked someone called Joseph Barrie out of a line-up, said it was him. That right?"

Shaw nodded, eyes seeking out McCoy's as if he would help him. McCoy just looked away, nothing he could do.

"Well, you were wrong. It wasn't Joseph Barrie."

Shaw went to protest, and Long drew his fist back, punched him in the face. Another cry.

"Do you understand what I'm saying to you, Brendan?"

Shaw nodded, tears and snot running down his face. "Please, son, just leave me alone . . ."

"You're getting on a bit, and you didn't have your glasses on that day, so you can't be sure it was Barrie you saw. Say it."

"I didn't have my glasses, I can't be sure."

"That's right. Good boy."

Shaw looked at them both, trying to work out what was happening to him. Five minutes ago he had been sleeping in his chair and now he was scared for his life.

Long stood up. Paced round the room. "Just in case you're stupid enough to think you can tell someone what happened here, let me put you right. Get down on the floor."

Shaw looked at him in terror. "Please, son, I'll do what you say! I promise! That's enough now. I—"

Long pulled him up and out the chair, slammed him down on the worn rug. He squatted down, spoke into his ear. "You tell anyone, then this will seem like a walk in the park. We know where you live, and we'll be back. You think I'm bad? My pal here's a fucking nightmare. He doesn't use his fists. He uses knives. You understand me?"

Shaw was crying now, just managed a strangled yes.

"Say it again," said Long.

Shaw managed to get it out. "I didn't have my glasses, I can't be sure who it was."

Long nodded to McCoy, and they walked out the flat, leaving Shaw on the ground sobbing away. They walked down the stairs in silence. Image of Long punching the old man in the face stuck in McCoy's mind.

They stepped out the close and Long lit up. Looked up at the pinkish clouds in the sky, exhaled. Turned to McCoy. "Next time, you're the heavy."

MONDAY
16TH JUNE 1975

McCoy was walking up and down outside the Saltmarket waiting for Phyllis. A queue had formed outside the fish market; day's catch chalked on the windows. Haddock, herring, mackerel. He walked round it, crossed the road and had a look in Golumb's camera shop. Didn't have much interest in buying a camera but he liked the window display. Jam-packed full of cameras, hundreds of them, wee signs with the name and price written in ink next to each one.

He looked back down towards the mortuary. Phyllis was walking towards him. Didn't know whether it was because she was tall or because of her slightly eccentric dress sense, but Phyllis always seemed to stick out in a crowd—especially round the Saltmarket. Looked like she belonged in some posh Edinburgh tea room, not making her way past the alkies standing at the corner of Steel Street.

"Glorious day," she said as she caught up with him. "Sure you don't mind?"

McCoy shook his head. Mortuary was busy today; Phyllis could only see him on her break and she needed to pick up a few things in town. Far as McCoy was concerned, anything was better than sitting in her office, even if it did entail shopping. The place gave him the heebie-jeebies. Smell of formaldehyde and horrible noises coming from next door.

"I may as well come out with it," said Phyllis as they walked up towards Glasgow Cross. "Callum Munroe died from methanol toxicity. Levels were very high in the blood, and in his tissue and stomach contents."

"Methanol rather than ethanol? So he was murdered?"

"It's not as simple as that. He drank the methanol, certainly, but whoever concocted the mixture could have been unaware it was poisonous, could just have been trying to make a very strong hooch or whatever they call it. Even methylated spirit contains a bit of methanol, and plenty of desperate people drink that."

"You sound like Wattie," said McCoy as they turned into the Trongate.

Phyllis sighed. "It's probably the most logical explanation, Harry. An accident. Things like this have happened before. There was a case in Govan a few years ago. Someone had made a mixture, shared it out at a house party. One dead, one blinded, three in hospital."

They stopped outside a pharmacy.

"Won't be a minute," said Phyllis.

McCoy lit up. Sat down in the bus stop to get out the sun. If it was methanol poisoning, then Gerry's story was looking a bit more convincing.

"Has the twenty-three been?" asked a woman with two big C&A bags as she sat down beside him.

"Not since I've been here."

"Thank Christ," she said and nodded at the bags. "Bloody weans grow out of everything so fast it's bankrupting me."

McCoy looked back at the pharmacy, wished Phyllis would hurry up.

"You got them?" the woman asked.

McCoy shook his head.

"Sensible man," she said, unbuttoning her cardigan. "Eat you out of house and home. My youngest, Terry? You wouldn't believe—"

"Harry?" Phyllis was standing there, paper bag in hand. "You ready?"

The woman's expression showed exactly what she thought of people who interrupted her conversations.

McCoy stood up, said "Cheerio."

"Marks next, I'm afraid," said Phyllis.

"If it isn't deliberate, why only fifty-something men, then? How do you explain that?" said McCoy.

Phyllis thought for a minute. "I'm not sure that's as significant as you think. Men in their mid-fifties who have been drinking for years are likely very short of money, more likely to drink a mixture, anything they can get. They also have a higher tolerance for alcohol, so the idea of extra-strong hooch probably appeals to them. They're just more likely to die this way."

"Maybe." McCoy didn't want to admit she was probably right.

"Are you worried about your father?"

He nodded. "The stupid bastard is an ideal candidate. Lives on the streets, right age, and Christ knows my dad will drink anything you put in front of him."

Phyllis pointed at one of the benches outside Marks. They sat down. "I don't want to pry," she said. "But Murray told me he was not the best of fathers."

McCoy smiled. "You could say that."

"You don't have to talk about it, Harry. I shouldn't have brought it up."

"It's okay. You know what's funny? No one ever talks about him; all they do is curse him out. He was a shit father, but once in a blue moon, when he wasn't too drunk, just happy, he could be great. Would play football with you in the street, buy you sweets, even took me to Parkhead once."

They watched a young woman put a squirming toddler down. Soon as she did, he started running, heading for a dog a man was holding. The wee boy shouted, "Doggy!" at it and started laughing. Dog looked less than impressed.

"Trouble with him was those kinds of things started

happening less and less. By the time I was five or six I was spending more time in a home than I stayed with him. He was pretty far gone even then. He'd sober up for a couple of days, but it never lasted. Then he'd say he was away out to buy the paper and you wouldn't see him for days. Drink was all he cared about. Whether I had food or clothes or anything to wear to school was way down the priority list."

"And that's where Murray came in?" asked Phyllis.

McCoy nodded. "I went to stay with him and his wife for three weeks as a foster and, somehow, I ended up never leaving. Followed him into the police force. He's been more of a father than my real dad."

"But you still care about your dad?"

McCoy shrugged. "I don't know. That's the honest truth."

"Murray said he would happily see your father dead for the things he did to you."

"I think Murray battered him a few times. Didn't tell me, but I always got that impression." McCoy grinned. "Isn't his biggest fan, let's put it that way."

"I imagine you don't want to accompany me on a fruitless search round the women's clothing department?" said Phyllis, standing up.

"Might leave you to it," said McCoy. "Should get back to the office, got an interview to go to."

Phyllis was walking towards the shop entrance when McCoy suddenly thought, called after her. "We can't exhume the other two, can we?"

"No point. The soft tissue will have broken down too much, and it won't really help. You still wouldn't know if someone gave them the hooch deliberately or if they drank it voluntarily."

"Fair enough," said McCoy. "Good luck."

Phyllis held up crossed fingers. "Maybe today the blessed St. Michael will have the red skirt of my dreams."

McCoy walked along Argyle Street. He had to admit Phyllis

was right. Munroe's death and the others were probably just a case of bad luck and too-strong hooch. Like Murray said, why would someone want to murder a bunch of down-and-outs? Didn't make sense. Trouble was, sometimes things like this only made sense to the person who was doing them. And they always had a reason, no matter how mad it was. *The man in the radio told me to do it. Drinkers are sinners and need to be eradicated. God told me to do it.* He stopped, remembered what that boy Hood had said when they discovered the body at the Clyde.

"A waste of space."

Maybe someone other than Hood thought the same thing.

TWENTY-EIGHT

McCoy pulled the door of the Possil station open just as Helen was coming out. She'd a pile of files under one arm, a shopping bag full of more of them in the other hand.

"I've just left a note on your desk," she said.

"Oh aye," said McCoy. "What did it say?"

She laid her bag on the ground, carefully balanced the other files on top of it. "There's no trace of the mysterious Jeremiah Michael West anywhere. No medical records, no school records, no birth certificate in Glasgow. I checked a couple of years either side of the date you gave me."

"Right," said McCoy. "So there's no chance he might exist but just not be in the system anywhere?"

"Unregistered children are as rare as hen's teeth these days, especially in a place like Glasgow. Might still get it way out in the country, the islands maybe, and it used to happen with Gypsy families, but even that's dying out, I think."

McCoy moved into the shade of the station door, was getting too hot to stand in the sun. "What about religious cults?"

She laughed. "In Glasgow? Don't think there're many of them."

"Say there was," said McCoy. "What then?"

Helen sucked the air in through her teeth, looked doubtful. "Possible but very unlikely. They would have to be born at home, never seen a doctor, never been to school." She shook her head. "I can't see it." She put the files back under her arm, picked up her bag. "Child protection services, here I come. Just where you want to be on a day like this."

Wattie was sitting at his desk reading something. Didn't look very happy about it. McCoy sat down, and Wattie held up Helen's note.

"Okay! Okay!" said McCoy. "No more missing kids. It's over. Malky and the half-brick in his coupon all the way. Let's go. You got the sister's handbag?"

Wattie opened a drawer in his desk, took out a normal-look-ing black handbag, handed it over. McCoy turned it upside down, emptied the contents on the desk. A jumble of paper, pens, make-up, hankies and coins. He picked up the receipts, started going through them. Stopped. Held one up.

"The bold Norma wasn't messing about. This is for a dinner at the Central Hotel."

"There's a couple of bills for Ferrari's in there too," said Wattie, going through them. "Steak dinner, bottle of red wine. Not the cheap stuff either."

McCoy sat back in his chair and tried to think. "So let's say she steals the money from Duncan Kent and runs through it at a rate of knots. Even buys her brother some posh messages from Marks and Spencer's. She's had fuck all money all her life—you'd think she'd keep some of it for a rainy day, wouldn't you?"

He pictured her lying there. Mouth going and saying noth-ing, wig half off. Seemed obvious now.

"Shite," he said. Sat down at his desk, dialled the phone. Waited.

"Need to speak to the doctor in charge of the care of Norma McGregor. Glasgow—sorry, Strathclyde Police calling."

He held the receiver in his neck while he waited for the hos-pital to find the doctor.

"Should have realised earlier," he said to Wattie. "She was wea—"

Phone back at his ear.

"Hello, doctor, Detective Inspector McCoy here. Your patient Norma McGregor, did she have something else wrong with her, something before the fit at the chapel?" Listened. Smiled. "That's great, thanks."

McCoy put the phone down. "She has cancer," he told Wattie. "Been getting chemotherapy, hence her hair falling out. Lung cancer. Heavy smoker. Doctor thinks the chemotherapy led to her having a pulmonary embolism."

"A what?"

"Blood clot on the brain."

"So she decided to go out with a bang?"

"Looks like it. Took her last chance at the good life before the cancer got too bad. She was probably as surprised to see Kent as I was. Didn't expect him to care enough to come after her. He spooked her and she ran." McCoy stood up. "You go through the rest of the stuff and we'll have our wee chat with Kent. I'm going for a piss. I'll see you in the car park."

McCoy was washing his hands at the sink when Rossi walked in. He unbuttoned his fly and stepped up to the urinal. "Hear you were out with Long last night."

"Yep," said McCoy. "Nothing too difficult. So that's what we do, is it? Sort out Archie Andrews' problems for him?"

"Sometimes," said Rossi. "Sometimes he sorts things out for us. You'll learn."

He stepped away from the urinal and buttoned up his fly. "A wee birdie told me Stevie Cooper is one of your pals. That right?"

No point in denying it. McCoy nodded.

"Well, maybe you can give him a message. Any more shite like the garage or the pubs last night, and he'll regret it. Andrews will come down on him like a ton of bricks, and he doesn't play fair. If he's a pal of yours, do him a favour and tell him to back off before what's done can't be undone."

McCoy watched him as he walked across to the sinks, started combing his hair in the mirror. Really, really wanted to punch the smug smile off his face.

"That's funny. According to you, Andrews torched his own garage."

Rossi smiled at him in the mirror. "Don't be a funny cunt, McCoy. You'll regret it, and so will your pal. So away and tell him like the jumped-up message boy you are."

TWENTY-NINE

W hat was your pal up to last night?" said Wattie as McCoy got in the car outside the station.

"Eh?" McCoy's mind was still on Rossi and what he had said.

"I've just been hearing from the desk sergeant about how Stevie Cooper and his troops went full tonto last night." He nodded at the dashboard. "Apparently the radio never stopped. The Royal is full of Archie Andrews' boys, most of them in bits, and two of his pubs got trashed."

"What pubs?"

"The Possil and the Round Toll." Wattie turned the engine over.

Knew the Possil was Andrews'; fact the Round Toll was his as well was news to McCoy. "That right? No idea."

Wattie sighed. Kept his temper. "If you don't want to tell me, that's fine, but don't treat me like my head buttons up the back. I'm not stupid."

Wattie pulled the car out into the road. McCoy rolled down the window, let some air in. Let Wattie cool off. He liked not driving, liked looking out the window at the world going by. There was always something to see in Glasgow. Today was no exception. A rag-and-bone man was coming up Saracen Street, horse ambling along, taking its time. Hadn't seen one for ages.

When he'd been a boy there had been loads of them. Coal carts, milk carts, all sorts.

They pulled up at the lights at the bottom of Craighall Road, and the Round Toll came into view. A couple of guys and a van were outside cutting up MDF to cover the broken windows, their feet crunching on the broken glass covering the pavement. A message had been spray-painted on the pebbledashed front of the pub.

TIMES UP ANDREWS

Car started up again, and McCoy watched the pub disappear in the wing mirror.

They were almost at St. George's Cross—or what was left of it, most of it seemed to be a building site for the new motorway—before Wattie spoke again. "Royal Terrace, is it?"

McCoy nodded. Knew he had to make amends. "It's about Possil. Cooper's trying to take it off Archie Andrews. Last night was the beginning of the war. And worse than that, he wants me to help him do it."

"Fuck," said Wattie. "How?"

McCoy shrugged. "Wants anything on Rab Jamieson and Archie Andrews, anything he can use."

"Are you going to give it to him?"

"Don't have anything to give."

"If you did, though, would you?"

They were coming into Royal Terrace. McCoy pointed through the windscreen. "Number forty-two, pull in over there."

Duncan Kent had come a long way since he'd run protection rackets in Bridgeton. Now he was a smart silver plaque beside the entrance to his office. KENT ENTERPRISES. Far as McCoy could work out, he did a bit of everything. Property development, commercial property, had just got into house-building, a big estate out near Riddrie. All kosher, all very above board, all very Rotary Club.

Wattie rang the doorbell.

A smartly dressed young woman appeared. "How can I help you?" she said.

He held out his warrant card. "Detective Watson and Detective Inspector McCoy to see Mr. Kent."

Five minutes later they were sitting in a boardroom sipping tea from Royal Doulton cups. Pale blue walls, white venetian blinds. Notepads, pens and water on the mahogany table. On a side table there was a model of what looked like a big shopping centre. McCoy wandered over for a closer inspection. Whoever had made it knew what they were doing: every detail was in place, even had wee people and cars parked on the street running along beside it. A small plaque was glued to the side.

Royston Shopping Centre
Gillespie Kidd & Coia Architects, 1975

McCoy was just about to ask Wattie if he'd heard anything about a new shopping centre when the door opened, and Kent came in. He was in suit trousers and shirt-sleeves, tie over his shoulder.

"Gents." He sat down. "Sorry for the wait. Expecting word on a big deal any minute." He nodded over at the model. "For that, as it happens."

"No problem," said Wattie. "Just an informal visit. We're here to see if you can shed any light on what happened to Norma McGregor?"

Kent looked pained. "It's not a very pretty story, I'm afraid. Norma worked for us for years, both here and at home."

"As?" asked Wattie.

"She started as a cleaner," said Kent. "But she'd become more than that over the years. She used to babysit the kids, became part of the family. Then a week or so ago a sum of money disappeared from one of the safes in the house."

"She knew the combination?"

Kent shook his head. "Either me or my wife must have left it ajar. She saw her opportunity and took it, I suppose."

"How much?" asked McCoy, sitting back at the table.

"Four hundred pounds," said Kent. "We didn't want to prosecute, just to get the money back. She hadn't been at home all week, so the church seemed the best place to see her. My wife knew she always went there."

He reached over to a carafe of water, poured himself a glass, took a drink and carried on. "I tried to speak to her, but unfortunately—"

"You grabbed her arm," said McCoy. "Hard."

Kent turned to look at him.

"I was there. I saw you. And you said something to her. What was that, Mr. Kent?"

Kent didn't flinch. "I asked her to be sensible and give the money back."

"Really? Didn't look like that from where I was," said McCoy. "Looked like you were threatening her. She pulled away from you and ran. She was terrified."

"Oh?" said Kent. "And where were you?"

"Just outside the church."

"So, in fact, you have no idea what I said. Too far away to hear, weren't you?"

McCoy shrugged. Had been caught out.

"May I ask why you were there?" asked Kent.

"No," he said. Sounded as petty as it was.

And that was enough for Kent. "Are we done?" he snapped.

"Just one more thing," said Wattie. "Her handbag was full of receipts from the Albany, the Central, the Grosvenor. She'd been staying at the best hotels in town instead of her flat. Why do you think that was?"

Kent shrugged. "Spending her ill-gotten gains, I would imagine."

He turned as the office door opened. A young guy in a suit stuck his head around the door. Grinned, stuck his thumbs up.

"Yes!" shouted Kent and punched the air. "Brilliant, Robbie. Bloody brilliant!"

He turned back to McCoy and Wattie, huge grin on his face. "Planning permission for the shopping centre has been granted. Was touch and go for a while."

"Maybe Norma McGregor was staying in hotels because she was hiding from you," said McCoy. "Why would she be doing that?"

Kent was too smart to rise to the bait or give anything away. "You really do have quite the imagination, Mr. McCoy. Hearing things you didn't, assigning motives you can't possibly know anything about." Turned to Wattie. "Because she had stolen my money, I would imagine."

McCoy stretched over the table, poured himself some water. Took a sip. Wasn't done yet. "So a beloved family servant suddenly steals a few hundred quid for no reason and decides to live the high life for a week. That make sense to you, does it, Mr. Kent?"

Kent didn't say anything for a minute. Was looking over at the model. Smiled. "Sorry, I'm a bit distracted. It's huge news for the company. What were you asking again?"

"Nothing important, Mr. Kent," said Wattie, standing up. "Thanks for your time. And congratulations."

They filed out, left Kent drinking his water, scribbling something down on one of the notepads. Walked out into the hall, more shouts of celebration from the staff.

McCoy almost made it to the car before he started. Couldn't hold it in any longer. "What was that about, Wattie? Could you have got your head any further up his arse? And that stuff about the hotels? Why hadn't you told me that?"

Wattie stopped, looked at him. "You never asked me, did you? Just left me going through everything while you sat there thinking about how to get Reverend bloody West and pretending you weren't. Well, now you know what it's like working in the dark half the time, waiting to see if the great Harry McCoy will deign to tell you what's going on or not. Not a lot of fun, is it?"

Wasn't a lot McCoy could say to that. He'd been caught bang to rights. "I deserved that, didn't I?" he said as they got in the car.

"Yep."

"I'll try and not be as much of an arse—how's that?"

Wattie drew the air in through his teeth. "Going to be difficult. You've been an arse for too long."

"I'll try."

Wattie nodded, started the car and pulled out into the traffic.

McCoy got his cigarettes out and lit up. "Say you're Duncan Kent, a bloody millionaire, about to build a bloody shopping centre. Are you going to chase all over town to try and get four hundred quid back?"

"Are you fuck. You either call the cops or you write it off."

"Exactly. So if Kent wasn't looking to get the money back, what did he want from Norma McGregor?"

"She stole something else as well?"

"Looks like it," said McCoy. "Now all me and you have to do is figure out what it is and where it is."

THIRTY

Whoever had done over Norma McGregor's flat had done a good job. McCoy and Wattie stood in the middle of the chaos and looked round. It was a single end in Govan, a one-room flat with a press bed recessed into the wall. What could have been picked up, examined, then thrown aside had been. What could have been turned upside down or broken had been.

"They've even taken the floorboards up over there," said Wattie, nodding over. "They weren't messing around. Must have—"

"So you finally turned up?"

A young woman with a baby on her hip was standing in the doorway. She couldn't have been more than seventeen, eighteen. Blonde hair, green satin blouse and wide denim flares.

"Only took you three bloody days," she said. "I called it in on Friday."

She was looking at them as if she was expecting an apology, so McCoy gave her one. "Sorry about that. And you are?"

"Lindsay Ross. I live next door." She moved the baby onto the other hip. "Do you know where Norma is?"

Wasn't much of a way around it. "Do you want to sit down?" said McCoy.

"Oh, Christ," she said, pushing a pile of records without their sleeves aside and sitting down on the couch. "I knew it."

The baby, sensing his mother's mood, started to whimper.

"Here," said Wattie, "I'll take him." He took the baby from

her, walked around the room bouncing him up and down on his arm, took a hanky from his pocket, wiped his snotty nose.

"What happened to her?" she asked.

"It was an accident," said McCoy. "She's in a coma. Not looking great, I'm afraid."

Lindsay looked round the flat. "So why all this? I don't understand . . ."

"That's what we're trying to find out. When did you first see it like this?"

"Friday afternoon," she said. "I heard noises in the flat, thought Norma must be doing spring cleaning or something. Hadn't seen her for a couple of days, so I waited until the noise finished. Thought I'd go and say hello, see if she could babysit Scott on Saturday night. Came round, the door was open, and all this had happened."

"Any idea what they were looking for?"

She shook her head, got a hanky out her pocket and wiped her eyes.

"Did you see who was in here?" asked McCoy.

Shook her head again. "What did Norma have? Nothing! Didn't have two halfpennies to rub together. She was just a wee woman, wouldnae hurt a fly."

And then the tears started properly. Wattie got the baby to look out the window, pointed at a dog crossing the street. Didn't work; he started crying too.

McCoy sat down beside Lindsay, put his arm round her, looked at the broken china ornaments, the pot plant on its side on the carpet, the Highland landscape that was hanging sideways now, and thought the same thing. What on earth did Norma and Malky have that was worth all this?

THIRTY-ONE

M cCoy was paying the taxi-driver outside the Waterloo when a middle-aged man appeared at the entrance to a nearby alley. He put his trilby on, looked right and left, and hurried up Waterloo Street.

"Looking for a good time, handsome?" said Sister Jimmy as he stepped out the alleyway, brushing the dust off the knees of his trousers.

"Very funny," said McCoy. "You got a minute?"

Sister Jimmy nodded. "C'mon, we'll go into the Wellington." Eyed the Waterloo. "It's like a bloody circus in there tonight."

They walked along Argyle Street, heading for the next pub. Sun was just about to go down, clouds a glorious shade of pink. Windows in the office buildings full of the colour.

"Who was your pal?" asked McCoy.

"Fuck knows," said Sister Jimmy. "More of a financial arrangement than an affair of the heart. Can't be too fussy these days."

Sister Jimmy still had the Rod Stewart hair, the silver jacket and the eyeliner, but like everyone else he was getting older. And in his business, that was the one thing you couldn't do.

The Wellington was quieter. Just a few punters watching the TV on the wall and a group of young lads all dressed up for a night out. Table in front of them a sea of pint glasses. Sister Jimmy got a seat at the back of the bar and McCoy brought the drinks over.

"How's the war wound?" he said, sitting down.

"Not too bad," said Sister Jimmy. "Scar healed pretty well and some of the punters like it. A stab wound makes you seem dangerous. Sexy. So I'm told."

"Speaking of which, you seen Paul Cooper lately?"

Sister Jimmy smiled. "Occasionally. Let's just say we run in different circles these days. His boot-boy pals aren't too fond of the likes of me. Doing okay, is he?"

"Working for his dad."

Sister Jimmy nodded. They both knew what that meant. He took a sip of his gin and tonic. "So I'm assuming you didn't come looking for me because you wanted a gobble?"

"Nope," said McCoy. "Need some information."

"That's fine by me. Costs the same and it's less messy."

McCoy reached into his back pocket, pulled out his wallet and put a fiver on the table. "You know a bloke called Jamieson? Works for Archie Andrews?"

Sister Jimmy raised his eyebrows. "I've heard tell. Right nasty piece of work."

They turned as the lads at the big table started shouting, one of them trying to sink a pint in a oner. Just managed it.

"You know anything about Jamieson?" asked McCoy.

"What exactly are you trying to find out?"

"I need something on him. Something Archie Andrews won't like."

"Do you now? And how am I supposed to know what his dirty little secret is?"

McCoy sighed. "Don't act all 'butter wouldn't melt,' Jimmy. It's me you're talking to. You hear things, you meet people. Need you to ask around."

Sister Jimmy had taken the lemon out his drink and was carefully nibbling around the peel. "What?" he said, dropping it back in the glass. "And Jamieson finds out and gets his boys to open my face?" He pushed the fiver back towards McCoy. "It's not worth it."

McCoy pushed it back. "Come on, Jimmy. You get me something and there's another twenty to come. After all I've done for you."

Sister Jimmy laughed. "What? Like get me stabbed? Thanks a lot."

He sat for a minute then reached over and put the fiver in his pocket. "Make it thirty."

"Good man," said McCoy. "It's a deal."

Sister Jimmy had his eyes trained on one of the lads who had gone up to the bar. Tight trousers and black curly hair. Turned back to McCoy. "I'm assuming you don't want to find out he's behind on his mortgage payments?"

"Nope. Need something that will make Archie Andrews turn on him."

"What if there isn't anything? What if he's pure as the driven snow, keeps his dick in his pants and shags the wife once a week?"

"I have confidence in you—you'll find something."

He left Sister Jimmy there nursing his gin and tonic, still watching the lads, and walked out the bar. Wondered exactly what kind of person he was turning into. He was supposed to be a polis and here he was doing a gangster's dirty work for him. Supposed that's how it worked: you ask someone like Stevie Cooper for enough favours and eventually he asks for one back.

Town was empty now, all the good citizens gone home to their dinner and their night in front of the TV. He started walking into town. He wasn't interested in them. He was looking for the other ones. The ones who had lost their place in the normal world, had given up pretending. The lonely souls.

THIRTY-TWO

It didn't take McCoy as long to find Liam as he'd thought it would. He struck lucky; he was in the second place he looked. Found him queuing outside the Wayside club in Midland Street, waiting for a bowl of soup and a couple of slices of bread just like everyone else.

"Found the murderer yet?" he asked as McCoy approached.

"Not yet," he said. "Need you to help me."

Liam looked up the queue. "Five minutes, and I'm all yours. I'm bloody starving."

McCoy nodded, leant against the wall of the railway tunnel and lit up. He recognised at least half the people in the queue. Had seen them in the same places over the years. Outside here, outside the Sally Army, lying unconscious in the waste ground opposite the Squirrel in Gallowgate. Maybe some of them had got out, stopped drinking, found a better life. None that he knew though.

Liam had for a while, but it hadn't lasted. His life was on the streets no matter how bad it was. On the streets he was someone, everyone knew him, asked for his help, trusted him. Living in the Great Northern and struggling to get work as a day labourer, he was just another nobody.

McCoy watched two women sit down on the kerb opposite, passing a bottle between them. He knew one of them, Annie Greene. Probably fortifying herself for going up to Blythswood later on to try to get enough money to start the whole thing over again tomorrow. Wondered how these women did it, kept going when they'd been dealt all the bad cards. Annie tipped the bottle of wine into her mouth and took a long drink. Too long for her pal; she tried to grab it back, but Annie batted her hand away, kept drinking. Same way his dad did, trying to fill a desperate need.

"So what's up, Harry?" asked Liam, wandering over. He wiped his mouth on the sleeve of his jumper, stuffed his last slice of bread into his mouth.

"You know Callum Munroe?"

Liam nodded. "He's a bit of a prick, to be honest."

"So people tell me," said McCoy. "But he's dead now, and guess what? He died of methanol poisoning."

Liam's face lit up. "So Gerry was right?"

"Not sure. Could be an accident or could be deliberate. Either way we need to warn people not to drink any hooch and that includes my dad. You seen him?"

"Alec? Saw him a week or so ago."

Familiar turn of the stomach he always got when he talked about his dad. "Where?"

"Was staying in some abandoned flat in Townhead, near the hospital. Him and a couple of his pals."

"How was he?"

"He wasn't good, Harry. Was drinking red biddy."

"Christ. Meths and red wine? That's brutal."

"And people don't last long when they start on that. Three or four months maybe." Liam looked back at the Wayside. "I'll go and spread the word."

McCoy watched Liam go up and down the queue telling everyone not to drink any hooch. Most of them nodded, said they wouldn't. Probably just doing that to be nice to Liam, but it was a start, at least. Liam reached the head of the queue and spoke to the two men behind the long wooden table. McCoy could see them listening, nodding.

McCoy had last seen his dad a year or so ago. He'd been bad

then, begging for money in the street. Hadn't even recognised him. Too far gone. Christ knows what he would be like now. He dropped his cigarette on the ground and stamped it out. Only one way to find out.

THIRTY-THREE

There wasn't much of McAslin Street left. Like the rest of Townhead it was being demolished. Now Townhead was mostly wasteland. A sea of mud, puddles and dumped rubbish. Continual noise of traffic thundering past on the motorway it had been destroyed to accommodate. Townhead was one of those places in Glasgow that was already becoming just a memory. Somewhere that just wasn't there any more.

One block of tenements had managed to survive the onslaught. Just. The windows and the front close had been boarded up, wooden planks nailed across them. Graffiti everywhere. A ripped safety notice still nailed to the boards.

Do Not Enter. Hazardous.

"This it?" said McCoy.

Liam nodded. "You get in round the back."

They walked round the building, through the courts and stood in front of the back entrance. Some wooden boards covering the bottom of it. Liam pulled at them, and they came away easily.

A dog wandered out, a dead rat in its mouth.

"You ready?" said Liam. "Not a pretty sight in here."

McCoy nodded. Wasn't sure if he was or not. Realised he was frightened, frightened of seeing what his dad had become. And more frightened of not being recognised again. Liam yanked the boards all the way off, and they crawled into the tenement. First thing that hit McCoy was the smell. Human shit. He put his hand over his nose.

"Be careful," said Liam.

It was hard to see, the only illumination the dim evening light seeping in through the cracks in the boards. Took a minute or so for his eyes to adjust. The floor of the close was covered in broken bottles, lighter fuel cans and balls of newspaper providing the smell. They stepped carefully, made it to the bottom of the stairs.

Liam shouted up, "It's Liam! Anybody there?"

Few seconds later there was a shout back, more of a grunt than anything else. They started climbing. Stairs were as bad as the entranceway. It was hard to avoid stepping on the dozens of rusting cans in the darkness. They got to the first-floor landing. Most of the doors were boarded up, but one was ajar. Liam pushed it open.

It was even darker in here than on the stairs. McCoy could make out three bodies sitting on the floor, but that was about it. One of them lit a match for his cigarette and his face was illuminated. It wasn't his dad. The smoker had probably been handsome once but not any more. His face was weather-beaten, a painful-looking scar going from his cheek right across his nose. Even in the matchlight McCoy could see that his skin was yellow.

As the light went out and his eyes adjusted, he realised one of the cigarette man's companions was a woman. She was bundled up in a duffel coat, thick specs. The third in the group was a young man, didn't look quite right, eyes vacant, tongue out his mouth, body held in a strange way.

The cigarette man gestured to a space on the floor as if it were a spare seat at a dining table. "Sit down, Liam, son—always nice to see you."

They sat down on the floor, McCoy praying he hadn't sat on one of the balls of newspaper. Could hear running water, a burst pipe somewhere. There were still a few traces of wallpaper on the damp plasterboard. Yellow with blue flowers. TOWNHEAD CUMBIE written on the other wall.

"Y'all right, Frank?" said Liam.

The man nodded. "Who's your pal?" he asked, peering over.

"This is Harry McCoy, Alec's boy. You seen him around?"

"Alec? He was here yesterday . . . maybe the day before? I cannae remember fuck all these days. Anyway, he stayed a couple of hours. Some posh wifey gave him a fiver outside Queen Street Station, told him to spend it on food." His laugh turned into a deep painful cough. "You know Alec—turned up with two bottles of wine and a can of Ronson. No food in sight. Made your day, didn't it, Jackie?"

The woman smiled, nodded. No teeth.

"Harry here is looking for him," said Liam. "If he comes by again, will you tell him? Tell him his son's looking for him and to go to the Possil police station?"

"I'll tell him," Frank said. "But Alec these days?" He tapped the side of his head. "Not much goes in. Not the man he was." Looked at McCoy. "No offence, son, but red biddy takes its toll."

McCoy was going to say thank you, tell them not to drink hooch, but realised if he spoke he'd start crying. He tapped Liam on the shoulder, pointed at the door and stood up.

"I'll tell them the rest," said Liam. "Off you go."

He managed to make it outside before the tears came. Wasn't quite sure what he was crying for. For his dad? For all the people like Frank and Jackie living in places like that? He wiped his eyes, lit up with shaky hands. Stomach in knots. He stood in the back court, could see the lights in the high flats at Dobbie's Loan. People watching television, laying out the dinner table, tucking up their kids. Only yards away, but they might as well be living in a different world.

"You okay?"

He turned and Liam was standing there. He shook his head.

"I shouldn't say this, but can we go for a drink?" McCoy said. "I really need one."

THIRTY-FOUR

A pint and a whisky later, McCoy and Liam were on the move again. They were following a route that wasn't on any map, the one people like his dad took across the town. From begging spots in the city centre to soup kitchens behind churches, from off-licences that took handfuls of dirty coins to bakeries that gave out stale bread at the end of the day. The places people like them went.

On the way they tried to tell people to avoid any hooch that was going about. Some of them had, but it was always the week before or a couple of days ago. Not much use. From what McCoy could see, times were harder than usual. The less money there was knocking about, the less of it filtered down to the streets. Wasn't sure if anyone was really going to turn down hooch if it was all they had. The DTs needed to be held at bay no matter the risk.

"You okay?" said Liam as they were walking over the suspension bridge.

"Aye. Just gets to you after a while, all these people living like that."

"They're just people," said Liam, "like you and me. Took a wrong turn somewhere and can't find their way back."

"What about you, Liam? How come you ended up here?"

Liam stopped, leant on the fence and looked out over the inky water of the Clyde. "You really want to know?" he asked.

McCoy handed him a cigarette, lit a match for him. Nodded.

"I don't know. I started drinking when I was fourteen and I've never really stopped. That's just the way my life went. I wasn't any better or any worse than anyone else, I just had a hole in me somewhere that the drink filled up. Made things better for a while, then it made things worse. But it's always there, the thirst for it. You understand? And I doubt it'll ever go away." He smiled. Tapped his cigarette ash into the river. "You're making me bloody maudlin. C'mon, one more stop and then we're done."

They passed the flattened-down grass and bushes where Callum Munroe had been found and headed towards the Salvation Army in South Portland Street. Was coming up for eleven. Town was quiet, pubs had shut, people were off the streets, gone back home. The streetlights were on, casting a yellow pallor over everything.

"You know the guy here?" said McCoy.

Liam nodded. "New bloke. Seems nice enough, better than the old fire-and-brimstone bugger that used to run it."

They turned the corner and found Kenny Lowell standing outside the entrance, uniform jacket undone, mug in one hand, cigarette in the other. He was talking to a uniform. Wasn't until they got closer that McCoy recognised Hood. The new boy from the station. He had a mug and a cigarette too. Looked a bit sheepish as McCoy approached.

"Sir . . ."

"Rest stop on the beat, Hood?" said McCoy.

"Can I get you two a tea?" said Lowell.

"Wouldn't say no," said McCoy. "Liam?"

Liam said yes, and Lowell disappeared back into the building.

Hood nodded down at the site where Munroe had been discovered. "I heard he'd been poisoned. Shame."

"Didn't you say people like him were a waste of space?" replied McCoy. "You had a change of heart?"

Hood had the good grace to look embarrassed. "Sorry about that. It was a stupid thing to say. Been talking to Lowell here. He sees things different. Trying to change my mind."

On cue, Lowell appeared with two mugs of tea, handed them to McCoy and Liam.

"Need you to do me a favour," said McCoy. "Need you to tell people coming for their soup to avoid any hooch that's going around. That's what killed Munroe."

Lowell nodded. "No problem. Although if I'm being honest, I'm not sure it will stop everyone."

"Probably not," said McCoy. "Speaking of which, can you keep an eye out for my dad?"

"What's he like?" asked Lowell. "Does he look like you?"

McCoy was about to say no when Liam spoke up.

"Aye, he does. Like an older, battered version."

"And he's got a scar here," said McCoy, drawing his finger across his right eyebrow. "A big one."

"Should be easy to spot. I'll just imagine you in a few years after you've got into a fight."

"You see him, tell him about the hooch and to come and see me at the Possil station. Tell him I'll give him money for a proper drink."

"Normally I'd advise trying to avoid drink of any kind," said Lowell. "But needs must."

Hood handed his mug back to Lowell and set off back down towards the river.

"Looks like you've made a convert," said McCoy.

"Not so much a convert, not yet anyway. Stops here most nights for a tea when he's on the beat. Seems to think the men who come here only have themselves to blame, tells me they're responsible for their downfall. Not very Christian, but I'm trying."

McCoy left Liam at the taxi rank at Central. Gave him a tenner for his help. Was the least he could do. Then he got in a cab and told the driver to take him to 66 Hamilton Drive. Margo would be back, and he wanted to see her, to lie beside her and drift off to sleep. To try not to think about his dad and Frank and Jackie and all the other lonely souls still making their way across the city.

He opened the door to the big house and went in. There was a note from Margo on the table in the hall.

Gone to see Laura. Don't wait up!

McCoy tried to remember which one Laura was, thought she was the one with the big house in Park Circus, old school pal. He went into the front room and got a bottle of whisky and a crystal glass off the trolley, poured himself a good measure. Sat on the couch and loosened his tie. Sombre face of Margo's grandfather staring down at him from the portrait above the fireplace. Sir John Lindsay.

He had a feeling Sir John hadn't spent much time with the likes of Frank and Jackie. Had been too busy making the family fortune. McCoy could never remember if it was shipbuilding or cotton mills, probably both. Seemed to remember he owned about half of Canada as well.

A fine, upstanding man. Wondered if he could have imagined how his grandson, Margo's brother, would turn out. Not sure anyone could have; monsters like him were rare, thank God. Remembered the atmosphere of fear in Glasgow when he and his private army were planting bombs all over the city. Turned out that was only the half of it. Lindsay went in for more personal damage as well. Brought the torture techniques he'd learned in the army back to Glasgow with him. McCoy took a sip of the whisky. Still wasn't quite sure how he had ended up in a place like this looking at paintings of ancestors on the wall. He'd never met his own grandfather; he'd been dead before he was born. His dad never spoke about him; fact he had left home at thirteen probably told you all you needed to know. Families. He yawned, got up and poured another measure, set off for bed.

TUESDAY
17TH JUNE 1975

THIRTY-FIVE

I don't even want the house. I always hated it, was always bloody freezing. Anyway, Rettie's think they can get some rich German to buy it. They like the hunting and stalking apparently. And then there's the tenant farmers, what am I supposed to do with them?"

No reply. Margo turned to McCoy, hit him with a pillow. "Are you listening to me, Harry?"

"Yes!" he said, although he wasn't really. "Tenants."

If he was being honest, Margo trying to get rid of her dead brother's Highland estate wasn't his number-one concern, but he enjoyed lying in bed with her, half asleep, listening to her rant about it.

"Won't the tenants just carry on as usual?"

"I don't know," said Margo, sitting up. "My brother knew all about this stuff—it was his job, not mine. I was never meant to inherit it."

"You ever think about him? Your brother?"

"I try not to. But if I do, I just try to remember him when he was a wee boy, when he used to make me laugh during supper. Before, you know, he became what he was." She stared into space for a minute. Turned to McCoy. "You've given me an idea."

"Oh aye, what's that?"

"The money from the house sale. I don't need it. Some of it can go to help running Innellan, but there'll be plenty left. So I'm going to give it away. My brother managed to brainwash those boys because they were lost, had nothing to do, no guidance. I'm going to use the money to try to change that. The places they live—there's nothing to do, nowhere to go. No wonder they drift into gangs or crime."

"Great idea," said McCoy. "How?"

"Youth clubs, activity camps, football clubs, that sort of thing. Run by people who really care about them, can help them find a path. What do you think?"

"Sounds good to me."

He reached for his cigarettes on the night table. Wasn't sure a couple of youth clubs were going to make much difference to the youth of Easterhouse and Blackhill, but no harm in trying. He lit up. "You sure this is going to work? You and me?"

"What do you mean?"

"Well, I spent yesterday trailing round every down-and-outs' hangout in Glasgow, and you spent it trying to get rid of one of—what is it?—six houses you own now. And you don't even need the money from it. I know opposites are supposed to attract, but we might be pushing it."

"Seven houses, actually, if you include this one. And this is the only one I like," she said. "And, yes, it will work if you stop thinking about it and just let it be."

"Fair enough," said McCoy.

They were in the big bedroom at the front of the house—sun flooding through the windows and a view of a garden that seemed to go on for ever. He wasn't quite sure how many bedrooms there were. Or bathrooms. Woke up this morning with one of Margo's hands down the front of his pyjamas. Nice way to start the day.

McCoy looked at his watch. Coming on for half seven. Needed to get up and get going. "What are you doing today?"

Margo sighed. "More of this shit. You?"

McCoy counted off on his fingers. "Trying to find my dad before he drinks some hooch that will probably kill him, getting nowhere with Malky McCormack's murder, buying a present for Wee Duggie, and trying to avoid getting incriminated in someone else's dirty work."

"Am I supposed to understand any of that?"

"Nope."

There was never going to be a good time for it, so this was as good a time as any. Cooper hadn't forgotten like he'd hoped. Decided to just blurt it out.

"My pal Stevie Cooper has a new girlfriend who's a model, wants to get into acting, so she wants to meet you. He's asked us out for dinner."

Margo's face fell. "When?"

"Tonight."

"You're kidding me," she said. "You have to be."

"Nope."

"Where?"

"Rogano's. Eight o'clock."

"And you couldn't have told me this before?"

"No," he said. "Because then you would have had time to find an excuse."

"Too bloody right I would." She thought for a minute. "This Stevie, is he a rich enough gangster to buy a country estate?"

"Not yet. Will be someday."

"Oh, well, a German with a rifle and bags of money it is. And, by the way, you owe me for this. I've got the perfect social occasion coming up to pay you back."

McCoy got out of bed, put his pyjama trousers on and headed for the nearest bathroom.

A shout after him. "I'm honorary president of the Hillhead Historical Society! They have an annual dinner dance coming up and—"

He shut the door, blocked the rest of it out. He'd worry about getting out of that later.

THIRTY-SIX

M cCoy could see Wattie standing outside St. Teresa's Church in Saracen Street, watching him climb the hill up to the entrance. McCoy took bites of his bacon roll every couple of steps, holding it out in front of him to avoid getting grease down his shirt.

"This your big idea, is it?" he said between mouthfuls when he reached Wattie.

"Could be," said Wattie.

McCoy took another bite of the roll, swallowed it over. Stomach seemed to be okay, so he kept going.

"Malky's sister had something valuable," said Wattie. "Wasn't in her flat and wasn't in her handbag. Let's say she saw the Kents sitting at the back waiting to pounce. She panics. Decides her best bet is to hide whatever it is in the church and come back for it later. But, of course, she doesn't come back. So—"

"So it should still be in there?" Wattie nodded. "That's the idea."

McCoy finished the last of his roll, looked for a bin, couldn't find one and put the rolled-up paper bag into his pocket. "Lead on, Macduff."

The church was empty but for one old man in a pew about halfway to the altar, head down, rosary in hands. No sign of the priest, just a crucified Jesus looking down on them with his usual disappointment at the foibles of mankind. They walked up the aisle, heels loud on the tiles, as McCoy tried to remember which pew Malky's sister had been sitting in. Decided it was either the second or the third one.

"You take the one in front," said McCoy, "and I'll do this one."

He sat down in the pew by the aisle. He wanted this done as soon as possible; the less time he was in a church, the better, as far as he was concerned. He had a rummage in the shallow storage space in the back of the pew in front of him. Hymnals, the paper from a caramel, nothing else. Slid a few seats along on his bum. Tried again. Just more hymnals. Another slide. More hymnals and an order of service for the funeral of one James McCann.

"Any luck?" asked Wattie.

"Not yet." McCoy slid along again.

More hymnals, a folded-over shopping list and then, in behind a Bible, an envelope. It was good-quality, heavy cream paper. No address. He slid his finger under the flap and opened it. There was a folded bit of paper inside. He got it out and unfolded it. It was a birth certificate.

Kathleen Garvie, born 23 June 1946.

"Got it." Handed it over the pew to Wattie.

He read it, looked at McCoy. "Who's Kathleen Garvie?"

"No idea," said McCoy. "But somebody murdered Malky McCormack to try and get a hold of her birth certificate." Looked at it again. Counted in his head. "She's almost twenty-nine. Born in Dundee. Mother a nurse, father a plumber. That ring any bells?"

Wattie shook his head. "All this for a birth certificate. It doesn't make any sense."

"Nope." McCoy put it back into the envelope. "Doesn't make any sense to us but must make perfect sense to someone."

"Duncan Kent," said Wattie.

"The very man. Let's see if he fancies another chat."

Thirty-Seven

According to his very snotty secretary, Duncan Kent was in London on a business trip and wouldn't be back until Wednesday. McCoy said he'd call back then and put the phone down. Looked over at Wattie, hidden by a pile of phone books and directories.

"Any luck?"

"Nope," said Wattie, peering round. "Got a Kenneth Garvie and a Kathleen Grieve, that's about as close as I've got."

"Maybe this is nothing to do with Malky," said McCoy.

"What do you mean?"

"Maybe someone brought it for a christening or a wedding or something, left it there accidentally?"

"But it was where she was sitting," said Wattie.

"Phone the church, see if the priest remembers anyone with the surname Garvie," said McCoy. "Quickest way to find out."

Wattie sighed, picked up the phone.

McCoy looked up as the main office door swung open and Rossi walked in, headed for his desk and sat down. He looked at McCoy and beckoned him over. Here, boy. McCoy felt the anger rise inside him. Little shit was probably going to ask him if he'd delivered his message to Cooper yet.

McCoy put the birth certificate back in its envelope, slid it into his jacket pocket and stood up. Figured he was in with Long now, no need to be so nice to his slimy wee lackey.

"All right, Rossi," he said, stopping at his desk. "You want me, do you?"

Rossi sat back on his chair, no doubt expecting the news that McCoy had delivered the message as instructed. "You do what I asked you to do yet?"

"Nope. Not yet."

"Why not?" Rossi sounded annoyed. "I told you to get it done."

McCoy smiled. Leant into Rossi's fat face. Could see the blackheads on his nose, bits of beard his razor had missed.

"I'll tell you why not. If you really think I'm going to do the bidding of a jumped-up wee cunt who thinks he's playing with the big boys, you've got another think coming. Comprende?"

Walked off before Rossi had a chance to reply. Little victories can sometimes be the most satisfying.

Helen was at her desk at the back of the office, piles of brown folders in front of her, another one on the floor beside her. She didn't look particularly happy to see McCoy.

"How's things?"

She nodded down at the piles. "Great. Just sitting here filing my nails, deciding what to have for my lunch. How about you?"

"Bit the same. Getting nowhere on the Malky McCormack case."

She looked puzzled.

"The old man killed round the corner," said McCoy.

"Ah, him. So let me guess, you want me to do something for you that you could quite easily do yourself? That it?"

"I can't do it this time. Honestly. Needs your expertise."

She rolled her eyes, and McCoy got the envelope out his pocket.

"It's a birth certificate. You deal with them all the time. Wondered if you could have a look, see if you can tell us anything."

He was just about to get it out the envelope when she nodded at the pile.

"Put it on there and I'll try to look at it today."

McCoy put it on the pile. Face must have told the story.

"I'm not being an arse, but I've got notes to prepare for this afternoon. Family with five kids of various ages. The mum and dad are about to be charged with sexual abuse of three of them."

"Shite," said McCoy.

"It is," she said. "It really is. Youngest one is only three. Let me get that out the way and I'll try to have a look."

McCoy said thank you, walked back to his desk. Rossi wasn't there any more, no doubt gone to tell tales. He didn't much care what Rossi did; he'd reached the end of pretending to be nice no matter what happened.

"No Garvies hatched, matched or despatched," said Wattie as McCoy sat down.

"So it was Norma McGregor who left the birth certificate there."

"Looks like it," said Wattie. "Not that it helps us much."

"Just have to wait until Kent's back, see what he has to say."

"So what do we do now?"

McCoy looked up at the clock on the wall. "I go into town and buy a bloody Matchbox car for my beloved godson."

THIRTY-EIGHT

McCoy was feeling very pleased with himself. In the space of half an hour he'd acquired one Matchbox police car set: a panda car, a van and a wee man on a motorcycle. Had even remembered to buy a birthday card. Poor wee bugger had had chickenpox on his real birthday, so the party had been delayed since then. He'd also gone to Forsyth's and treated himself to a new suit he couldn't really afford and three new shirts. He hated to admit it, but Wattie was right: Forsyth's was a cut above. Soon as he put the suit on, even he could tell the difference.

The town was busy, office workers using their lunchtime to go for a wander in the sun or sit on the benches in George Square. It had been a while since he'd been there last—seemed to be more shops opened. Shoe shops, boutiques, that sort of thing. He was just weighing up whether he should go to the Litebite for a roll or treat himself to an open sandwich from the Danish Food Centre when he saw them.

The first one was the tiny woman with the callipers. She was standing in the middle of Buchanan Street handing out tracts. Didn't seem to be having much luck. Most people just shook their heads and hurried by. Second was a man wearing a sandwich board with REPENT BEFORE IT IS TOO LATE painted on it in red letters. Wasn't long before McCoy heard the booming voice of Reverend West. He was standing on a wooden box outside Fraser's department store, Bible in hand, most of the congregation McCoy had seen on Sunday around him, armed with more tracts.

"Listen to what the Bible says, ladies and gentlemen. Listen to Peter—*Therefore, since Christ suffered in his body, arm yourselves also with the same attitude, because whoever suffers in the body is done with sin.*"

A few bored passers-by were watching the show: two wee boys nudging each other and laughing, an elderly couple looking interested, two hippies, one of them making "wanker" signs with his hand.

West zoned in on the elderly couple. Gave them both barrels. "Learn this and learn it now, my friends. Our time here is short, and we must suffer as Christ did if we want to ascend to heaven and be bathed in the glorious light of his love. Thank you and God bless you, one and all."

He stepped down, and the little crowd dispersed, elderly couple with tracts in hand. McCoy had hoped West wouldn't see him but no such luck.

West waved at him, walked over. "Mr. McCoy, did you come to hear me speak?"

"Just passing."

West looked disappointed. Rallied. "Oh, well, you still heard the word of the Lord. Did you get anything from it?"

"Told you before," said McCoy. "Wasting your time with me."

West looked round at the dearth of new followers. "Think I'm wasting my time here too. Not exactly a big crowd, but I need to keep trying. Never give in."

"It's lunchtime," said McCoy. "People are busy, not much time to stand and listen."

West nodded. "I'll leave it a couple of hours, then try again. The message has to get through somehow. These people are sleepwalking towards a journey to hell. Unless they repent, there is no hope for them."

That was probably why he was back at work just days after the death of his wife, thought McCoy. Before she was even in her grave. West believed with all his heart that he was fighting against evil. If conviction was enough to save you, he had it in spades.

"So," continued West, "if you haven't come to hear the word of the Lord, what brings you into town?"

"Something much less noble, I'm afraid." McCoy held up the Woolworth's bag. "Needed to buy a birthday present for my partner's wee boy. Matchbox cars, as instructed."

"Excellent."

McCoy suddenly realised talking about kids maybe wasn't the best idea, given Judith's obsession. "Sorry. Not very sensitive of me to talk about kids."

"Nonsense," said West. "Our misfortune with children doesn't—didn't—prevent us having joy in other people's. Judith loved kids, despite the hand we were dealt."

"Does your church still do a soup kitchen?"

"Thursday evenings. Why?"

"There's some very poisonous hooch going about, a few deaths already. Be good if you could spread the word not to drink it."

West nodded.

The lady with the callipers approached them, elderly couple in tow. "Reverend West? This couple were hoping to learn more about our church."

God help them, thought McCoy. "I'll leave you to it," he said and started to walk away.

There was something about West that didn't ring true. Maybe it was just McCoy's inbuilt distrust of any sort of clergy, but West bothered him. He knew it shouldn't, but the story of the never-was boy still nagged at him. He turned back, and West was smiling at the elderly couple, reaching out to put a friendly hand on the woman's shoulder. Another convert in the making.

THIRTY-NINE

C arlo, Rogano's maître d', greeted Margo like a long-lost sister. He took her hands, leant in and kissed her cheek. Raised his voice to make sure the other diners heard who was in the restaurant.

"Miss Lindsay, it's been too long. How are you?"

"Good, thank you," said Margo. "Glad to be back, as always."

"Your usual table?" said Carlo, whisking a couple of menus from a hovering waiter.

"Not tonight. We're joining friends. A Mr. . . ."

"Cooper," said McCoy.

Carlo tried and failed to disguise his surprise. "Ah. I can move the party to your usual table if you'd prefer?"

"Not at all, Carlo. We'll be fine," said Margo.

"As you wish. This way, please."

They walked through the bar, past the booths, people trying not to stare at the film star, and into the restaurant proper. It was hushed, comfortable, no real change since it had been built in the thirties. All art nouveau curves and bird's eye maple.

Stevie Cooper and his girlfriend were seated at a booth at the back. Not the best table in the house by any means, but they looked happy enough. Stevie was resplendent in suit, tie, black eye and stitches across his eyebrow. Gail wore a black sleeveless maxi dress that showed off her figure. Blonde hair reached halfway down her back.

After the introductions they ordered some drinks. Beer for

the boys, champagne for the girls. After Cooper had finished ribbing McCoy about his new suit Margo took a sip of her champagne and smiled at him.

"I'm sorry, Stevie, but I have to ask, what on earth happened to your face?"

"An accident," said Cooper. "I was swimming and didn't realise how fast I was going, bumped right into the side of the pool. No great damage done."

My arse, thought McCoy. Took a drink of his beer.

"Where was it you were swimming?"

"Arlington," said Cooper. "Go every day."

Margo looked delighted. "No! My father was a founder member. He loved that place."

And there it was. Having established Cooper was an "Arlington man," Margo decided the sun shone out of his backside. They chatted through the starters while McCoy made small talk with Gail. Apparently, auditions were a nightmare and she was sick of being treated as a dumb blonde by casting agents. Listening to her complain wasn't his idea of a great night out, but he had to admit it could be a lot worse.

Carlo materialised, took the plates away and filled up their glasses. Red wine that he insisted they try. McCoy sipped the little measure in his glass, pretended to be savouring the taste and pronounced it fine. Had no idea what it was supposed to taste like, but it seemed all right. Margo put her hand over her glass and announced that she and Gail were going to the powder room to have a little chat.

Soon as they were out of earshot, McCoy started. "Accident, my arse. Was that a gift from one of Archie Andrews' boys? The big fight?"

Cooper nodded. "Should have seen *him* though. Got him with one of Paul's Stanley knives."

"Jesus," said McCoy, trying not to picture the poor guy's face. "All go well, did it? Was all over the police radio, apparently."

"Yep. Only two of our boys in the hospital compared to most of his. Two pubs smashed to fuck. Andrews'll be on the back foot now."

"I saw the Round Toll. What a mess."

Cooper took a deep swig of his wine. "Other one was worse."

"Is Jumbo okay?" asked McCoy, dreading the worst.

"Right as rain. Pulled some big bugger with a knife off me before he could use it. Got him some *Commando* comics and a Chinese takeaway for tonight, he's a happy boy."

"Paul?"

"Not so good. Some bugger battered his shin with a hammer and broke it in two places. He's got a stookie, sitting in the armchair with his leg up, Iris flapping about."

"Don't know what's worse," said McCoy. "A broken leg or Iris looking after you."

Cooper looked around the restaurant, at the plush interior, at the gleaming glassware, the silver platters and the cream of Glasgow society enjoying a night out. No scars on their faces, no wary stares.

"Never thought you and I would end up in a place like this." Cooper sounded happy in a way he seldom did. Content.

"Not bad for two nobodies from the children's home."

"Speaking of which, I want you to come out with me after we drop the girls off."

"Where?"

"Out. Someone's trying to sell me Clouds. Want to go and have a look."

"What do you need me for? I was looking forward to an early night."

"I bet you were. She's some woman, your Margo," said Cooper, watching her walk across the restaurant, heads turning in her wake. "Still got no bloody idea what she sees in you."

"Would you believe it?" said Margo, sitting down. "Gail

here graduated from the Royal Scottish Academy of Music and Drama! Same as I did."

So that was Gail a great pal too, now. All was well. McCoy sat back, ate his dinner and drank his wine as the three of them got on like a house on fire. It was the last thing he'd expected, but it was better than them sitting in polite silence. He was just about to tuck into his baked Alaska and order another bottle of wine on Cooper's bill when he looked up and found Wattie standing there, Carlo behind him.

"Sorry, sir," said Wattie. "There's been another one, thought you'd like to know."

McCoy's stomach dropped. "It's not . . ."

Wattie shook his head. "No. It's Charlie the Pram."

FORTY

"Why him? Of all people?"

McCoy looked down at Charlie's body. Was like the others: head stretched back, mouth open, green bile drying on his chin.

Charlie the Pram had had it all once. A house, a wife, a good job. Then he had started hearing voices, hiding from people who weren't there. Had ended up wandering all over Glasgow, pushing his belongings in an old pram. Charlie saw parts of Glasgow most people didn't, disappeared into the background, kept his eyes out for McCoy. Had been more than a tout, had been a kind of a pal.

McCoy walked away from the body, and from Wattie and the circus beginning to assemble. He leant back on the bonnet of a panda and lit up. They were just off Alexandra Parade, in a yard behind a Masonic lodge in Wood Street. It was quiet and sheltered, the perfect place for Charlie to settle in for the night and drink a bottle in peace.

He could see Wattie giving out instructions to the uniforms, telling the ambulance van where to park, doing his job. McCoy knew he should be helping but he couldn't bring himself to—just wanted to sit there and wish it hadn't happened.

He could see a figure approaching, could tell who it was by the shuffling walk alone. Gerry. Big black suit, white shirt, gloves, left leg trailing.

"What you doing over here, Gerry? This isn't your normal patch, is it?"

"I found him. Charlie's here most nights, thought I'd better check on him. Try and warn him about the hooch. But—"

"Too late."

Gerry nodded. Looked about as sad as McCoy felt.

"Was he a pal of yours?"

"Sort of. Sometimes he was okay, sometimes you couldn't get through to him, was away with the fairies. Good days and bad days."

McCoy knew exactly what he meant. Looked back over at the crowd and saw Wattie was waving him over. "Be back in a minute."

"You all right?" asked Wattie as he approached.

McCoy nodded. Wasn't. "What's up?"

"Couple of things. There's no bottle. We've looked everywhere, all through his pram as well. If he died alone, it should be beside him, shouldn't it?"

"Unless someone took it to hide the evidence."

"And if you're doing that, then it's no innocent accident with dodgy hooch. It's murder."

"What's the other thing?"

Wattie glanced past McCoy. "Your pal over there."

"Gerry?"

"Don't you think it's a bit weird that he's always around when these bodies are discovered? He reported them, and here he is finding Charlie. Bit of a coincidence, isn't it? Plus, this is the back arse of nowhere, not a usual hangout for alkies. Not like he would be walking past."

"Said he came to check up on Charlie."

"Did he now? Makes a habit of tucking up Glasgow's alkies for the night, does he? Maybe he came here to give him something. Like a nice big bottle of hooch that was going to kill him."

"Come on, Wattie, it's not like—"

"Like what? Just because they live on the street doesn't

make them bloody fallen angels, you know. Some of them are right bastards. You just don't want to believe it."

Wattie was right: Gerry's presence might well be more than a coincidence. If there was a bottle, he could have taken it and hidden it before he called them in.

"Why would Gerry be murdering down-and-outs? And why would he be drawing attention to the killings none of us found suspicious till he told us about them?"

"Some killers want to be noticed. If the crime doesn't get attention, they'll find another way."

McCoy sighed. Couldn't argue with that. "Let's get him in tomorrow. Get a statement. See what he's got to say."

Wattie nodded, went back to the scene.

McCoy walked over to Charlie's pram. Was full of stuff that meant nothing to anyone but Charlie himself. Bits of paper with spidery writing on. Some pebbles. Half a loaf in a paper bag. Three notebooks full of drawings of devils and angels. And a photograph folded over and over. McCoy unfolded it, white cracks crossing it. Looked like Aden or Malta, somewhere like that. A group of young soldiers, sleeves rolled up, arms around each other smiling for the camera. A young Charlie in the middle, huge grin on his face. Not a care in the world.

McCoy put the picture in his pocket, wasn't sure why. Just didn't want it going to the dump with the rest of Charlie's stuff. Wattie was talking to Gerry, writing down the address of the Possil station. Could imagine what he was saying. *Just routine because you discovered the body, nothing to worry about.*

Gerry put the paper in his pocket and wandered off.

Poor bugger had no idea what he was in for.

FORTY-ONE

McCoy needed a drink. Too wound up by what had happened to go home and sleep. He got Wattie to drop him off at Lauder's in Sauchiehall Street, got there just in time for last orders. Walked in, and Cooper was holding two pints, passed him one.

"Girls went home in a taxi. Going back to Margo's for another drink, chatting away like old pals. Who's Charlie the Pram by the way? Another of your dead alkies?"

McCoy nodded.

The pub was slowly emptying, customers heading home or off for a fish supper or a night at the dancing. Barman rang the bell, shouted, "Let's be having you." McCoy and Cooper sank their pints, put the glasses on the bar and followed everyone else out. They started walking up the hill to the Apollo, squeezing past the lines of people waiting for their buses.

"Why do you want to buy a disco?"

"I don't know if I do," said Cooper, "but the accountant thinks it's a good idea. Cash business. Helps hide the money I'm not supposed to have."

McCoy stopped. Ahead of him was a queue of a hundred-odd people waiting to get into the disco above the Apollo. All of them dressed to the nines, good few of them passing quarter-bottles back and forth. "Fuck sake. It's going to take ages to get in."

"Is it fuck," said Cooper. "Just follow me."

He walked straight to the front. Ignored the complaints from the queue. A young guy about the size of Jumbo in a too-tight dinner suit was standing by the door looking bored. Suddenly sprang to life when he saw Cooper.

"Mr. Cooper," he said. "Welcome to Clouds. Mr. Dunbar is upstairs."

He held the door open—immediate distant thump of music. Cooper put a couple of quid in the guy's pocket and they went in. The actual disco was a couple of flights up, music getting louder as they ascended the stairs. A young guy was standing in the entrance at the top of the stairs: moustache, huge flares, corduroy bomber jacket, big smile.

"Mr. Cooper, come away in."

Was hard to see anything at first, just dry ice and pulsing green and red lights. There was a dancefloor, booths up the side. The clientele were young, good-looking. Satin bomber jackets with Vietnam army stuff embroidered on the back or tight cap-sleeve T-shirts for the boys, boob tubes and tight shiny trousers for the girls. Music was loud, bass thumping in their chests. McCoy was amazed that he recognised the song, "The Love I Lost." Had heard it on the radio a few times in the car.

Dunbar guided them to a booth, shouting over the music as they sat down. "Got a bit of a celebrity in tonight," he said, nodding at the opposite booth.

McCoy looked over, expecting a Miss Scotland or some Celtic player. First person he saw was Sister Jimmy, second was Jake Scott, the singer of Holy Fire. As befits a celebrity, Jake was sitting in the centre of the booth, someone very skinny and very good-looking with an arm draped round him. Black suit, black shirt, silver tie, black lipstick, blonde hair slicked back. No idea if they were a he or a she.

"All right, Mr. McCoy. Didn't expect to see you here," said Jake sleepily as he approached the booth. "Bit young for you in here, isn't it?"

"Thought you were living it up in America, Jake?"

"I was. Had a few days off, and Sam here wanted to see Glasgow."

Sam smiled. Bright white teeth.

"Harry McCoy, friend to the stars," said Sister Jimmy. "Who'd have thunk it. Glad you're here though, saves me a trip to the wilds of Possil." He stood up, eased his way out the booth. "Come to my office."

Sister Jimmy made his way through the dancers to a fire exit at the back, McCoy following. Jimmy pushed it open and held it for McCoy. They stepped out onto an iron staircase. The door closed behind them, and it was suddenly silent, no thump from the big speakers. Glasgow was laid out below, lights twinkling in the darkness. Could even see the Red Road flats silhouetted against the night sky in the distance. The view made McCoy realise just how high up they were.

"This why they call it Clouds, is it?" he said.

"Yep," said Jimmy, leaning against the railing and staring out. "You notice how out of it your singer pal and his chum are?"

"Not really, was hard to see anything in there."

"The both of them, eyes pinned—that give you a clue?"

"Ah. Smack?"

Jimmy nodded.

"Par for the course for rock stars, is it not?"

"Yep. It's where they got it that's interesting."

"How's that?"

Jimmy turned to McCoy and smiled. "Did you see a guy in there, tall, reddish hair, yellow Simon shirt on?"

"Might have done. To be honest, it sounds like every bugger in there."

"Well, his name is Teddy. Teddy Jamieson, to be accurate. Rab Jamieson's son. Always out and about, face on the scene—always in here, Cinders, the Arms. Good-looking boy, and he knows it. Wouldn't say no, myself. Anyway, he's starting to deal to a select clientele. Smack, hash, even has coke sometimes. All comes up from Liverpool. There's no way his dad doesn't know, has to have set him up with the contacts and the initial buy money."

"His dad who works for Archie Andrews, who has a strict no-drugs policy?"

"Yep. Did Andrews' son not die of an overdose or something?"

"His nephew. You sure about this?"

"Oh yes. Jake thinks he's too famous to be involved with a drug dealer, doesn't want his hands dirty. Gave me the money and a decent tip to sort it out for him. Teddy Jamieson was out here with me half an hour ago handing it over, telling me anytime Jake needs anything to let him know."

McCoy got his wallet out, handed Jimmy fifty quid.

"Was only thirty," said Jimmy.

"You can give me the twenty back if you want."

"Aye, right," said Jimmy, putting the money in his pocket. "Glad to be of service."

Cooper was sitting in a booth with Dunbar and a few others when McCoy got back in. Even with the smoke and the coloured lights, McCoy could tell by the look on his face that he was bored. Looked like he wasn't going to be joining the nightlife industry after all. He saw McCoy and stood up, said a hurried goodbye and came over to him.

"Where have you been? Let's get going, waste of a bloody night."

"I wouldn't say that. Far as you're concerned, it's been your best night out for a while."

Cooper looked at him. "Fuck you on about, McCoy? Been smoking the wacky baccy with Sister Jimmy, have you?"

McCoy smiled. "I'll tell you on the way home."

WEDNESDAY

18TH JUNE 1975

FORTY-TWO

The desk sergeant stuck his head around the office door, shouted across the office, "Gerry Lewis is here for his interview."

McCoy gathered up his notes, his jotter and his pen.

Wattie put his hand out. "I want to do this one myself, Harry."

"How come?"

"I don't want you in there, in the interview. You'll be too soft on him. Okay?"

McCoy nodded. Watched Wattie gather up his notes from his desk and go. Felt a bit peeved. He should be happy—it showed Wattie was becoming his own man, a proper polis. Didn't feel that happy though, felt like he was being left out of things. Was so lost in feeling sorry for himself he didn't notice Helen standing in front of him until she spoke.

"I need to talk to you."

"What's up?"

"I showed your birth certificate to a friend of mine, works in the registry at Martha Street. Deals with them every day. She wants a word." She looked at her watch. "She'll be in the Press Bar for the next hour. Go and see her."

"That sounds ominous."

"You're telling me. I've never seen her so excited."

"What's her name?"

"Audrey Gibson," said Helen. "She's tiny. Black bob and red lipstick. You can't miss her."

The Press Bar was next to the newspaper offices, always packed with journalists and blokes who worked on the big presses. McCoy had never been in there and it not be busy, and today was no exception. A sea of middle-aged blokes in shirt-sleeves drinking pints and, sitting at the bar, just as Helen had described, Audrey Gibson.

McCoy sat on the stool next to her, held out his hand and introduced himself.

Audrey turned to him, looked him up and down. "You know what a functioning alcoholic is, Mr. McCoy?"

McCoy nodded. "I think so."

"Good, then you won't mind me ordering what I want. For you?"

McCoy asked for a pint and Audrey asked for a triple vodka. Straight. No ice. The drinks were put down in front of them and she swallowed over half of hers. Grimaced.

"Now that's out the way, where did you get this birth certificate?"

"Found it in a church," said McCoy. He wasn't lying but he wasn't exactly telling the whole truth either. "Why?"

"What do you know about it?"

"Nothing. That's why I'm sitting here."

Audrey looked from side to side as if she was scared of someone listening in. She took an envelope out her bag, wiped the bar with a towel, took the birth certificate out and smoothed it out in front of them. "There's a problem. A big problem."

"What's that?"

"The paper that birth certificates are printed on changed in nineteen fifty-one. Something to do with supplies being difficult to get a hold of after the war. Not something that anyone but an expert would notice."

She rooted around in her bag and brought out a folded piece of paper. Waited until the man sitting on the next stool finished his pint and moved off. "This is my birth certificate," she said, laying it beside the other one. "Audrey Anne Gibson. Born nineteen forty-nine."

McCoy looked at them. Looked exactly the same to him. "I don't get it. What's the problem?"

"Look at them," said Audrey, knocking back the rest of her vodka. "Closely."

He did. Was still none the wiser.

Audrey put her finger on the certificate McCoy had found. "The one you have is printed on different paper to mine. It's printed on the new paper, but it's dated nineteen forty-six. It should be on the old paper, same as mine."

"Maybe it's a duplicate?"

Audrey shook her head. "The duplicates are easy to spot, printed on cheap paper by the post office. This isn't a duplicate."

McCoy was lost. "So what is it then?"

"It's an official birth certificate, all right, but I've never seen one like it. One like this is only produced when someone is given a new identity by the government. Made my day to see it, sad as that is."

"Eh?"

"Say you're an important witness to some terrible crime and you agree to testify even though you know it's basically a death sentence. Whoever did it will take their revenge no matter how long it takes. The government, very occasionally, will give you a new identity to protect you. New name, new birth certificate, new driving licence. A new life with no connection to your old one. If whoever the criminal was is still after you, this would be worth a lot of money. Once you have this? It's a guarantee of who they are now, their new identity. You could find them easily."

Audrey looked at her watch, swore, put her own certificate back in her bag and eased herself off the stool. She really was tiny.

"Need to go. Need to open the hellhole up again."

"Thanks for that," said McCoy.

"Just be careful. A birth certificate like that is always going to have someone looking for it."

He watched her go, sipped at his pint, sat there trying to think. Only one person he knew of who was apparently interested in this birth certificate: Duncan Kent. Maybe somebody did the dirty on him, went to the polis and started talking for the promise of a new identity. Then Duncan Kent was still so angry about it he wanted to hunt them down. Maybe it was the wife of someone who had been a bit too loose with his pillow talk.

He still didn't understand why Malky's sister had the birth certificate though—she was far too old to be Kathleen Garvie herself. Maybe she'd overheard something at the Kents'? Stolen the birth certificate, wanted money from Kent for it and overplayed her hand. Didn't work out, so she decided to steal some of his money from the safe and run. Kent must have thought she gave the certificate to her brother for safekeeping and tortured him to find out where it was.

McCoy took another drink of his pint. A paper boy had appeared, big bundle under his arm, walking round the bar. Doing good business. The journalists were keen to see their words in print, he supposed.

It almost made sense. Far as he could make out, Kent still wouldn't have a clue to the person's new identity. There was one big question sitting in the middle of the whole thing. Who was Kathleen Garvie? And, more importantly, who had she been before?

FORTY-THREE

McCoy took his time walking back to the station. He had a lot to think about. Plus, he wanted Gerry's interview out the way before he got there. Saracen Street was its usual jumble of buses heading north or back into town. There was a queue outside the bakery, guys in dirty work clothes and boots waiting for their rolls and pies.

As he turned the corner into Bardowie Street he saw Long and Rossi walking out the station entrance, deep in conversation. Rossi was no doubt telling Long what a naughty boy McCoy had been. Maybe he should give Murray a call tonight, keep him up to date. The pair got into an unmarked car, still talking away. Thick as thieves.

He pulled the station door open and just about walked into Gerry coming out. He looked glum, head down, muttering to himself under his breath.

"Gerry? How did it go?"

Gerry looked like he was about to burst into tears. "He thinks I'm a liar. Your pal, he thinks I killed those men. He thinks I gave them poison to drink. Why would I do that? All I ever tried to do was help people."

"Wattie? I'm sure he doesn't think that at all. He has to ask these questions though; it's his job. It's nothing personal."

Gerry didn't seem convinced.

"What did you tell him?"

"I told him the truth. That I came to check on Charlie and I found him dead. No bottle, nobody else there. I didn't kill him."

"If you didn't, then you're fine. Did you explain that to Wattie?"

"Yeah. Then he asked me about the other dead men. I told him that's what I do. I walk around at night, try to make sure everyone's okay. I don't think he believed me. I told him over and over but . . ." Rubbed his eyes, stood there like he had the weight of the world on his shoulders.

McCoy dug in his pocket, handed him a couple of quid. "Away down to the Lido, get yourself something to eat, eh? Make you feel better."

Gerry took the money. "Thank you," he said. "I'm sorry about Charlie. I know he was your pal. He used to talk about you, said you were one of the—"

"Gerry!"

Wattie was standing at the door, clipboard and pen in his hand. "Glad I caught you," he said. Saw the expression of terror on Gerry's face. Smiled. "It's nothing to worry about. I just forgot to get your full name for the statement. Is it Gerald or Gerard?"

"Neither. It's Jeremiah."

McCoy looked at him. Stomach rolled over. "What did you say?"

"My name is Jeremiah."

"Do you know Reverend West?"

Gerry stood for a minute. Looked at McCoy. Nodded. "Oh, I know him all right. He tried to crucify me."

FORTY-FOUR

Y ou're never bloody out of here," said Tony as they walked
into the Lido. "You no got a home to go to?"

McCoy went to the counter, let Wattie and Gerry find
a booth. "Can only boil a kettle. Three teas, please."

"Coming right up," said Tony.

McCoy walked to the booth at the back of the cafe. Radio
was on as usual, sounded like the Beach Boys. Summer weather
must have inspired the DJ. Gerry was as far away from Wattie
as he could get and still be sitting in the same booth. No wonder, thought McCoy. Wattie was still the villain.

He sat down and watched as Gerry took a sugar lump from
the silver bowl, unwrapped it and ate it. He was wobbling in
the seat, face white.

"When did you last eat?" said McCoy. "Properly, I mean."

Gerry shrugged.

"Right. You sit there, we'll get you something, you eat it in
peace and then we'll have a chat? That okay?"

Gerry nodded.

McCoy turned to the counter. Called out, "Full breakfast
over here and lots of toast, Tony, eh? Soon as you can."

"No worries, Harry," said Tony and shouted the order back
into the kitchen.

McCoy and Wattie left Gerry waiting for his breakfast,
stepped outside and lit up. Sun dazzling them after the dim
cafe. McCoy took his jacket off, loosened his tie. Across the
street a man in a vest was drinking a can of Tennent's, happily

serenading the passers-by with a version of "Little Green Apples."

"Crucified?" said Wattie, taking out his last fag and dropping the empty Regal packet in the wire bin attached to the lamppost. "He can't be serious, can he? Wouldn't he be dead?"

"Fuck knows. How did the interview go anyway?"

Wattie shrugged. "Pointless. He stuck to his guns. Says he goes round checking on people and that's why he found Charlie. Even if I don't believe him, there's nothing I can do to take it any further. Short of us finding a bottle of the stuff with his fingerprints on it, he's free as a bird."

"He say anything else?"

"Did say one weird thing. He said, 'If you don't believe me, then ask Mr. Hood. He sees me all the time.'"

"Hood? Our Hood? From the station?"

"Yep."

McCoy couldn't believe it. "Well, he's changed his bloody tune. From thinking all down-and-outs are a waste of space to becoming a living saint wandering the streets. What's that about?"

"I'll check with him, see what he's got to say to it."

McCoy dropped his cigarette end on the pavement and stood on it. "Better go in. Get it over with."

McCoy and Wattie squeezed past the queue of punters waiting for a table and made their way back to the booth. Gerry was looking less fragile, empty plate in front of him.

"Feeling better?" asked McCoy.

Gerry nodded.

"Right, Gerry. Need you to tell us about Reverend West. Start at the beginning and just take your time. Okay?"

Gerry kept his head down, started talking. "My mum joined his church when I was wee. Just went occasionally at first, then as time went on, she became a proper regular, used to take me with her. Then she started giving out the leaflets in town, attending special prayer meetings with Reverend West. That sort of thing. Changed my name to Jeremiah in honour of the church."

He raised his head, looked at McCoy. "She wasn't always well, my mum. She got ideas in her head, and they wouldn't go away."

"Like what?"

"She stopped me going to school, said it was ungodly and that all I needed to know was in the Bible. Made us fast for days at a time, said it was an offering to God. And then"—a pause—"and then Reverend West started talking about suffering being the key to holiness. How we should offer up suffering to honour the Lord. And my mum took it all in. He told her the suffering of an innocent was better than a sinner. That it meant more. That it would help show us the path to enlightenment."

Gerry's hands were shaking; he'd gone white again.

"In West's church, Midsummer's Day is like Easter. It's the big occasion. It's the longest day, the day we can spend longest suffering to reach God. For three or four days before it, my mum didn't give me anything to eat. I kept passing out, wasn't quite sure what was going on. Think maybe there was something in the water she gave me to drink. The only thing I really remember is waking up in the attic of his house. It was pitch-black, and he was leaning over me. Saying, 'In two minutes, the sun will rise. Midsummer, the longest day. Prepare to carry us home.'"

He rubbed his eyes again. Kept going. "And I realised I was lying on a cross, tied onto it."

"What?" said McCoy. "Are you sure? Maybe you were hallucinating, if you hadn't eaten for days, like—"

He stopped, realised Gerry was shrugging his jacket off, starting to unbutton his white shirt. The girls in the next booth started to giggle.

Gerry pulled his shirt off, and McCoy gasped, could hear

Wattie swearing under his breath. Girls weren't giggling any more.

Gerry's arms were grotesquely misshapen. The left one was just skin and bone; the right one had what looked like another elbow poking out beside the original one.

"'As soon as the dawn light comes through the skylight and hits us,' he said to me, 'one of us must suffer so all of us may find Christ.' And I was the one that suffered. He hit me with an iron bar, my arms and legs."

He couldn't stop the tears falling onto the Formica tabletop. He wiped his eyes with the shirt. "And then he hammered the nails through my hands and I passed out."

"Son, you don't have to put yourself through this," said McCoy. "If it's too much, just—"

"Yes, I do." Gerry nodded at Wattie. "Because this guy doesn't believe what I say."

Gerry peeled off his left glove, then the right. Laid his hands on the table, palms up. There were two dark circles of scar tissue in the middle of each palm, each a couple of inches across. They were purple, livid against his pale skin.

"Do you believe me now?" he said.

FORTY-FIVE

Twenty minutes and another round of toast later, Gerry was beginning to look normal again. McCoy and Wattie left him dipping his toast into his mug of tea and stepped outside. Needed to talk, to try and make sense of what he'd told them without him hearing.

"So what do we do now?" said Wattie.

"We go and speak to the Reverend West. See what he's got to say for himself."

"About what?" said Wattie, stepping aside to let a young woman with an excited toddler blabbering on about an ice lolly into the cafe. "A nutty story from an unreliable witness about something that supposedly happened years ago? Where is that going to get us? He's not—"

Wattie stopped. It dawned on him. "Oh, for fuck sake. You still think there's a missing boy, don't you?"

McCoy nodded. "There might be a chance—"

"Of what? That West had a kid and kept him secret for nine years, so one day he can half-kill him for the glory of God without anyone knowing? Are you nuts, McCoy? This is Glasgow, not the bloody wilds! He couldn't do it. It's impossible."

"I just want to ask him a few questions." McCoy sounded more petulant than he intended.

"And you're going to use what that nutter Gerry said as an excuse to do it?"

"You saw his hands. Do you think he's lying?"

"I don't know," said Wattie. "And neither do you. Fuck

knows what happened to him. I don't think even he knows half the time. But the way you look at it, you've won the pools. Another excuse to have a go at someone you don't like, who, funnily enough, just happens to be a bloody minister. Even better. I told you before, McCoy, you need to have a good look at yourself. See what you're really doing."

"And what exactly is that?" said McCoy, starting to get annoyed.

"You try and punish every minister or priest you come across because of what happened to you as a wee boy. What you're doing isn't even policework any more, it's just a personal vendetta."

"That right, is it, Detective Sergeant?"

"Christ, I thought you were better than that. You think reminding me you're the boss is going to make me shut up? I hate to say this, but ever since we came to Possil you've been acting as much of a prick as all the other fuckers here." He went to walk off, but then turned back and faced McCoy. "You know what? Maybe you've found your ideal station after all. Tell me this, Detective Inspector McCoy: how was it intimidating a witness? Get in a few kicks as well as Long, did you? Nice one."

"How did you know about—"

"How did I know? Because I'm not stupid, Harry! People talk, and I sit there looking like a big stupid lump staring into space, and meanwhile I'm taking it all in."

"There's a reason I was there," said McCoy, trying to calm him down.

"Maybe there is. But I wouldn't know because you don't tell me anything any more."

Wattie's face was getting red. Breathing heavy. Looked like he'd like nothing more than to punch McCoy in the face.

"Let me go in and ask Gerry a few questions," said McCoy.

"Send him on his way. Then I'll talk to you. Talk to you properly. Tell you everything that's been going on. Okay?"

Wattie didn't say anything, still looked furious. McCoy took it as a yes, went back into the cafe.

He sat in the booth opposite Gerry. "Full up?"

Gerry nodded. "For once."

"Does West have a son?"

"Not that I know of. But me and my mum left the church ten years ago, and I've never been back. He could have, I suppose."

"Keep your eyes open. Keep telling people not to drink hooch. Find Liam or me if anything else bad happens."

He left Gerry there with another cup of sugary tea. He knew he was going to have to tell Wattie everything, even the stuff Murray had expressly told him not to. He owed him. He pushed the cafe door open, was going to suggest going for a pint, but there was no one to suggest it to. He looked up and down the street, but Wattie had gone.

FORTY-SIX

Y ou just missed him," said the desk sergeant, looking up from his paper. "Said he'd be back in a couple of hours."

"Shite," said McCoy.

"Did he not tell you? Thought you two were as thick as thieves."

The door to the office swung open and Hood appeared. Even dressed in his civvies, jeans and short-sleeved shirt, he still looked like a polis. He'd a gym bag over his shoulder, wet hair combed into a side shed.

"Sir . . ."

"The very man," said McCoy. "You seen that wee guy Gerry around when you're helping at the soup kitchens and stuff?"

"Saw him yesterday," said Hood. "At the Sally Army by the Clyde. He was in the queue. That's about it, I think."

"You've certainly changed your tune," said McCoy.

Hood shrugged. "Lowell's a good guy, said I'd help as a favour to him, that's it. They're still a waste of space as far as I'm concerned."

McCoy let him go and stepped back out into the street. If Wattie had left the station, he must be in a bigger huff than he'd realised. Probably taking a couple of hours to walk it off.

He started up the hill towards Whitburn Street. Figured he may as well speak to West today, get it done. It was hard to believe Gerry was telling the truth, but his body hadn't lied: something bad had happened to him at some point. Whether that was West or not, he couldn't tell.

He passed the Vogue cinema and kept walking. Was glad of the chance to speak to West without Wattie knowing. Wattie's words had hit home. Probably because they were at least half true. Maybe he had gone over the edge, started seeing every priest or minister as someone to be investigated, not to be trusted. Maybe he was becoming some sort of modern Witchfinder General like in the film. So caught up in his own beliefs, he couldn't see that he was the problem. Maybe.

West was in the garden when he got there, down to his shirtsleeves, hoe in hand. Looked up as McCoy approached. "Weeds. The garden was Judith's department. Trying not to let it go to rack and ruin. This a social call?"

"'Fraid not."

West put the hoe down. "In that case we'd better go inside."

McCoy sat at the kitchen table while West busied himself making tea. The table was covered in piles of leaflets, all black and red, all the same message of doom. *Suffer to Know Christ.* Cheery stuff.

West pushed a few aside, set the two mugs on the table and sat down. "So, Detective Inspector, what can I do for you?"

"I've been talking to Gerry Lewis," said McCoy.

West rolled his eyes, shook his head and grinned. Not quite the reaction McCoy expected. "Oh dear," said West. "What is it I've done this time?"

Even as McCoy said it, it sounded ridiculous. "He says you crucified him."

"Did he?" West looked genuinely interested. "That's a new one. I only broke his leg before. I'm going up in the world." He took a sip of his tea. "How much do you know about Bobby Lewis, Inspector?"

"Bobby?"

"Yes, Bobby's his real name. My middle name is Jeremiah; his mother changed his as some sort of tribute."

"I don't get it."

West sat back in his chair. "Let me try to explain. Elaine Lewis, his mother, is a very troubled person. She'd been in and out of state institutions before she had Bobby. Should probably still be in there, if I'm being honest. She started coming to our church many years ago. I think she'd been through a few others before us. The Jehovah's Witnesses, Plymouth Brethren. At first, she was quite sincere about her belief, quite stable. Then things went off track."

"How do you mean?"

"She fundamentally misunderstood the idea of suffering, how we perceive it in our church. We see it as suffering from a lack of God's love, nothing else. She got it in her head somehow that it meant physical suffering. She started hurting herself. Came and showed me the scars on her arms and head where she'd been cutting herself with a razor. Poor woman thought I'd be pleased. She stopped eating for days, drank only water, half delirious most of the time. I tried to help her, but her illness was beyond my help."

"I thought you didn't believe in psychiatrists? I thought prayer would solve everything?"

"I don't, but this was different. It was clear there was something physically wrong with her brain. It wasn't functioning properly. She needed professional help of some sort."

"So what happened then?"

"She disappeared for a couple of years, and I thought that was that. I thought she must have moved on to another church. But then she came back." West looked serious. Sad, even. "She looked much better than she had before, but the reason for that was because she had transferred all her madness onto poor Bobby. It was a January day, cold, and she came to the door with a big coat on, Bobby standing behind her. He looked half emaciated. His face was grey, pinched, and he had bandages on both arms. She presented him to me as any other proud mother would do. Said she was doing the Lord's work."

West stood up, went to the cupboard and got a bottle of whisky out, splashed some into both mugs.

"Sorry, I don't like thinking about this." He smiled. "Even a man of God needs earthly help sometimes. Anyway, my face must have told the story. I was horrified, I couldn't hide it. I tried to get her to come in, so I could get the boy some help, but she sensed something was wrong. She picked him up—couldn't have weighed more than a few stone—and ran. I called the police, but they weren't much help. They told me to speak to the social, so I did, but nothing came of it. Seemed like Elaine and her boy had disappeared again."

Another sip of the tea.

"And that was that, until a couple of years ago. One Sunday I looked up from the altar and Bobby Lewis was sitting in a pew."

"Did you speak to him?"

West nodded. "He told me he'd lost contact with his mother, he thought she was in an institution, and that he was living on the streets. I gave him a few pounds, told him he was always welcome at the church. Obviously, that wasn't enough. He was back again the next week, except this time he stood outside the church telling the congregation not to go in, that I was an evil man, that I had hurt him. That went on for a few weeks, every Sunday, and then he disappeared again."

"And you never hurt him?"

"I'm a man of God. Why would I do such a thing? The only person I know who hurt him was his mother."

"He's got terrible scars on his palms," said McCoy.

"I don't know anything about that. I'd guess either he or his mother are responsible."

"You think he hurt himself?"

"Look, I don't want to speak ill of a young man who is clearly disturbed, struggling with life, but Bobby says and does things sometimes to get attention, to get sympathy. There were a few incidents when he was younger."

"What kind of incidents?"

"First time, he was playing with the other children round the back of the church. He appeared in the church with Simon, a lad aged two or so, in his arms. Simon was howling, blood coming from a cut on his head. Bobby said a bad boy from over the houses had thrown a stone at him and he'd chased him away. Naturally the congregation were very pleased with him for doing such a brave thing and saving Simon."

"But . . ."

"A couple of days later, Andrea, a very timid wee girl, finally told her mum she'd seen Bobby hit Simon with the stone himself. He'd made the whole story up."

McCoy sat back in his chair. Didn't want to admit it, but what West was saying made sense. "Have you seen him lately?"

West shook his head. "But I think he's up to his old tricks. He came to one of our soup kitchens a couple of months ago. Told Judith that I'd broken his leg when he was younger. And then Bill, a member of our congregation, met him in the street. Told Bill he was working for the police in a top-secret capacity. That they'd asked him to help them solve a series of murders. And that if he did well, they were going to offer him a proper job."

McCoy left West at the kitchen table still sipping his tea. Walked out the house and up the path. West's story made more sense than Gerry's. Seemed like Wattie was right—he had been blinded by Gerry and his stories, too eager to believe them.

He stopped at the gate, got his cigarettes out and lit up. Wondered about how eager Gerry was to be in the centre of things, to be important. If he was eager enough to poison people and then "find" them? Didn't seem outwith the realms of possibility. Maybe Wattie should have another go at him.

He walked out the gate onto the pavement, turned to shut the gate behind him. Saw the flicker of movement in the attic window of West's house. Someone walking across the room? He stopped, waited for a while to see if he saw it again, but the figure didn't appear.

Must have imagined it.

FORTY-SEVEN

S o let me get this straight," said Wattie, counting on his
fingers. "Duncan Kent is after someone who fucked him
over, Gerry has been telling porky pies, and we're here
on an undercover mission to find out how corrupt Long is?
That it?"

"Pretty much," said McCoy.

"So how come you didn't tell me why we were coming here
at the beginning?"

The question McCoy hoped he wasn't going to ask. "Murray
thought it would be better if we had different viewpoints. Me
looking for trouble here and you just being normal, seeing if
anything stuck out."

Wasn't that convincing of a lie, but Wattie seemed to take it
on board.

He hadn't reappeared until just before the end of the day.
Still looked a bit huffy to McCoy, but at least he was talking to
him again. They had walked up to the Glen Douglas for a pint,
and McCoy had spilled the beans as promised.

"Sure there's not anything else? Rossi's a space alien? You've
won the pools? We're being transferred to Edinburgh next?"

"Very funny. Nope, that's it."

"So where does that leave us?"

"Not much further on than we were before. We can go and
see Kent, but that's going to be a dead end. All Kent has to
do is say he has no idea about any birth certificate and that'll
be pretty much that. Norma McGregor's not expected to hang

on much longer, zero chance of regaining consciousness, Malky McCormack's murder will be unsolved, and the world will move on. We still don't know who's poisoning the down-and-outs—"

"If they even are."

"And I need to get some more evidence on Long that's not just beer money on a Friday. Can't use the old guy, would just be my word against his. Plus, the old guy will be too scared to say anything."

"Great," said Wattie. "All going well then. Another pint?"

He stood up and made his way through the tables of tea-time drinkers towards the bar. The Glen Douglas was one of those pubs where there always seemed to be something going on. People whispering in corners, people watching the door and pretending not to. Word would have gone around that there were two cops in as soon as they arrived.

"Where did you go anyway?" asked McCoy when Wattie got back with the drinks.

"Went for a walk," said Wattie, sitting down. "Then I went to see Lowell at the Salvation Army."

"What did you go and see him for?"

Wattie took a drink of his pint and one of McCoy's cigarettes from the pack on the table. "I ended up that way, so I thought I'd drop in, see if he'd heard anything."

"And had he?"

Wattie shook his head, wiped away his foam moustache, stuck the cigarette in his mouth. "Nope, thinks the message about not drinking the hooch might have filtered down. Most of the guys they talked to knew to look out for it."

"That's one thing, then," said McCoy. "Who knows? Maybe it was just a rogue batch and it's over now."

"Let's hope so. So what do we do about Long?"

"Not sure there's much I can do—just have to wait for him to come to me. Can't look too keen."

"You think he will?"

McCoy shrugged. "I bloody hope so. The sooner he does, and I have something concrete for Murray, the sooner we can get out of here."

Wattie chucked the rest of his pint over. Nodded at the half-pint left in McCoy's glass. "Drink that, and I'll give you a lift home. The wee bugger should be asleep by now."

Wattie dropped McCoy off in Dumbarton Road at the bottom of his street. He wanted a pee, which was all the excuse he needed to go into Victoria's instead of walking up the hill. He pulled the door open, nodded to Jimmy behind the bar and headed for the toilets. He came out a minute or so later and sat at the bar, was just about to raise his pint to his lips, when he heard a voice behind him.

"They said I'd find you in here."

He turned. Long was standing there, car keys in hand.

"C'mon," he said, "we've got work to do."

FORTY-EIGHT

L ong drove. Didn't tell McCoy where they were going. Didn't say much at all. He kept his eyes on the road, cigarette in the corner of his mouth. Headed through the West End and up towards Maryhill. Light rain had come on, blurring the streetlights. Long switched the windscreen wipers on. A gentle chug-chug.

"What are we doing?" asked McCoy.

"I'll tell you when we get there."

McCoy gave up, leant his head against the car window and watched the world go by. A glimpse of in-focus street every so often as the rain ran down the window. Smell of Long's No. 10 and the quiet chatter on the police radio.

Twenty minutes later they were in Lambhill. Long drove past St. Agnes' Church, slowed the car down and reversed into a narrow road that led to a garage. *MOTs for Less!* sign above the entrance. They were pretty well hidden from the passing traffic by a clump of bushes and a big chestnut tree, but they still had a clear view of the row of shops on the other side of the street.

Long pointed. "See that post office? That's why we're here. Tonight the owner shuts it, but he stays in there working late."

"Okay," said McCoy.

"And tonight it's going to get turned over."

McCoy's stomach lurched, had visions of himself with a sawn-off shotgun threatening some terrified pensioner. "By who?"

"Don't need to know that."

"Right." McCoy gave an inward sigh of relief.

Long pointed at the post office again. "The old boy in there isn't daft. He's got an alarm button under the counter, and soon as they burst in, he's going to try to press it. If he does, that's where we come in."

McCoy nodded, although he wasn't quite sure what was going on.

"If he does, there'll be a call on the radio saying there's a raid. We make sure we answer first and say we're in the vicinity and we'll be there in two minutes."

"So we go in?"

"No," said Long. "We sit here until they've gone."

"And we've said we're on the way to stop any other cars coming?"

"Exactly. Not our fault if we turn up too late, is it?" Long looked at his watch. "Ten minutes."

McCoy had smoked a cigarette, watched a dog sniff at an overturned bin and some kids pass on their bikes, all the while with a gnawing feeling in his stomach. Was about to light up another when Long sat up in his seat.

"Here we go."

A navy-blue Cortina estate drove up the hill from Cadder and pulled over in front of the post office. The back doors opened, and two men dressed in dark clothes, balaclavas on, got out and hurried into the doorway of the post office. Sawn-off shotguns held vertical, close to their bodies. McCoy couldn't see what happened next, but a few seconds later the door was opened and they disappeared inside.

"Shouldn't be long now," said Long. Leant over and turned up the police radio.

It wasn't. Couple of seconds later the radio came to life. *"Possible robbery at Lambhill Post Office. Need unit to respond immediately."*

Long counted to three then picked up the receiver. "Blue four two. We're just coming down Balmore Road. Be there in under two minutes. We've got it covered. Out."

"Roger that. Out."

Long put the receiver back.

The Cortina had done a U-turn and was now parked outside the post office facing back to Cadder. It was a big housing scheme, easy to get lost amongst too many streets that looked the same, if there was a chase.

McCoy heard it before Long. Sat up. "What's that?"

"What's what?" said Long, and then he heard it too. A distant police siren. And it was getting louder.

FORTY-NINE

L ong's face went white.

"Who the fuck are they? They shouldn't be coming."

"Maybe just passing by, decided to help," said McCoy.
"Maybe we should—"

"Fuck!" Long started the car, jammed it into gear, stood on
the accelerator and pulled out into the road. McCoy was flung
against the window as Long hit the siren and the lights. Barely
had time to register what had happened when Long steered the
car straight at the Cortina, pressed down hard on the accelerator, shouting "Watch yourself!"

McCoy could see the Cortina driver put his arms up over his
face. He braced his legs against the floor and was flung forward
as they rammed into the front of the car. McCoy didn't manage
to get his hands up in time, head bouncing off the dashboard
before he was flung back into his seat.

"You okay?" said Long.

McCoy put his hand up to his face. Wet, warm blood.

The man in the Cortina was slumped in his seat, eyes closed,
blood pouring from his head. The siren was getting louder now,
police car couldn't be far. They were almost at the post office
when there was a low boom from inside and the glass panel of
the door exploded, showering them in fragments.

McCoy turned to Long, shouted, "Need to—"

He didn't have the chance to finish what he was going to
say before Long rugby-tackled him. He pulled him down onto
the ground just as there was a second, louder explosion and

something whistling over their heads and blasting into the Cortina, the car door suddenly buckling as it was peppered with dozens of tiny holes. McCoy rolled back onto the pavement, got up, ran behind the Cortina. Long scrambled up, but he slipped and fell, a loud moan as his hands crunched down onto the broken glass.

The post office door banged open, and the two men stood there, guns up.

The siren was getting louder and louder. The first man took in the smashed Cortina, the noise of the police car approaching. He pointed the gun at Long's head.

"Run!" shouted McCoy. "You've still got a chance."

The gunman looked over at him.

"Just go!" McCoy shouted over the siren.

And they did. Came out the post office holding bags and guns and ran round the back of the shops and up into the warren of Cadder's streets.

A panda car screeched in beside the Cortina and three uniforms jumped out. One ran to McCoy, asked him if he was okay. McCoy wiped the blood from his face, told him he was. Could see another uniform kneeling down by Long. Long's hands were a mess of blood; he could see the glass sticking out from them even from where he was standing. Could hear more sirens now, an ambulance, crackle of the car radios.

The old man came through the smashed door, stood there in his cardigan and slippers, face pure white, looked like he was about to pass out. The third uniform put his arm round him, sat him down on the kerb.

The ambulance pulled up, and two medics got out, ran over to Long. McCoy leant on the side of the smashed police car, got his cigarettes out, tried to light up. Couldn't strike the match, hands were shaking too much. He gave up. Closed his eyes, listened to the sirens and the shouts and the wailing from the old man and wondered how the fuck he had got himself into this mess.

FIFTY

M cCoy yawned, searched his pockets and realised he had run out of fags. Swore. Felt his forehead, a bump was already coming up. He looked at his watch. Eleven fifteen. The doctor had said Long would be done in half an hour or so, and that was at half ten. Needs must. He walked up to the bus stop opposite the Royal and asked a happily drunk man if he could spare a smoke. The man obliged, McCoy thanked him and walked back to the entrance of the A&E.

He'd given his statement at Central, finished an hour or so ago. Long had had to give his in the hospital while he was getting his hands stitched. Last thing he said to McCoy before he'd been driven away in the ambulance was "Stick to the story."

So McCoy had. Lied through his teeth. Told the investigating officers they were on the way to Cadder to see a tout when the call came through; they had responded immediately, driven to the post office. Made a quick decision to immobilise the getaway car, then confronted the robbers. Had been lucky to escape with minor injuries.

Heroes.

The getaway driver was still unconscious, under armed guard at the Western. Both of the gunmen had been lost in the back-streets of Cadder, but that was someone else's problem now. Interviewers sent McCoy on his way with congratulations and talk of a bravery medal.

McCoy couldn't get out of there fast enough. Refused the

offer of a celebratory whisky with the boys in the station. Said he needed to get home, get some sleep. More lies.

The double doors to the A&E swung open, and Long walked out. His left hand was in a big mitten of bandages, right one covered in stitches, tape and plasters. He walked towards McCoy, looking anxious.

"I stuck to the story," said McCoy before he was asked.

"Good man," said Long, relieved. Held up his bandaged hands. "Christ, do I need a drink."

They walked down the hill and turned into Duke Street. McCoy pointed up ahead at a low building with no windows by the high flats. The Lamppost.

"If we go round the back, Big Al should let us in."

"Let's hope so. My hands are starting to really hurt."

"They give you anything at the hospital?"

Long grimaced. Nodded. "Whatever it was, it's starting to bloody wear off."

They walked round the back of the pub, weaving their way between the metal barrels and crates of empties, and McCoy knocked three times on the back door.

"This a regular thing, is it?" asked Long.

"Used to be when I lived in Castle Street—been a few years now. Hope Big Al's still here."

They stood back at the noise of locks being turned. Door opened a crack and a head appeared.

"Fuck sake," said Big Al. "Thought you were a West Ender now."

"I am," said McCoy. "Too good for a shitehole like this, but needs must."

Big Al pulled the door open. Stood there in what looked like the same clothes McCoy had last seen him in. Suit trousers, black slip-ons and a blue shirt with rolled-up sleeves. FUCK THE POPE in blue ink on one arm. NO SURRENDER on the other. He bowed.

"Welcome to my humble abode," he said. "Even if you are a dirty Pape."

Long moved to go inside, but McCoy stopped him.

"Thanks," he said. "For outside the post office. If you hadn't got me down fast, chances are I wouldn't be standing here now."

"I'm a cop. It's what I was trained to do," said Long. Smiled a sad smile. "Used to be a good one as well, once upon a time, before it all turned to shit."

FIFTY-ONE

Rossi?" said McCoy. "No way."

Long sat back in his chair and nodded. They were in a corner of the pub, sitting under some horse brasses, lights dim in case any police passed. They were a few whiskies in. McCoy had given Big Al a twenty to keep them coming.

McCoy shook his head, couldn't believe it. "That wee shite's the one in charge?"

Long swallowed over some whisky. "Started just after I got to the Possil station. I was taking every shift I could get, trying to pay for the family down south and the new one on the way. Didn't take Rossi long to notice I was always looking for money. So it started the same way you did."

"The Friday Club?"

Long nodded. "Beer money and a few quid to put away. I knew it wasn't right, but it didn't seem to be doing that much harm. Letting the adult shops stay open, looking the other way at hotels like the Arlington. But it was the tip of the wedge. Once you start getting money for nothing, you can persuade yourself that almost anything you do is fine." He smiled. "So I did."

"What happened then?"

Long swallowed back another whisky. Flinched as the pain in his hand hit him. "Rossi comes to me, tells me he's got a proposition, needs something doing for a pal of his."

"Let me guess," said McCoy. "Archie Andrews?"

A nod.

"Some guy's getting out of prison, Andrews wants him back

in there. Day after he gets out, me and Rossi go to his flat and magically find a revolver in his bedroom drawer. The guy tells anyone who'll listen it was planted, but nobody listens. It's his word against two upstanding officers of the law. We get fifty quid through the post the next week."

Long took another drink. Looked like he didn't want to keep talking but seemed like he needed to tell someone. "Couple of months later I tell Rossi I'm done, I want out. He says to me it doesn't work like that. I work for Archie Andrews now, not the polis. I tell him to fuck off. Think that's the end of it. Until . . ." He fell silent, stared into space.

"Until?"

"Until I come into work the next day and he comes into my office, shuts the door and takes out a brown envelope."

"What was in it?"

"Pictures," said Long. "Pictures of me on every job we've done. Whoever took them was good, managed to just get me in the photos, not Rossi. A complete record of every illegal thing I did for money."

"Christ."

"And then it got worse. Takes out another envelope. More pictures, this time ones of my kids down south waiting at the bus stop to get to school, playing in the garden. Rossi makes it perfectly clear that if I don't keep playing ball, he'll either give the photos of me to Pitt Street or something will happen to my kids."

"Bastard."

"And what an idiot I was falling straight into the trap." Long took another drink, sat there and smiled. "So, as you can see, McCoy, I'm fucked. Royally fucked."

McCoy could see his point. Long was stuck between the devil and the deep blue sea. One thing he wasn't so sure of though. Had to ask. "What are you telling me this for?"

Long sighed. Picked at one of the stitches in his hand. "Because

I've always heard you were a good cop—no team player but a decent guy. There's still time for you to get out before Rossi gets his claws into you. You should do it. Do it before what happened to me happens to you."

"I still can't believe Rossi's behind it all."

"He grew up in the same street as Andrews. The two of them are joined at the hip. This deal works for them both. Andrews gets a pet polis and Rossi gets protection."

McCoy didn't want to think about how familiar that set-up sounded.

Big Al appeared with an empty bottle of Bell's in his hand. "Right, gents, you've tanned the bottle and I need my beauty sleep. So beat it."

McCoy put Long into a taxi, walked down the High Street to look for one for himself. He felt sorry for the man. He'd made a couple of wrong moves, and now his fate was in the hands of a pair of bastards like Rossi and Andrews. What would happen to him? Either McCoy would spill the beans about Long to Murray, and he'd go away for a very long time, or Andrews and Rossi would keep bleeding him dry until he couldn't take it any more. Poor bastard didn't look that far off from it as it was.

He stopped, lit up, watched a fox cross the road, head up, sniffing for something.

Something else Long had said was gnawing at him. Was that really all he was? A Rossi to Stevie Cooper's Andrews? He didn't think so, but he knew what it could look like from the outside. And what was he doing? Helping Cooper to take over from Andrews. Had to admit there wasn't that much difference at all.

He saw a taxi, whistled, and it turned round.

He was going to have to do something about Rossi before this assignment at Possil turned out to be the worst move of his life. If Rossi got pressure put on him from above, he would go down fighting, flailing, naming names. Murray had made it very clear McCoy was there to observe and report back, nothing more. Turned out that wasn't as easy as he'd thought it would be, especially when they were trying to drag him in, make sure he was one of the boys. McCoy thought of the old man being punched in the stomach, the post office. Knew that one of the first names Rossi would blurt out would be his.

THURSDAY

19TH JUNE 1975

McCoy was still bleary-eyed when he sat down at his desk. His stomach hurt, and a nasty headache was settling in behind his eyes. Served him right, he supposed—too much whisky.

He yawned, reached for the phone, and dialled Duncan Kent's office. Same snotty secretary. No, Mr. Kent could not see him today; he had back-to-back meetings.

"Tomorrow?"

"The same, I'm afraid," she said with a distinct note of satisfaction in her voice.

That pushed McCoy over the edge. "Well, why don't you tell the very busy Mr. Kent that I have a birth certificate he might be interested in seeing?"

Put the phone down. Immediately regretted it. He'd given away his hand for nothing. Perils of working with a hangover—too quick to react, to get annoyed. Nothing he could do about it now.

The morning moved slowly. McCoy nursed his hangover, made useless notes, tried to sort out some old paperwork. He got a pint glass from the kitchen, filled it with water from the tap and took it back to his desk. Drank half of it in a oner. Felt marginally better.

"What have you been doing all morning?" asked Wattie as he walked into the station.

"Trying not to throw up," said McCoy. "You?"

"A load of shite. Buying a cake and lucky bags for the kids' party. You're still coming, aren't you?"

"Wouldn't miss it for the world," said McCoy, already thinking how he could make the shortest appearance possible.

"Good man. I'll keep you a lucky bag. The wee bugger is up to high doh already, knows something's up. God knows what he'll be like tomorrow."

"Duncan Kent is in back-to-back meetings until the end of time, apparently. Can't see us."

"There's a surprise," said Wattie. "Got a feeling we're on a hiding to nothing with that one."

"Looks like it."

"What's this I hear about you and Long foiling the crime of the century last night? Want to buy me my lunch and tell me all about it? I'm starving."

McCoy was just about to suggest they went into town for something when his phone rang. He picked it up. Desk sergeant, telling him there was someone for him in the front office and hanging up before he could ask who.

"Must be my dad," he said. "You want to come and meet him?"

Wattie shook his head. "Not after what Murray told me about him. Be more likely to lamp him than anything else."

"Fair enough," said McCoy. "I'll no be long."

He walked into the front office and stopped dead. It wasn't his dad. It was the very elegantly dressed figure of Kathy Kent, Duncan Kent's wife. She was dressed to the nines: pale blue suit, gloves, slingbacks and handbag the same tan colour, make-up immaculate.

"Mr. McCoy?" she said. "I wonder if we could have a chat?"

FIFTY-THREE

They stepped out the station door into the sunshine, sunshine that was reflecting off a black Daimler parked across the street, crowd of curious kids surrounding it. A chauffeur stepped out the front seat, held the back door open.

"You're kidding, aren't you?" said McCoy.

"I can't drive," she said. "What do you want me to do? Get the bus?"

"Suppose not."

Five minutes later he was sitting in the back seat of the car driving down Saracen Street heading for town. The car was brand new, still smelt of leather and polish. He pressed a button and the window slid down. Never seen that before.

"Lunch?" Kathy Kent asked. "Are you hungry at all?"

McCoy couldn't help himself, nodded.

She leant forward and spoke to the driver. "George, can you take us to the Ubiquitous Chip?"

A nod in the rear-view mirror.

"Have you been? It's very good."

McCoy shook his head. He knew about it though; Margo had been. Was some new place off Byres Road, big thing was that it served Scottish food. Not pies and beans and fish suppers, but prawns and venison, that sort of thing. The kind of Scottish food that Scottish people never ate.

"Why do we need to have a chat?" asked McCoy as they drove along Great Western Road.

"Do you mind if we wait until we get there?" said Kathy Kent. "It's a long story, and I need a glass of wine in my hand to tell it."

Ten minutes later she had a glass of Sauvignon Blanc in her hand and McCoy had a pint of Bass in his. They seemed to be in some sort of covered courtyard. Tables and chairs laid out, tablecloths and napkins. There was a fish pond surrounded by plants at the entrance, more plants painted on the walls. McCoy had ordered Cullen Skink, thought it would be good for his stomach. Kathy Kent had gone for langoustines in garlic butter, whatever that might be. The clientele looked like arty types from the university or the BBC up the road. All tweed jackets, beards and earnest expressions. Waitresses just looked like students. No black dresses or white frilly caps—they wouldn't know what silver service was if it hit them in the face. Talked about where the food had come from, this loch or this farm. Couldn't have been further from Rogano's if it had tried.

McCoy put his pint down, faced Kathy Kent. She was a looker, all right. Dark hair and eyes, pale skin. Hard eyes though, like she took no shit. Time to find out.

"Does your husband know you're here?"

She grinned. "If he did, he would be here now dragging me out. This is a solo visit."

"I told your husband I had a birth certificate this morning. That why we're having this chat?"

She nodded. "Where to start . . . where to start . . ." She took out a packet of Dunhill and a gold lighter. Lit up. "Can I trust you, Mr. McCoy?"

He nodded.

"I don't mean just not to tattle, but to keep a very important secret."

He nodded again, and she smiled.

"Good. Didn't think you looked the type to tell tales." She took a sip of her wine. "The reason I ask is that what I am about to tell you could ruin me, ruin my husband, ruin everything we have built these past ten years or so."

McCoy sat back in his chair. "In that case, are you sure you want to tell me? I'm a polis. I can't keep everything secret."

"I have to, Mr. McCoy. No choice. I have to roll the dice, see what happens."

"I don't follow you. Why is there so much at stake?"

"Maybe we should start at the beginning. Do you remember the killing of the little girl in Dundee back in the mid-fifties? Josie Barr?"

How could he not? Nobody would ever forget it. A six-year-old girl strangled and her body left in a playground. Killed by another little girl, her neighbour Fiona Thomson. The press had gone nuts. The devil amongst us, the bad seed, all that sort of stuff. Men and women outside the court screaming for Fiona Thomson to be hanged. Suddenly thought. Stared at Kathy Kent.

"What are you telling me?"

"It was me. I'm Fiona Thomson."

FIFTY-FOUR

W e lived at the foot of Law Hill. Me and my mum. A single room with a press bed. No toilet, no hot water, peeling wallpaper and the stink of damp all the time. That's where my mum used to 'entertain,' as she called it."

Kathy Kent wasn't looking at McCoy any more. She was looking somewhere past his head, lost in her story, lost in the past.

"When I was about five or six, I started to get included in the entertaining. The men had to pay more for that, so my mum always pushed for it. I'd be sleeping on the settee, and she'd wake me up. 'C'mon, hen, time to play a wee game,' she'd say." She took a sip of her wine, hands trembling. "Soon I wasn't going to school much, just staying in the room helping my mum with her work. Slowly that room and everything that happened in it became my world."

"That's awful," said McCoy. "I'm sorry."

She shrugged. "When it's all you know, it's all you know."

She put her glass down and looked at him. "I didn't mean to kill that little girl, you know."

"No?"

"It was one of the rare days I was out of the room. I was playing with Josie, down at the swings, and all of a sudden, she was shouting at me, calling me names, calling my mum names. I asked her to stop, didn't want the other kids to hear what my mum was, but she wouldn't. She just kept screaming at me, calling me a dirty wee whore, stuff like that."

She looked McCoy in the eye.

"So I put my hands round her throat and choked her until she stopped. I didn't think I'd killed her; I didn't really know what that was. I was just doing what my mum did with some of the men. Strangled them while they were playing with themselves. They went quiet for a few minutes and then they were fine. I thought that was what was going to happen, but the girl never woke up."

A waiter brought their food to the table. Both of them ignored the plates. No appetite any more.

"What happened then?" asked McCoy.

"Remand homes, secure units, juvenile detention. I don't remember a lot of it. I was drugged up most of the time. They kept the other kids away from me in case one of them attacked me. I spent most of my time in solitary, eating food the wardens had spat in. And then when I was eighteen a man from the Home Office came to see me. Told me I was going to be released and I was going to be somebody else so nobody could find me."

"Kathleen Garvie," said McCoy.

She nodded. "A few years after that, I met Duncan one night in a club in Glasgow. They say there's no such thing as love at first sight but . . ."

She fell silent, then ordered another glass of wine from a passing waiter.

"I knew who he was, what he did for a living, but that didn't matter. He loved me, loved me even after I told him. The only person who ever has."

"What did he say when you told him?"

"I can't really remember. I was so petrified I thought I was going to pass out. I just remember him taking me in his arms and saying none of it mattered."

"You were lucky. Not many men would have done that."

"Don't I know it."

"So is that what all the charity stuff is for? Atonement?"

She shook her head. "Honestly? I don't think I've much to atone for. I was eight years old and I made a mistake, that's all."

McCoy wasn't sure if she was telling him or telling herself.

She carried on. "As I said, I know what my husband does, how he makes the stupid amount of money he does. So I try to give away as much of it as I can—children's charities, mostly—to try to stop any other wee girls having the life I had."

"Very noble," said McCoy.

"Not the word I'd use. If I've learned anything about what happened to me, it's this: it didn't have to be that way. Poverty will make people do terrible things."

"So will trying to get a birth certificate back." Couldn't help himself.

"Touché," she said. Finished her wine in one gulp. "Now I need a proper drink."

FIFTY-FIVE

McCoy stood in Curlers waiting for the barman to finish serving a group of half-cut businessmen. Was glad of the couple of minutes to think. Kathy Kent hadn't been joking when she said it was quite a story. What she had told him was hard to believe, but he had no reason to think she was making it up. Why would she?

Question was, what was she telling him for? For all she knew, he could stop at a phone box on the way home, dial the *News of the World* and make himself a couple of thousand quid. Would be lying if he didn't think it had a certain appeal. When he looked up he realised the barman was staring at him.

"Sorry, pal, miles away," he said. "Pint of Bass and a gin and tonic. Double."

Whatever had happened to Kathy, whatever she had gone through, one fact remained: her husband had paid someone to batter Malky McCormack to death. All the charity work in the world didn't make up for that. The drinks arrived, and he carried them over to the table and sat down. Kathy Kent took a long draught of hers, lit up another Dunhill.

"So how did Norma McGregor fit into all this?"

"Norma." She shook her head. "I know I shouldn't speak ill of the dead, but Norma McGregor was an evil old cow. I used to get a letter from the Home Office every year, checking up, telling me when I had to go in for an interview, make sure I was still on the straight and narrow. Seems she "accidentally" opened it, figured out who I was. And that's when it started, the blackmail. Started off as a twenty every week, then it grew and grew. And always the threats. You don't pay me, I'll go to the papers; you and Duncan will be ruined."

McCoy took a sip of his pint, wiped his mouth. "I don't want to sound callous. But we both know what your husband does. Why didn't he just get rid of her?"

"She told us she had a letter at a lawyer's that would be opened if anything happened to her. Another lie, as it turned out."

"So what did she steal? I'm assuming it wasn't four hundred quid."

"She stole the birth certificate and twenty grand from the downstairs safe."

McCoy let out a low whistle.

"Gambled most of it away, as far as I can make out. Duncan said she'd piles of bookies' lines in her flat."

A woman approached the table, asked for a light, sensed the atmosphere, and lit her cigarette as quick as she could before scuttling off.

"And how would he know that?" said McCoy after she'd gone.

Kathy narrowed her eyes. "Don't be coy. It doesn't suit you. He knew because my husband and some employees rolled her flat over, as you well know."

"What about her brother?"

She blew out a cloud of smoke, waved it away. "What about her brother?"

"Your husband arranged for him to be battered to death. Thought he knew where the birth certificate was. Stupid old bugger hadn't a clue."

She looked genuinely shocked. The colour drained from her face, hand with the cigarette in it started to shake. She stubbed it out. "I didn't know that. He never told me."

McCoy sat back in his chair, unsure whether to believe her or not.

"Mr. McCoy, my husband is a violent man, always has been, always will be, despite all the Daimlers and country houses. You know that as well as anyone. Maybe he could see everything he had—me, the business—on the verge of falling apart. You think anyone would do business with him if they found out who he was married to? He must have panicked. Done something stupid."

"So that's why you're here, is it? To make the case for your husband getting away with murder?"

"No. I don't need to. If I know my husband, and if he did do this thing, then you will have zero chance of pinning it on him. He's too sharp. If you could have, you would have done it by now. That's not why I'm here."

"So why are you?"

"My husband tells me you have a certain reputation as a friend of those less fortunate. So I'm begging you to give me the birth certificate back and to keep quiet about what I've said here today. I can't give my husband's money away if he isn't making any. Do you want to cut off that supply to the charities I support? What's more important, Mr. McCoy? Exposing me as Fiona Thomson, guilty of an act committed twenty years ago by a disturbed child, ruining my life, ruining my husband's life—or making sure there's less chance of little girls growing up like I did?"

McCoy clapped a few times, sat back in his chair.

"That was a good speech," he said. "Flatter me, pull my heartstrings, pretend Malky McCormack's death never happened. Take you and Duncan long to think it up, did it?"

She picked up her drink and threw it in his face. "I tried, Mr. McCoy, really tried, to make you understand, to tell the truth, and what did it get me? A cheap comeback. Seems I was wrong about you, very wrong." She stood up. "Do whatever you're going to do, Mr. McCoy. Just, please, make it quick."

And with that she walked out the door.

FIFTY-SIX

McCoy wiped his face with his hanky. It wasn't the first time he'd had a drink chucked in his face, probably wouldn't be the last. He finished his drink and walked out the pub. Needed to go and see Stevie Cooper, needed time to think. Decided to walk there. Byres Road was busy: students, some Hari Krishnas dressed in orange banging a drum and chanting, school kids in uniforms walking home. He passed the library, stopped and lit up, dropped the spent match onto the ground and started walking again.

Trouble was, something in the way Kathy Kent spoke about her childhood had got to him. His childhood hadn't been anything like as bad as hers, but he knew what it was like to grow up in poverty, neglected and unloved. Knew what that could do to a person. Knew what it had done to his dad, knew what it had done to him.

If Kathy Kent was going to keep giving away as much of her husband's money as she could, then maybe he should just give the birth certificate back and let her get on with it. She was right when she said they'd never be able to pin Malky's death on her husband. There was no chain of evidence, no witnesses, and Duncan Kent's lawyers would tell him where to go if he tried to bring him in for questioning.

He turned into Great Western Road and walked round two women with prams taking up the whole pavement. Realised he had no idea what to do about Kathy Kent.

Iris opened Cooper's door, looking less than delighted to see McCoy.

"He's on his way out," she said.

As she spoke, Jumbo and Cooper appeared in the doorway.

"McCoy!" said Cooper.

"Need to speak to you," said McCoy.

"Sounds serious. In that case you can come with us. Need to be somewhere."

Five minutes later McCoy was sitting next to Cooper in the back of his new car. Jumbo was driving, happily humming along to ABBA on the radio.

"Had a wee chat with some people about Teddy Jamieson," said Cooper. "Glad I did. For two reasons."

"Oh aye, what are they then?"

"Fact Jamieson and his son are dealing behind Andrews' back is enough for Andrews to blow a gasket. No way they're going to be pals after he finds out. And Jamieson is the only handy boy Andrews has."

"And the other reason?" asked McCoy.

"Because now I know why our takings are down. You know what your Angela used to do—supply the high rollers, bands, all that stuff? Well, some wanker called Clive—"

"Clive?"

"Yep, Clive has been doing it. Or not, as the case may be. Takings have been going down, so I got the stupid bastard in last week. Not his fault, he says, town's been quiet, no bands on tour. Real reason is the stupid bastard is too thick to realise Teddy fucking Jamieson has been stealing his clients."

McCoy looked out the window. "Where are we going anyway?"

"We," said Cooper, "are going to buy some ice-cream vans."

FIFTY-SEVEN

There were about twenty vans on the lot behind the speed-way track. All pale blue. All with badly painted cartoon characters on them. Mickey Mouse with too-small ears. Tom and Jerry except Jerry looked like a rat. Superman with a face like Hitler and a kiss curl.

"Why on earth does he want bloody ice-cream vans?" asked McCoy, sheltering his eyes with his hands so he could see. They were watching Cooper and the salesman walk up and down. Occasionally stopped at a van, went inside. Wasn't only ice-cream vans they sold. The lot stretched out behind them. Ice-cream vans, Transit vans, fish vans, chip vans. A sort of hut thing off at the side that seemed to serve as an office.

"Don't ask me," said Jumbo. "Mr. Cooper doesn't tell me much."

McCoy lit up, and they kept watching. At least the information on Jamieson had gone down well. Felt like he had paid his debt. Get me something on Jamieson, Cooper had said, and he had certainly done that. Sister Jimmy had come through big time.

"I don't like ice cream," said Jumbo. "It makes your teeth hurt."

"That right?" said McCoy. "Maybe you need to go to the dentist."

Jumbo shook his head furiously. "No, no. I'm fine, thank you."

Cooper was shaking the salesman's hand now. Looked like the deal had been done.

He walked back towards them, all smiles. "Sorted."

"How many did you buy?" said McCoy.

"Twelve. Should be enough to cover Royston. That's where we're going to start."

"Start what? Selling ninety-nines and bottles of Red Kola?"

"That and something else," said Cooper. "Paul's idea."

"What something else?"

Cooper tapped the side of his nose. "I'll let Paul tell you himself. Jumbo, let's go."

Paul was sitting in an armchair in the kitchen, plaster-cast leg up on a stool in front of him. Besides that war wound he had a black eye and a nasty cut just above his wrist. He looked perky enough though, smiling as Iris arranged the cushions behind his back.

"Would you look after me if I broke my leg?" said McCoy, watching her.

"Would I fuck," she said, not missing a beat.

"Forget it, McCoy," said Cooper, sitting down at the table. "She hates you. Can just about stand me on a good day and thinks the sun shines out of Paul's bum. That right, Iris?"

"Near enough," said Iris, picking up some mugs from the table. "Think I'll change all the bedding today."

"You only changed it yesterday!" said Cooper.

"Jumbo, you can help me. Come on."

They waited until Iris left, Jumbo lumbering after her. McCoy realised Cooper and Paul had big grins on their faces.

"It's working," said Paul. "She washed all the floors this morning as well."

"Anyone going to tell me what's going on?" said McCoy.

"Okay. You know as well as I do half the bloody housewives in Glasgow are addicted to bloody Askit Powders, just like Iris," said Paul. Grimaced as he moved his leg further onto the stool.

"Always running to the van for them or sending their kids

to the shops. Supposed to be for headaches, but they take them for a wee pick-me-up. They're full of painkillers and caffeine, keeps the motor running. But we're going to make it run even faster."

"I don't get you."

"We buy the Askit Powders in bulk, take all the powder out and cut it with a bit of amphetamine, then package it as an 'export' variety, super-strength, not really meant to sell them in Scotland—and we charge more. Treble the price. Once they've had an export Askit, they aren't going to want anything else. They'll be standing in the street, ignoring all the others, waiting for our vans to turn up. And while they're there, they'll be buying their fags and an ice cream for the kids."

"Can you make that much money from an ice-cream van?"

"You kidding? You seen those places? Easterhouse, Ruchazie? Hundreds and hundreds of houses, and not a bloody shop in sight. Vans are the only way to buy anything. Going to sell groceries, papers, all sorts. We're going to make a fortune."

Paul sat back in his chair, big grin on his face. McCoy had to admit it wasn't a bad idea.

"Not just a pretty face, eh?" said Cooper. "Brainy, chip off the old block."

"I didn't know his mum was bright."

"Very funny." Cooper looked at the clock on the wall. "Time for my swim. Fancy coming?"

"I can't. Got to get back to the station. Work to do."

"That'll be a first," said Cooper. "C'mon, you can walk me down to the Arlington."

They stepped out the front door, Cooper chatting away, still full of Paul's big idea. McCoy was half listening, couldn't really get his mind off Kathy Kent. Suddenly realised Cooper had stopped. He looked up. Saw him.

"Who's that?" asked Cooper.

"He's here for me," said McCoy. "You go on."

Gerry was across the street. Looked like he'd had a rough night. Suit was dusty, hair sticking up at all angles. He crossed over, stood in front of McCoy.

"You following me?" said McCoy.

Gerry nodded. "I need to tell you something. You were right. Reverend West has a son."

FIFTY-EIGHT

T hat right?" said McCoy.

Walked round Gerry and continued down the street. Heard the shuffling behind him as Gerry caught up.

"That's what you asked me to find out. Do you not care any more?" He looked disappointed, like he'd expected a lot more.

"I spoke to Reverend West," said McCoy. "Had a long chat."

Suddenly Gerry didn't look so sure of himself. "He's a liar."

"Funny, that's exactly what he said about you. So which one of you is it? Who's lying and who's telling the truth?"

"It's him," said Gerry, voice rising. "He tried to crucify me. I told you, I showed you the scars."

"Not according to him. He says either you did it yourself or your mum did it."

Gerry didn't say anything, just stood there.

"Thought so," said McCoy. Started to walk away.

"He's got a son called Michael," Gerry shouted after him. "A woman that my mum knew that goes to his church told me. Nobody's seen him for a couple of years."

McCoy kept walking. Had only gone a couple of steps when he heard the familiar shuffle again, and suddenly Gerry was tugging on his arm, turning him around.

"The longest day of the year is on Saturday. The longest time in daylight we can offer suffering up to God. He's going to hurt him then, I know it."

For a minute McCoy was tempted to believe him, but he knew he shouldn't. He was a fantasist, not right in the head.

Tried to let him down gently. "Gerry, I'm sorry, but I just don't believe you. I've no reason to and every reason not to. There's no trace of a son. No birth certificate, no photos, no school record, no medical records. It just doesn't add up. Either someone's playing a trick on you or—"

"Or what?" said Gerry. "I'm mad? You believe that, don't you? Just like your pal does and all the other fuckers that put me in homes or hospitals did." He spat on the ground by McCoy's shoe. "Fuck the lot of you."

Turned and walked back up the road.

FIFTY-NINE

The minute McCoy opened the station door and saw the look on the desk sergeant's face he knew.

"I'm sorry, Harry. Wattie's looking for you. He's at the site."

He handed McCoy a bit of paper with an address written on it in blue ballpoint pen.

26 McAslin Street, Townhead.

McCoy said thank you, put it in his pocket and walked out the station. Stood for a minute in the dying light of the day. There'd been times, loads of times when he was younger, that he'd wished for this day. Now he didn't know what he felt. He didn't feel happy, didn't feel sad. Didn't feel anything much. He held out his hand, stopped a taxi and got in.

Wattie was standing outside the close in Townhead when he got there. They'd removed the corrugated iron and the danger sign covering the front close and were using that way to get in and out. He walked towards him as McCoy got out the cab. McCoy wasn't expecting it, but Wattie hugged him. Held him tight.

"I'm sorry, Harry, I'm really sorry."

That set him off; could feel the tears welling.

Suddenly all he wanted was his dad back, the good times, when he took him to the park or bought him an ice cream, pretended to be a horse and put him on his back and circled the flat on all fours. Wattie let him go and McCoy stepped back, wiped at his eyes.

"You okay?" asked Wattie.

"Is it—"

"Exact same as the other ones. But there's a bottle this time."

McCoy could see the uniforms setting up the ropes looking at him, the photographer looking at him. Everyone looking at him. Didn't want to start crying in front of them all.

"I want to see him."

"Come on, Harry. That's not going to help. Don't put yourself through it."

Maybe Wattie was right. He didn't know what to do with himself. Didn't want to be here, couldn't be anywhere else. Tried to act like it was any other crime scene.

"Who found him?"

Wattie nodded over to the police van. Frank, the man he'd met in the flat before, was sitting on the kerb beside it, head in hands. The boy who had been there before was there too. Eyes up at the sky, tongue lolling in his mouth, somewhere else.

"Said he went out to the shops and when he got back to the flat your dad was dead. They said he didn't have the bottle when they left."

"So someone must have gone up to the flat and given him it?"

"Looks like it."

They turned as a car pulled up just along the road. Murray's Rover. He got out, slammed the door behind him. Walked straight up to McCoy.

"You okay?"

McCoy tried to say yes, but the tears came. Murray hugged him, pulled him into his coat. McCoy could smell the sheepskin, the pipe tobacco, the Ralgex. The smell of home. Finally let himself go and started sobbing.

"Watson," said Murray, talking over McCoy's shoulder, "you know what you need to do here. Make sure you do it to the letter. I want a report first thing in the morning, and I want those fingerprints fucking fast-tracked. Do me proud."

Wattie nodded. Watched Murray walk McCoy towards the car and put him in the back seat. Turned to one of the uniforms and told him to get the bottle to the lab now. Walked back towards the flat. Work to be done.

FRIDAY

20TH JUNE 1975

McCoy woke up, didn't know where he was for a few seconds, remembered he was in a bedroom in Phyllis and Murray's house. Light blue wallpaper, a dresser, some pictures of horses and hounds. He lay there and tried not to think about his dad. Couldn't. Couldn't remember much about last night either. He'd drunk a couple of whiskies with Murray, then Phyllis had given him something to help him sleep.

He'd woken up a couple of times before he'd finally fallen asleep properly. Heard them talking downstairs, Wattie too. Seems they were worried about him. Remembered Murray going on a rant about how bad a father Alec McCoy had been and what he had done to his own son, Phyllis shushing him, trying to calm him down, saying McCoy might hear.

He sat up. Head didn't feel too bad. Sun was coming in through a gap in the curtains. He looked at his watch. Half seven. Time to get up.

But he didn't. He lay there for another half an hour or so listening to the sounds of the house waking up. Kettle whistling, steps on the stairs, Murray coughing, Phyllis asking if she should go and wake him up. Got up eventually, got dressed and went downstairs.

Murray and Phyllis were sitting at the table, breakfast things laid out.

"How are you feeling this morning?" said Phyllis.

"Fine."

Sat down and realised he was starving, hadn't eaten anything since yesterday's breakfast. Took a couple of pieces of toast from the rack sitting on the table. Could feel the tension, Murray trying to stop himself. But he couldn't.

"I don't want you tying yourself in knots for that bastard," said Murray, red-faced. "You hear me? He's not worth it. That man—"

"Hector! For God's sake, leave him alone," said Phyllis.

Murray harrumphed, went back to his paper.

McCoy ate his toast, drank his tea, stared at the trees in the garden. Said cheerio to Phyllis when she went off to work. Felt like he was on autopilot.

"Wattie'll be over in an hour or so," said Murray. "He's standing over the fingerprint boys, making sure they're working as fast as they can."

McCoy nodded, took another slice of toast and started buttering it.

Murray closed his paper, put it down on the table. "Any more on Long and that bloody disgrace of a station?"

McCoy wasn't sure why, but he lied without even thinking about it. "Nope. Got a feeling it's just a bunch of blokes thinking they're high rollers because they get some beer money on a Friday night. Small-time stuff."

Murray looked puzzled. "I was sure there was more to it than that."

"Not sure any of them are bright enough to take it any further than that."

"Might be right. Should we let your mum know what's happened?"

McCoy shook his head. Thought of her in the hospital, mind gone, staring into space. "She won't understand, best just leave her. Besides, the last time she saw my dad he broke her nose with a gin bottle."

Finished buttering his toast, suddenly didn't feel like it, put it down on his plate. "I know you want me to hate him. And I want to hate him too. Christ knows I've got every right to, but I don't. I can't. Whatever he was, whatever shit he did to me, he was my dad and some part of me is sad that he's gone. Sad at what he became. I don't think he was all bad. Just weak and selfish and stupid. Do you know what I mean?"

Murray nodded. "I never told you this. But I used to run into him every so often, before he got too bad. He thanked me each time, said you were better off away from him and to tell you he was sorry." He smiled. "And then he'd ask me for a couple of quid."

"Sounds like him," said McCoy.

The doorbell rang.

"That'll be Watson," said Murray, and got up to answer the door.

McCoy watched the trees in the garden sway in the wind. Took a drink of his tea. Waited.

Sixty-One

Y
ou sure you want to hear all this?" asked Wattie, sitting down at the table.

McCoy thought for a minute. Knew he had to. "Yes."

"Okay," said Wattie. "The bloke you spoke to before in there? Frank? I had a word with him. Like he said, he leaves your dad in the flat and he goes out to buy whatever he can get with the change they'd made begging that day. Gone half an hour or so, comes back and . . ."

Wattie stopped, looked like he didn't know what to say.

"Go on," said McCoy.

"And your dad's dead. Same as the others. Looked like he's had a fit of some kind, dried greenish foam around his mouth. And there's a lemonade bottle beside him, bit of brown liquid left in it. Smelt like methanol and some kind of sherry or tonic wine, something sugary to help it go down. Frank swears the bottle wasn't there when he left."

Just as he said it, the phone started ringing. They all looked at each other. Murray got up, picked up the receiver.

"Murray," he said. Listened. Held out the phone. "It's Margo. For you."

McCoy stood up, took the receiver. "It's me," he said.

"Christ, Harry," said Margo. "I'm so sorry. I'll be back to-morrow—you okay until then?"

"Where are you?"

"London. The audition, remember? The director you don't say no to even if you're retired."

"Sorry, my head's all over the place. Of course."

"You sure you're okay?"

"No," he said. "Not today I'm not, but I will be by tomorrow."

"I love you," said Margo.

"I love you too." He said it before he even thought. Realised he meant it.

He put the phone down, came back to the table and sat down. Suddenly thought. "Why didn't they take the bottle this time?"

Wattie shrugged. "Frank said he heard a noise in the flat as he was coming in, thought it was just another alky, but maybe it was the guy. Maybe he panicked when he heard Frank, ran and forgot the bottle."

"Frank knew not to drink any hooch. Did he tell my dad?"

"He did, but he said your dad had been on the red biddy for a while, wasn't quite sure if anything was going in or not."

"Probably not," said McCoy. "That stuff is brutal."

Wattie looked unhappy. "There's something else."

"What something else?"

Wattie rubbed at the stubble on his chin. "There was a note on your dad's body, tucked into the collar of his jumper. Addressed to you."

"A note? What kind of a note? What did it say?"

Wattie looked over at Murray. He nodded.

"It said, *Now you know how it feels.*"

McCoy sat back in his chair, felt like the air had been punched out of him. "I don't understand. What does that mean?"

"Probably doesn't mean anything," said Murray.

"Of course it means something," said McCoy. "Did someone kill my dad to get at me?"

He tried to stand up but suddenly felt dizzy, couldn't breathe. Head was spinning. "Is that what it means?"

Murray and Wattie just looked at him.

"Will you fucking answer me!" he shouted.

And then the phone rang again. It was for Wattie. When he came back to the table they could see something had changed.

"We've got to get to the station. It's Frank," he told McCoy. "He's saying he wants to confess."

SIXTY-TWO

I just don't get it," said McCoy. "Frank? I thought he was my dad's pal?"

"He's been crying in the bloody van all the way here. Telling everyone how sorry he is. Look, you stay there. I'll see if I can get any sense out of him."

McCoy watched Wattie walk off towards the interview rooms. Why would Frank want to kill his dad, all those other blokes as well? Made no sense. And the note, what was that about? He'd only met Frank that one time before—had Liam even told Frank his first name? He couldn't remember. All he could do was wait for the answers.

He decided to make a mug of tea while he waited. Had a couple of Valium that Phyllis had given him. Might be time to take one, try to stop his mind from racing. He got up, noticed Rossi was sitting at his desk, must have just come in. The last person he needed to see today. He headed towards the kitchen, and Rossi got up and followed him.

He pushed the door and held it open.

Rossi walked in, sat at the table, pushed the bag of sugar and some empty mugs out the way, gave himself some room. "Long's in the hospital," he said. "Got an infection in the cuts in his hands. Going to be out of action for a couple of weeks, so it's over to you. You fucked up the post office, so as far as Archie Andrews is concerned, you owe us. Better not fuck up next time. Archie won't be happy."

"That right?" McCoy pulled out a chair and sat down opposite him.

"Yep," said Rossi. "You really don't want to make Archie Andrews unhappy."

McCoy spoke slowly and calmly. "You know what, Rossi? You and Archie Andrews can fuck right off."

Rossi's eyes narrowed. "You can't say that to me."

"I just did."

Rossi stood up. "I'm going to fuck you over, McCoy. You're dead." He mimed taking a photograph. "Click. Not just Long that's in black and white."

McCoy's stomach rolled. If they had photos of him, he was in trouble, big trouble.

"Dead as a doornail," said Rossi. "Just like your alky father."

McCoy was on him in seconds. Grabbed him by the collar and put his face in his. Rossi looked scared, eyes darting everywhere. McCoy let him go, pushed him away, and he fell onto the kitchen floor. He left him there.

Wattie was back at his desk when McCoy walked into the office.

"Frank wants to talk to you," he said. "He's in some state. Can't stop crying."

Frank was sitting on the bed in the cell at the back of the station. Bucket at his feet. He was shaking, sweating, twisting a corner of the blanket in his hand. If ever a man needed a drink, it was him.

When McCoy came in, he started crying. "I'm sorry, son, I'm so sorry."

"Just tell me what happened, Frank."

His face crumpled. "I've been telling lies."

"That's okay, just tell me the truth now."

Frank nodded, tried to pull himself together. "I went out to get something to drink, what I could get. Left your dad. He couldn't come anyway. He was in a bad way."

"What do you mean?"

"Your dad was at the end, son. Been on the red biddy for months. His skin was all yellow, kept seeing things coming out the walls, his middle had all swollen up like a balloon. He was in agony. Wouldn't let me get an ambulance, said his time was up."

McCoy tried not to think of his dad dying in that ruin of a flat, smell of shit everywhere, rain leaking in through the roof.

Frank went on. "I comes out the off-sales and this lad comes up to me. He's got a bunnet down over his face, couldn't really see him in the dark. Gives me the bottle and twenty quid." He wiped his eyes. "And the note, he gives me the note. Tells me to give the bottle to your dad and put the note on his body.

"So I think I'll be fly. I'll just take the money and forget giving the bottle to your dad, but when I got back, oh, son, he was bad, so bad, screaming in agony, clutching on to me, so help me God I gave it to him. He wisnae going to survive the night. I just wanted to help him. Do you know what I mean?"

McCoy did. At least his dad hadn't died alone in that dump. If he had to go, it was better than dying like a dog in the street. The feelings for his dad kept coming and going, needed to keep on working before they had a chance to engulf him.

"He died with a pal beside him," he said. "That's important. Would mean a lot to him. You did the right thing."

Frank looked like he had been forgiven by God himself. Face changed completely. "Thanks, son, that means the world to me."

McCoy sat down on the bed, put his arm round him. Tried to think as Frank cried and told him how sorry he was. No matter Frank's intention, he had given his dad a bottle of poison to drink. In the circumstances he'd be charged with culpable homicide, minimum two years' prison. There was no way Frank would survive that, no way that boy he looked after would either. Had to stop it happening.

"Frank, you need to listen to me."

Frank wiped his eyes on his sleeve. Nodded.

"I'm going to tell you what happened," said McCoy. "You went back to the flat and told my dad about the man giving you the bottle, told him you were going to keep the money for tomorrow and fuck the bottle. Chances were it might be poisoned, so you weren't going to drink it. Okay?"

Frank nodded again.

"You put it down on the floor, left it there, you went off for a piss and when you came back my dad was drinking it. Told you he needed it, the DTs were so bad that he was going to take the chance. He drank most of the bottle, seemed okay for a few minutes, and then he had a fit. You got that? It was my dad's choice to drink it, right?"

McCoy wasn't sure how much of it Frank had taken in, but if he told that story, he had no case to answer, no criminal intent.

"You were still drunk when you made your first statement to the officer, confused, upset about the death of your pal, but you remember now. Remember everything clearly. Okay?"

"Thanks, son," said Frank.

"Can you remember anything about the man that gave you the bottle?"

Frank shook his head, looked apologetic. "My eyesight's no that good, especially at night. He was a big lad though, looked twenty-odd."

"If you remember anything else, you let us know, eh?"

He turned to go, and Frank called him back.

"I remember one thing," he said. "When he walked away, I could see he was wearing shiny black boots. Like the kind the polis wear."

SIXTY-THREE

That get us anywhere?" said Wattie as McCoy sat back down at his desk.

The office was quiet, lunchtime. Apart from Helen sitting at her desk eating a sandwich, there was no one around.

"Not sure," said McCoy, stifling a yawn. "The poor bastard was all over the place. Story makes more sense now, think he'll give you a decent statement."

Wattie looked at him.

"What?"

"Let me guess. This statement means he won't end up in prison."

McCoy shrugged, and told Wattie about the man who had given Frank the bottle. As he spoke, Wattie started rifling through his drawers, vanishing below the desk as he hunted.

"What are you doing?"

"Need a Mars bar. Sure there's one in here somewhere. Ah!" Wattie reappeared, smashed-up Mars bar in hand.

McCoy looked at him. "Who have I fucked off enough that they're going to kill my dad?"

"You'd know better than me," said Wattie, chewing away. "Remember, you only tell me half of what's bloody going on."

"Trouble is, I can't think of anyone. I've put people away, had fights with them, but nothing so bad it would make someone want to do something like that. And why my dad? It's not like we're—*were*—close."

"He was out there and he's vulnerable, I suppose. Maybe it's

someone so nuts they think something trivial you did is justifi-
cation."

"Who do I know that's a bit nuts?"

"Every nutjob that lives in Glasgow, as far as I can see," said
Wattie.

Dawned on McCoy. "Gerry. I told him where to go yesterday. Maybe it's him."

Wattie shoved the last of the Mars bar in his mouth. "But
Frank's description doesn't fit: he's no exactly a big lad, is he?
And I've never seen him in anything but they bloody ruined
slip-ons."

"Okay, so what about the shiny boot thing? Who wears
boots like a polis does?"

"Lots of people if you start thinking about it," said Wattie.
"Firemen? Paramedics? Soldiers, maybe? They're just black
boots—the bloke could be anyone."

"Or he could be a polis," said McCoy. "Like Hood."

"Hood? You're joking, aren't you?"

"He's helping out at the soup kitchen, been at a couple of
the murder sites. Before he became a bloody saint he hated
down-and-outs, didn't he?"

"What's he got to do with you or your dad though?"

"No idea." McCoy stood up. "Let's ask him."

SIXTY-FOUR

Turned out Hood had a day off. McCoy got his address from the front desk. Some bedsit in Govan. They got a car from the yard, drove round to the front of the station, waited for a gap in the traffic. McCoy was smoking, running through a list in his head of all the people he'd put away, trying to find someone with reason enough to kill his dad to get back at him.

"Your pal's here," said Wattie.

McCoy looked up and saw Gerry walking towards the front door of the station.

"Shite. Get moving before he sees us. I don't need another lecture about Reverend West."

Wattie did, and soon they were heading south towards Govan and Hood.

"Suppose you think the fact your dad's been killed is enough of an excuse to avoid the wee bugger's party, do you?" said Wattie as they drove over the Kingston Bridge.

Hadn't crossed McCoy's mind, but now it was the perfect excuse. "I'll come and see him in a few days, eh? Bring him his police car thing."

Wattie nodded. "That's fine. I'll just tell him his Uncle Harry's poorly and he'll visit soon."

"You trying to make me feel guilty?"

"Why would I do that?" Wattie flicked the indicator on and turned into Blackburn Street. "You're just his godfather, after all. The only one he has. Here we are."

*

Hood looked surprised to see them when he answered the door. He'd a cheese sandwich in one hand, book in the other, civvies on. Shorts and sandshoes, checked shirt.

"Mind if we come in?" asked McCoy.

Hood swallowed over the sandwich, held the door open.

The bedsit was tiny. A bed with a faded blue candlewick spread taking up most of the space. A small table and chair, a sink and a gas burner next to it. Ancient striped wallpaper with damp stains in the corners of the ceiling.

McCoy sat on the chair and Wattie eased himself onto the bed.

"What can I do for you two?" said Hood. Wasn't happy about them being there, not happy at all.

"What's that you're reading?" asked McCoy. Hood held up the book he was holding and McCoy peered at it.

"*Atlas Shrugged*," he said. "Any good?"

Hood nodded.

"Collect empty bottles, do you?" asked Wattie, his eyes on the two empty wine bottles sitting on the windowsill. "Use them for something?"

"Not really," said Hood. "They were from a special night. A souvenir."

"Of what?" asked McCoy.

"That's my business," said Hood. "What are you doing here?"

"Sir," said McCoy.

"What are you doing here, *sir*?" recited Hood.

"That's not very friendly," said McCoy. "We were in the area. Just thought we'd drop in."

Wattie stood up. "Mind if I use your toilet?"

"Across the hall," said Hood. "Blue door."

"Cheers." Wattie walked past him and out the door.

"You know much about me?" asked McCoy. "Or my dad?"

Hood looked puzzled. "Don't know anything about you,

and the only thing I know about your dad is he's a down-and-out."

"Was. Somebody killed him yesterday."

"Sorry to hear that," said Hood. No trace of sympathy in his voice. "Still, a life like that. Some would say you'd be better off dead. In God's hands."

"Is that what you'd say, Hood? That what you think?"

Hood shrugged. "It's no life. Wasting police time, ambulance-men's time, pissing yourself, sleeping in the street and asking people for money. If it was me? I wouldn't want that, to be a burden on society. I'd kill myself, be better off."

Wattie opened the door, walked back in holding a dark brown bottle by the cap.

"Any reason there's a bottle of methanol in your bathroom?"

SIXTY-FIVE

M cCoy was watching the clock above the office door. Wattie had been in with Hood for forty minutes. Must have got something from him. Was just about to go out and get some more fags when the door to the office opened and Wattie walked in. Didn't look happy. Dumped his notebook and pen on the desk, stretched.

"How did it go?" asked McCoy.

"It didn't," he said. "Blanket denial of everything. Said he'd never given any down-and-out anything to drink, never seen the bottle your dad drank from and never seen the methanol. He's going to brazen it out. Apart from the bottle of methanol, we've got nothing to connect him to your dad or any of the other dead men. He could claim the methanol was for a camping stove or something. Or he can just say, since it was found in a communal toilet in the bedsit, that it's got nothing to do with him. Maybe it belongs to one of the other people staying there. There's five of them—finding them and interviewing them'll take days."

He put his head in his hands. Didn't look up as he spoke. "We're going to have to find something else and quick, or we'll have to let him go. According to Murray, we don't have enough to charge him with anything."

"Where is he?"

Wattie sat up. "He's still in the cell. We can hold him for another few hours."

McCoy got up, walked towards the office door. Ignored Wattie calling him back.

*

McCoy pushed the eyehole cover to the side and looked in the cell. Hood was sitting on the bed, shoes gone. He was staring into space, muttering something too quietly for McCoy to hear.

McCoy opened the door and Hood looked at him.

"What are you doing?"

"Praying."

"You better. You're going to need all the help you can get."

"I didn't kill your father. I didn't kill anyone."

"Spare me," said McCoy. "You know, I came in here expecting to feel something, see some kind of twisted killer, but I don't. I'm just looking at some cunt sitting on his bed praying for his mammy. Whatever he was, my father was still twice the man you are. You're nothing, just a puddle of piss on the floor."

He turned to go, and realised Hood was smiling.

"That it, McCoy? That all you've got, is it? You came in here just to call me names?" He shook his head. "I thought you were a useless cunt the first time I walked into this station. Full of yourself. The great Harry McCoy. Looks like I was right. I lied earlier. I know all about you, Harry McCoy. Know who you are. Know the things you've done."

"You don't know anything about me," said McCoy, suddenly unsure.

Hood smiled, like he was pitying someone too stupid to argue with. "Fuck off. And tell your pal he's got two more hours, then I'm walking."

McCoy had his fists bunched, tensed up. Wanted nothing more than to punch the smile off Hood's face. Knew if he did, Hood would use it against them and he would have yet another excuse to be let go. He walked out the cell, closed the door behind him, stood in the corridor trying to breathe slowly, get the anger out of him.

A couple of minutes and a fag later he was breathing normally again, hands unfurled. There was something else he needed to take care of. He'd let Rossi needle him and that was bad, wasn't fitting in with the plan he had half-formed in his mind. Time to fix things. Time to crawl.

"Rossi?"

Rossi looked up from his typewriter.

"Got a minute?"

Rossi looked doubtful, but he stood up and followed McCoy out into the corridor.

"Sorry," said McCoy. "I was upset about my dad, and I took it out on you."

Rossi raised his eyebrows.

"I'm in. The next job. I won't fuck it up this time."

"Glad to hear it," Rossi said. "I'll be in touch."

McCoy watched him walk back down the corridor towards the office. No matter what he did, he was going to destroy that wee shite if it killed him.

"You okay?" asked Wattie as he returned to his desk. "You look like you're going to blow a gasket."

"I'm fine," said McCoy. "Going to nip out for some fresh air."

Wattie nodded, went back to his typing.

McCoy needed time out the station, needed to think. Everything was starting to pile on top of him. His dad. Long and Rossi. Kathy Kent. Duncan Kent. Stevie Cooper and Archie Andrews. All of it swirling around in his head. Needed to get some clarity, decide what he was going to do next.

The desk sergeant stopped him on the way out. "Some guy left a note for you."

McCoy took the folded-over paper, stepped out into the sunshine and started walking towards Saracen Street. Unfolded the paper and began to read. Gerry's familiar scrawl.

I told you someone was killing those men. You didn't believe me and now you know it is true. You need to believe me about something else. Tomorrow is Midsummer's Day. The longest day. Reverend West is going to hurt someone tomorrow, hurt them bad. You need to stop him. He is going to hurt his son. He exists. You know he exists. You have always known. Gerry.

McCoy folded the paper over. Started walking towards Saracen Street again. Started to think. Things were becoming clearer. Maybe there was a way out of this mess. Now all he had to do was find it.

SATURDAY

21ST JUNE 1975

SIXTY-SIX

Y ou saw my wife."

McCoy nodded.

"And she told you the story," said Kent.

He nodded again.

"So the ball's in your court."

"Looks like it," said McCoy.

This time Duncan Kent's secretary had put McCoy straight through. No meetings. No "not available" this time. So now they were sitting in Epicures in West Nile Street. Popular lunch spot for businessmen like Kent. Small tables, waitresses in uniform, big windows overlooking the busy street outside.

Kent was pushing the remains of his prawn salad around his plate. Hadn't eaten much. Had drunk two glasses of white wine though. The strain was showing.

"I told her not to go and see you," he said.

"She said as much," said McCoy, finishing the last of his soup. He wiped his mouth with his napkin and sat back. "But she did. So now we have to work out what to do."

"We?" asked Kent. "I imagined this as more of a blackmail situation."

"I'm not a thief," said McCoy.

Kent held his hands up. "Point taken. In that case, what are we going to do?"

A waitress appeared, cleared away the plates, asked them if they wanted coffee. A yes from McCoy and a no from Kent.

"I don't really give much of a fuck who your wife is," said

McCoy after she left. "Seems to me she's paid the price for whatever she's done." He got his cigarettes out, lit up and blew the smoke away. "If I'm being honest, it's you that bothers me."

Kent raised his eyebrows. Wasn't expecting that.

"You got one of your goons to torture and kill Malky McCormack—an old man who knew nothing about nothing— so you'll forgive me if I don't quite buy into you and Mrs. Kent as lord and lady of the manor dispensing alms to the poor."

Kent went to speak, but McCoy got in first. "I don't imagine I'll ever be able to pin Malky on you, will I? Too many expensive lawyers and too many degrees of separation. Am I right?"

Kent smiled, showing off a row of even white teeth. "You haven't a hope in hell."

McCoy's coffee arrived and he took a sip. "I don't much care what you do either, Kent, just when it happens on my patch, and Malky McCormack was on my patch. I've probably got just about enough to get you into the station for an interview. It'll come to nothing, but I'll make sure the photographers from the *Record* and the *Evening Times* are there. Should knock a bit of a shine off your halo. Make me feel a bit better about poor Malky."

"You could, but you're not going to."

"Why do you say that?"

Kent twisted the signet ring on his pinky round and round. "Simple. You've won the golden ticket. You've got the birth certificate. You know exactly who my wife is. You're not going to throw that kind of opportunity away to try and shame me in two shitty provincial papers that'll be wrapping fish suppers tomorrow. You're not that stupid." He leant forward. "So why don't you stop all this fucking around and just tell me what we are going to do?"

McCoy put his coffee down. Grinned. "Funny you should ask."

SIXTY-SEVEN

McCoy sat down on the steps of the High Court, took out his cigarettes. Stone he was sitting on was pleasantly warm, sun had been shining on it all day. Across the road Glasgow Green was full of kids and young families. An ice-cream van was parked by the gates, long queue waiting. Made him think of Paul and his Askit plan. Wondered how it was going.

Now that the meeting with Kent was out the way and the plan set, he started to think about Hood. Evidence was pretty damning. He'd the motive, the opportunity and the weapon. Only one thing that made absolutely no sense. Why would Hood hold so much of a grudge against him that he would kill his father? He'd only spoken to Hood once or twice; granted, he hadn't been the pleasantest to him, but that was nowhere near enough of a reason.

Still couldn't think of anyone who did. Suddenly struck him. Maybe the note wasn't for him at all. Maybe the note was for his dad. *Now you know how it feels.* How it feels to die? Had his dad done something so bad to somebody that they wanted to kill him, wanted him to suffer?

It was a possibility, but what could his dad have done to Hood? According to Frank, he'd been in a bad way for months. What could a terminal alky have done to a big strong guy like Hood? Nothing physical anyway.

He stubbed out his cigarette and stepped on it, saw Wattie coming out the door of the mortuary. He waved, and Wattie walked up to the steps.

"Like a home from home for you, these bloody steps," he said. He sat down, stretched his legs out, yawned. "Been standing for two bloody hours. I'm knackered."

"How'd the party go, by the way?" asked McCoy.

"Great," said Wattie. "Trapped in a flat with twenty screaming toddlers, best day of my life."

"Did the wee bugger enjoy it?"

"The wee bugger was having a whale of a time until the girl from upstairs took his bit of cake off him and ate it. All hell broke loose after that. You would've loved it."

"Was he asking after me?"

Wattie nodded. "Yep. Kept asking where his Uncle Harry was."

"Did he?" said McCoy, feeling a bit touched.

"Did he fuck. Didn't notice you weren't there, didn't even notice I was—it was all about the cake and the crisps. Got a fag?"

McCoy handed him the packet and Wattie lit up.

"You sure you want to hear all this? It's not pretty."

McCoy nodded.

"Up to you. The cause of death was acute alcohol poisoning. The way Phyllis was talking, that bottle of hooch was just the icing on the cake. Even without it he would have been dead in a couple of days apparently. He was only fifty-nine?"

McCoy thought. Nodded.

"Christ, he looked more like seventy-odd, Harry. He was in some state."

"Anything else?"

"Cirrhosis of the liver, some brain damage. She thinks he had a fall at some point, bashed his head."

"He got hit by a car."

"I'm surprised he made it to fifty-nine," said Wattie. "You okay with all this?"

He was. Whatever he felt now, it wasn't really grief, more

like regret at the waste of it all. Time to make amends. "Will you help me do something?"

Wattie looked doubtful. "Like what, exactly?"

"Don't go mad," said McCoy. "This is Midsummer's Day. I want to have one last look at Reverend West's house. Gerry's convinced he has a son and that today's the day West is going to do something to him."

"Gerry? That wee liar? Are you serious?"

"I told you not to go mad. It'll only take an hour. Gerry left me a note. He was right about the poisonings, wasn't he? He deserves a chance on this."

Wattie shook his head.

"I'll buy you a drink afterwards," said McCoy. "Two drinks, three drinks. And I promise I'll never mention it again."

"If, *if*, I say yes, you have to do me a favour too."

"Okay," said McCoy. "What is it?"

"You have to babysit the wee bugger, or, as you know him, your beloved godson one night, so me and Mary can go out. Haven't had a night out since he was born."

McCoy held out his hand to shake. "Deal."

SIXTY-EIGHT

Wattie got out the car, loosened his tie and rolled up his shirtsleeves. McCoy locked the car up, and they started walking down the hill. Hillend Street was empty, a couple of other parked cars and the noise of kids playing in the adjacent field. It was hot, sticky. Clouds of tiny flies circling in the air. Smell of cut grass.

"Tell me again," said Wattie.

McCoy sighed. Started again. "Gerry says Midsummer's Day is today. The longest day of the year. The day when they can give up most suffering to God. For West it's the biggest date in the calendar. So, if West is going to do anything, he'll do it today."

"What a load of bollocks. Catholics and Protestants are bad enough, never mind all this shite."

"Don't have to convince me."

"You really think West has some sort of secret son and he's going to torture him or whatever today?"

"That's what Gerry thinks."

"Where is he anyway?"

"He'll be here somewhere, don't worry."

They continued walking, then McCoy stopped. "Speak of the devil."

Gerry stepped out onto the street from behind the hedge of the house next to West's. Usual black suit, gloves, hair everywhere.

Looked very pleased with himself. "I knew you'd come. I knew you'd believe me."

"Knew more than I did, then," said McCoy. "Only decided to come half an hour ago. And let's say it's more to satisfy myself than because I think you're right."

Gerry grinned. "Doesn't matter. You're here now. Let's go. We should hurry."

They walked up the path of West's house, and McCoy rang the bell.

"What are we going to do?" said Wattie. "Ask him to hand over the nonexistent boy?"

McCoy rang the bell again.

"Doesn't look like anyone is in," said Wattie.

"Round the back," said Gerry.

McCoy shrugged, and they followed Gerry round the side of the house. The garden looked a bit neglected. Grass needed cutting, weeds in the flower beds. Gerry looked around, picked up a brick from a pile by the hut.

"Gerry," said McCoy, "what are you going to do with that?"

Got his answer straight away as Gerry threw it at the kitchen window. It shattered, noise seeming very loud in the quiet residential street. Gerry pulled his sleeve down over his hand, knocked the remaining bits of glass out the frame and climbed in. Reappeared a few seconds later in the window of the back door. Noise of a key turning, then the door was pulled open.

"Great," said Wattie. "I've always wanted to be done for breaking and entering."

It wasn't only the garden that had been neglected; the house was suffering too. Looked like things had gone downhill since his last visit. There were dishes piled in the sink, bluebottles hovering round a piled-up bin.

"Anybody home?" McCoy shouted.

Nothing.

"We need to search the place," said Gerry. "He's here somewhere. He has to be."

McCoy nodded. They were here now, may as well do it

properly. Half an hour later of opening cupboards, looking under beds, tapping walls for secret rooms and a ladder climb up to an empty and dusty attic they hadn't found anything. Or anybody.

McCoy called them all back into the kitchen, slapping the legs of his suit to get the dust out. Gerry was growing increasingly agitated, muttering to himself, tugging at his hair. Wattie just looked tired.

"There's no one here, son," said McCoy.

"It's Midsummer. There has to be," said Gerry. "I know what he's like." Then something seemed to dawn on him. "He'll be at the church."

"Hang on," said Wattie. "This is getting ridiculous. We've gone along with you—against my better judgement, I may add—torn this place apart, and there's nobody here. No mystery, no Reverend West. Nothing. Need to call it a day."

McCoy was about to agree with him when Gerry opened a kitchen drawer, took out a carving knife and held it up to his neck. "We need to go to the church right now, or I'll stick this knife in my neck, so help me I will. I mean it."

A bead of blood appeared at the tip of the knife.

"Gerry," said McCoy, moving towards him, "don't be daft. Just put the knife down and—"

Gerry pushed the knife further in, eyes locked on McCoy's. Blood started flowing down his neck.

"Gerry! For fuck sake! Okay! Okay! We'll go to the church!" shouted McCoy.

Gerry kept the knife there for a few seconds, then pulled it away. Wiped at the blood with his sleeve.

"We better hurry," he said.

SIXTY-NINE

They arrived at the Church of Christ's Suffering to find the doors shut, no noise of singing, no sign of any activity at all. Gerry still had the carving knife in his hand, tea towel wrapped around his neck to stop the bleeding, still muttering to himself. McCoy coughed up some of the dust from the house, spat on the ground.

"So," said Wattie, nodding at the little green building. "Breaking and entering charge number two, is it? I'm going to fucking kill you, McCoy."

"Let's just get it done," said McCoy. "We've wasted enough bloody time as it is." He turned to Gerry. "This is it, son—the end. If we search it and there's nobody there, then we walk away, okay? And you don't do anything stupid. Agreed?"

Gerry nodded.

"Right." McCoy started walking towards the church door. Was a couple of feet away, about to ask Gerry if there was a back way in, when the door banged open.

The woman with the callipers stepped out, blinked in the light. Her face was white, eyes red from crying. She staggered off to the side, fell onto her knees, eyes rolled back in her head, and she passed out.

McCoy started running down the path, Wattie and Gerry behind him. He got there first, pulled the church door open. Couldn't see properly at first, dramatic change from the bright sunshine outside to the gloom of the church. Dust was spinning in the air, a smell of old damp wood and paper. He could hear someone talking, sounded like Reverend West. As his eyes adjusted he saw him.

He was standing by the altar, leaning over something. His tie was gone, shirt gaping open, manic look in his eyes and a long kitchen knife in his hand. He looked upwards and shouted, "But even if you should suffer for what is right, you are blessed."

McCoy ran round the pew to see what was happening and stopped dead in his tracks. There was a woman lying on the church floor, arms and legs tied to a rough wooden cross. Reverend West, kneeling beside her, shouted again: "Do not fear their threats; do not be frightened."

And he raised the knife, metal shining in the light from the windows. The woman turned her head to McCoy just as West brought the knife down into her stomach. She didn't flinch as it went in. Just looked at McCoy and smiled. Empty eyes meeting his.

McCoy's stomach lurched. He tried not to look at the blood and ran at West. West brought the knife down again just as McCoy wrapped his arms around his neck and pulled him to the floor. West fell on top of him and McCoy felt a pain in his back, like a hard punch. He pushed West over, tried to get on top of him. Had just about got him down when Wattie appeared and kicked West. Hard. He flew back and his head battered off the floor.

Wattie stamped on his wrist, took the knife from him and put it down on the pew. "You okay?" he asked.

McCoy nodded. He was winded, heart racing, but other than that he was fine. West lay there, seemed a bit dazed by his head hitting the floor. Seemed to be reciting something under his breath. McCoy stood up, suddenly felt a sharp pain. He put his hand behind him to feel what it was and his hand came away red. He swore, looked up, and Gerry was standing at the church door.

"Gerry," he shouted. "Don't come in here."

Gerry dropped his knife, started walking down the aisle.

"Fuck," said McCoy under his breath. He tried to move to

stop him, but the pain in his back hit hard and all he could do was sit down on the pew, try to breathe. Gerry walked past him and up to the woman on the floor. She was still smiling, eyes up to the sky, looked like she was in some kind of ecstatic trance, bright red blood starting to pool all around her.

Gerry fell to his knees. Reached out for her hand. "Mum," he said. "Mum, are you okay?"

West tried to sit up, but Wattie had a hold of him, had his arm around his neck in a stranglehold. "Stay the fuck down," he hissed.

West wasn't listening. He looked straight at Gerry. Smiled. Seemed happy to see him.

"Hello, son," he said. Nodded at the woman. "That could be you too, Jeremiah. It's not too late. You too can bring us closer to God by your suffering, fulfil your destiny at last."

McCoy had never seen Gerry move so fast. One minute he was kneeling by his mum. The next he grabbed the knife from the pew, ran at West and stuck it straight into his throat. Force of the blow knocked West and Wattie backwards, and they sprawled on the floor.

West's neck gaped open, pumping blood up into the air.

Gerry moved back to his mum, lay down beside her and cuddled into her. "It's okay, Mum, I'm here, it's okay . . ."

McCoy tried to stand up, to get away from the blood, but he had no strength. He stumbled and fell onto the wooden floor. He lay there, watched Gerry cuddle his mum, talk quietly as the life slipped out of her, saw Wattie get up and come towards him. Heard "Harry, fuck sake, are you okay?"

He tried to say yes but he couldn't get the words out. Tried to get up again. Fell again. Heard Wattie telling him to just lie still and that he would get help. Nodded his head. Closed his eyes, didn't want to see West any more. Gerry's mum. No more blood, no more pain.

WEDNESDAY

25TH JUNE 1975

There was a scattered round of applause when McCoy walked into the office. He bowed, headed for his desk. Familiar cloud of tobacco smoke over everything, clatter of typewriters, some radio playing Alvin Stardust. Seemed like not much had changed in the few days he'd been off. His back still hurt a bit, but other than that he felt fine. He sat down, winced a bit. Took out his fags.

"Still sore?" asked Wattie.

He shook his head. Started looking in his drawer for matches. "Not too bad. Just the stitches, itchy as hell."

"How many did you get?"

McCoy found a box of Swan Vestas with a few left in it. "Twelve. My back's fine, but my new suit's fucked. Big hole in the back, bloodstains all over it. Why can't I have been wearing the old one when the bastard stabbed me?" Lit his cigarette, waved the match out. "So what have I missed?"

"A lot," said Wattie. "Don't know if you know, but West died in the ambulance."

He didn't. Wasn't very sorry about it. "Gerry's in Leverndale—"

"The mental hospital?"

Wattie nodded. "He's not great. Hasn't spoken since the church. They're keeping him in for observation. He's on suicide watch."

"Christ," said McCoy. "Poor bugger."

"The woman . . ."

"Gerry's mum?" said McCoy.

Wattie nodded. "Died yesterday. Never regained consciousness." He shook his head. "Still can't believe she was smiling when he stabbed her. Gave me the creeps. So all fucking religious loonies present and accounted for."

McCoy was about to speak but Wattie beat him to it. "And before you ask, they did another full search of the house and the church. No sign of a boy. No clothes, toys, paperwork, anything. Looks like he never existed after all. What they did find was a false wall in the attic. Looks like the mum had been staying there. Blow-up mattress. Some clothes. A Bible."

"So that's who it was," said McCoy.

"What?" said Wattie.

McCoy shook his head. "Nothing."

"Is Gerry West's son, do you think? Is that right?"

"Not sure," said McCoy. "Might have just meant it in an older guy speaking to a younger one way. With the mum dead we'll never know. Doesn't really matter, I suppose. Not any more." He blew out a cloud of cigarette smoke and looked round the office. Had things he had to get done. "Rossi been around?"

Wattie shook his head. "Not much. Seen him a couple of times. Apart from the religious loonies it's all been a bit quiet. Writing all that up was a fucking slog though, took me most of the week." He looked at McCoy. "You know Hood is out?"

McCoy shook his head, but he wasn't surprised.

"Couldn't hold him. Not enough evidence for a conviction according to the Crown Office. Can you believe it? Worse than that, he even wanted to come back to the station, but Murray told him to get to fuck. He's sent him to Tobago Street. You okay with that?"

McCoy shrugged. "Nothing I can do about it. Besides, I'm not even sure he did it. The note thing still makes no sense."

"I've been thinking about that," said Wattie. "Maybe your dad had another son. Maybe it's all to do with him?"

"Could be. I don't know. We'll probably never know what it's about."

"Probably not. You still staying at Margo's?"

"Yep, she's supposed to be looking after me, but she's got a buyer for the estate, been up there going through stuff, seeing what to leave for them, seeing what she wants to keep. Hardly been there."

"Poor you," said Wattie. "Maybe we could drop the wee bugger off there and you could look after him?"

McCoy shook his head. "Are you telling me that amongst all this death and stabbing, not to mention my own personal injury, your main concern is me remembering that I promised to babysit?"

Wattie nodded. "Yep. Mary's all excited. How about tomorrow?"

McCoy nodded. May as well get it over with.

"Good man," said Wattie. "I'll away and phone her."

McCoy watched him go, then looked at the pile of files on his desk. Sighed and opened the first one. Started to read it and drifted off. No matter what he told Wattie he was still bothered about the note left on his dad's body. Still wondering what it meant. Was just about to start on the file again when the office door opened and Rossi walked in. Usual greased-back hair, usual kipper tie, usual smug smile on his face.

He nodded at McCoy and pointed at the toilets. "You're back," he said as McCoy walked in. "About bloody time."

"Nice to see you too," said McCoy. "What's going on?"

"You heard about Long?" asked Rossi, taking out a comb and starting to sweep his hair back in the bathroom mirror.

McCoy shook his head.

"He's fucked. The infection spread. Had to get the left hand amputated and lost two fingers on the right one. He'll no be back."

"Poor bugger," said McCoy.

"Fuck him," said Rossi, putting his comb away and turning round. "Shouldn't have fucked the job up." He walked across to McCoy, prodded him in the chest. "What it does mean is you're in prime position. Time for you to step into his shoes. Make a bit more money."

"Sounds good," said McCoy. "When do we start?"

"Tonight," said Rossi. "You up for that?"

McCoy nodded. "What is it?"

"Archie wants to meet you. Suss you out. See if you're up to the job."

"No worries," said McCoy. "When and where?"

"Anchor bar in Tollcross," said Rossi. "He's visiting his sister. She lives next door. Eight o'clock."

McCoy nodded, went to go.

"And, McCoy? Archie hasn't forgotten about Cooper. He needs you to deliver."

McCoy saluted, walked out the toilets. Sat back down at his desk and picked up his phone. Dialled. The snotty secretary picked up.

"Need to speak to Mr. Kent," he said. "Now."

SEVENTY-ONE

I f there were stranger situations McCoy had been in, he couldn't think of any offhand. He was sitting in the passenger seat of a clapped-out Cortina, Duncan Kent in the driving seat and Joseph Monaghan in the back, whistling through his teeth and flicking through a copy of the *Evening Times*.

"Where'd you get the car, Joe?" asked Kent.

"Some street in Ibrox."

Kent moved the rear-view mirror so he could see Monaghan's face. "I told you to get a car no one would notice, didn't say get a bloody jalopy. I'm probably getting fleas off this bloody seat."

McCoy should have guessed Monaghan would be with Kent. Didn't make him any happier to see him though. Wasn't keen on small talk with the man who had battered Malky McCormack to death. Still, if you chose to dance with the devil, you couldn't be too choosy about your dancing partner.

McCoy looked at his watch. Five to eight. Taxi was coming down the road. "This could be us."

The taxi stopped, Rossi stepped out, then it was gone, back on the hunt for fares. McCoy heard the back door of the car open as Monaghan got out. Watched through the windscreen as he walked over to Rossi, holding out a fag like he was looking for a light. Rossi put his hand in his pocket to get the matches, and Monaghan headbutted him. Rossi's nose burst, and blood started pouring down his face. He staggered back, and Monaghan followed the headbutt with two haymakers to the side of his head. Rossi started to drop. Monaghan caught him under the arms and dragged him back towards the car.

McCoy heard the boot opening, a thud, felt the car lowering a bit before it was slammed shut again. Back door opened, and Monaghan sat down, picked up his paper again. Whole thing had taken less than a minute. Much as he had no time for Monaghan, he had to admit he was bloody good at his job.

"What's the address again?" asked Kent.

"Kingsacre Drive," said McCoy. "Number seventy-eight."

Kent turned the key, engine started, and they were off.

SEVENTY-TWO

Rossi's house was a semi-detached bungalow on the Southside of Glasgow. It was neat and tidy: swirly patterned carpets and anaglypta wallpaper, wee picture of Christ with a hollow for holy water under it by the front door. Rossi also had quite a collection of pictures of Glasgow in days gone by. Twelve or thirteen of them framed and hanging on the walls of his living room. McCoy looked at each one, trying to work out where they were and trying not to listen to the sound of Joseph Monaghan being very good at his job again.

Kent moved over to the radiogram and started flipping through the records piled beside it. "Anything you want to hear?"

McCoy shook his head. Just wanted anything but the sound of Rossi trying to scream through the pair of socks stuffed in his mouth. Socks, because after Monaghan had tied him to the chair he'd got from the kitchen, he took Rossi's shoes off and then his socks, stuffed them in his mouth, then rammed a screwdriver through each foot, effectively pinning Rossi's feet to the floor.

Kent picked up a record and smiled. "Haven't heard this for ages." Seconds later, the sound of Rod Stewart's "Gasoline Alley" filled the room.

McCoy went into the kitchen, poured himself a glass of water and drank it over, hand shaking. What had been a good idea in principle was turning into a nightmare. Get Kent to threaten Rossi—and make him surrender the photos—in return for Kathy's birth certificate had sounded neat and tidy.

What he hadn't realised was how much people like Kent and Monaghan enjoyed hurting people. It wasn't a side effect of their job: it was why they had got into it in the first place. Heard his name being shouted, put the glass back on the draining board and walked back through.

The socks were out Rossi's mouth. He looked absolutely terrified. Eyes wild, sweat running down his face, hair everywhere. Had even pissed himself.

"Say it again," said Kent.

"The spare bedroom, under the bed. There's a lockbox. Key's under the encyclopaedia on the shelf. Please don't hurt me any—"

Monaghan stuffed the socks back in.

"Off you go, McCoy," said Kent.

McCoy got the key from the shelf and knelt down by the bed. The room was cold, smelt a bit damp, like it never got properly aired. He pulled the box out, tried not to think about what was happening in the living room. He got the key in, wouldn't turn at first, jiggled it, and eventually it gave. He lifted the lid up and stared.

There were a dozen large brown envelopes, glassine bags of negatives beside them. That wasn't all. There was money, lots of it. About thirty thick rolls of twenties. Rossi's share of all the jobs over the years. He grabbed them, started stuffing them in his pockets, had to leave a couple there were so many. No more room in his pockets. Picked up the envelopes and the negatives and headed back through.

Monaghan and Kent were standing in front of one of the framed pictures on the wall arguing as to whether it was Shettleston Road or Tollcross Road. Turned when McCoy came back in.

"Got them?" asked Kent.

McCoy nodded. Didn't say anything about the money.

"Could be easier to just end this all permanently, if you know what I mean?" said Kent. "Joseph's got rid of enough bodies in his time."

McCoy shook his head. Last thing he wanted. "He'll be scared shitless. That's enough."

Kent shrugged. "Up to you."

Rossi was still tied to the chair, blood pooling out from his feet, seeping into the swirly carpet. He looked broken, huge sweat stains under the armpits of his shirt. Kent walked over and stood in front of him. Rossi immediately recoiled, started shaking his head, trying to talk through the gag.

Kent put a finger to his lips, said "Shh," then leant over and took the socks out Rossi's mouth. "You going to behave yourself?"

Rossi nodded.

Kent squatted down so they were face to face. "This is how it's going to work. Tonight never happened. If I ever hear that you have so much as breathed a word about it, Joseph here is going to come back and he is going to kill you. And before you die, he will torture you so badly death will seem like sweet relief. Do you understand?"

Rossi nodded.

"And when you see McCoy in the station you will nod politely and say hello, enquire after his health and that is all. Do you understand?"

Rossi nodded.

"I don't give a fuck how you tell Archie Andrews you're not going to work for him, but you're not. Again, mention me, Joseph or McCoy to him, and Joseph will come back. Do you understand?"

Rossi nodded again.

"Good boy." Kent pushed the socks back in his mouth and pulled the screwdrivers out of Rossi's feet.

His face contorted in agony.

Kent pointed at the painting. "Shettleston?"

Rossi managed to nod.

Kent grinned, stood up. "You owe me a fiver, Joseph. Now let's go."

They walked out the house and to the car. McCoy couldn't face getting back in with them.

"I'm going to walk for a bit," he said.

Got the birth certificate out his inside jacket pocket and handed the envelope to Kent, who took it, put it in his pocket. "That's the end of it," he said. "I never saw it, don't know what it says, don't know who it belongs to."

"You know what happens if it's not?" said Kent.

McCoy nodded. Knew all too well. Joseph would come for him, and he wouldn't stop until McCoy was in the ground.

Kent held out his hand to shake. McCoy hesitated for a second, then shook it. Watched them get in the car and drive off. Had a look up the road. He seemed to remember there was a pub called the Beechwood up the way. He started walking. He needed a drink and he needed to wash his hands. Pretend to himself he was still different to people like Kent and Monaghan.

SATURDAY

28TH JUNE 1975

SEVENTY-THREE

The nurse pointed down the corridor to the day room. "In there," she said.

McCoy thanked her, walked down the corridor. He'd a carrier bag with him. Had the photos of Long, a bottle of Lucozade, bag of grapes and £32,000 of Rossi's money in it. He opened the day room and went in. It was a large room, big windows overlooking the new motorway, armchairs with cushions, coffee table with well-thumbed magazines on it.

Long was sitting by the window in pyjamas and dressing gown, fast asleep. Both his arms ended in bandages, the left one a good bit shorter. McCoy sat down beside him, listened to him snore, and looked out at the cars driving past. He decided to let Long sleep for a while, took out his cigarettes and lit up. Had some thinking to do.

He'd ended up in the Beechwood until closing time, drunk as a skunk. Couldn't face going to Margo's and having to explain why, so he went back to his own flat. Woke up in the morning lying on the bed fully clothed, bag with a roll and chips leaking grease onto the bedside table. He'd got up, had a bath, made a cup of tea and sat at the table with the photo envelopes.

McCoy's own photos had been easy to find—the thinnest one. Him pictured outside the old man's flat, sitting in a car in Lambhill, and one that surprised him—sitting with the envelope of money in the Arlington bar. Hadn't even realised it had been taken. Long's was much thicker. The photographer had even managed to get one of him in action, kicking some guy lying on the floor of what looked like an empty pub. He opened the others. People he didn't know doing the same sort of things.

He opened the last one, held it up, and the photos slid out onto the table. He looked at them for a minute, not believing what he was seeing. Archie Andrews and Murray sitting at a table in Rogano's. Archie Andrews and Murray playing golf somewhere. Archie Andrews and Murray at the rugby. Archie Andrews and Murray sitting in the back of the Glen Douglas, deep in conversation.

He sat back, took a sip of his tea. Could maybe say most of them had been taken at charity events. Andrews and Murray moved in the same circles. It was the one in the Glen Douglas that bothered him. They didn't tend to hold charity events in shitty pubs in Lambhill.

The photos didn't prove anything but a casual acquaintance, he supposed. Nothing too untoward. Just prominent Glasgow citizens having a chat. He peered at the one in the Glen Douglas again. Earnest faces leaning into one another. Thick as thieves.

He picked the Murray photos up and walked over to the bin, started ripping the first one into tiny pieces. Did the same with the next few. The Glen Douglas one was last. He looked at it, folded it in half, and slipped it in between the pages of a copy of *Jaws* sitting on the bookshelf.

He finished his cigarette, stubbed it out in the tin ashtray on the coffee table of the day room. Decided to just let Long sleep. Tucked the carrier bag in beside him and left.

SEVENTY-FOUR

I'll get it!" McCoy shouted up the stairs. He opened the front door of Margo's house. Wattie and Mary were standing there, both dressed up, Wee Duggie in Mary's arms. Wee Duggie saw McCoy, stretched out his hand to him, McCoy took it and blew a raspberry into his chubby palm.

"Hello, Smiler," he said. "You come to visit your Uncle Harry?"

Wattie handed him a bag. "All his stuff's in there. He's been running about the park all day, so hopefully he's knackered. If you put him down about eight, he'll cry for a few minutes, then he'll fall asleep. It's what he always does. We're going to Ferrari's, so if anything happens, you can phone us there. Okay?"

"All good," said McCoy, taking the bag and Wee Duggie.

"See you about half ten," said Mary. "Thanks for this."

"No bother," said McCoy. "Margo's looking forward to it."

He said goodbye, walked through to the living room, took Wee Duggie's anorak off and set him down on the floor, dug in the bag, took out three Matchbox cars, put them down in front of him.

"There you go."

Wee Duggie smiled at him and started running the cars up and down the carpet. McCoy sat down on the couch and looked at the boxes and boxes of stuff Margo had brought down from the estate. Pile seemed to be growing by the day.

"Look at him!" said Margo, walking in. She sat down on the

couch, started talking nonsense to him. Wee Duggie toddled over, climbed into her lap, car in each chubby hand.

"What are you going to do with all this stuff?" asked McCoy.

"Go through it," said Margo, not taking her eyes off Wee Duggie. "See what's worth keeping. There should be some more photos of my mother in there somewhere. I'd like to keep those."

McCoy got up, walked over to the table where she had started. Half emptied box on the floor, two piles of photos. Keep and bin. He picked up a photo of a good-looking young woman. Held it up. "This her?"

Margo peered over. "Yes, at her coming-out, of all things. Think there's one of her and Princess Margaret somewhere. See if you can find it."

McCoy sat down at the table, grabbed a pile of photos from the box and started going through them. A line of men firing guns at a shoot. Two Jack Russells sitting on an apple crate. Next one was Margo's brother, back when he was young, good-looking, sitting in military uniform in a studio. McCoy looked at it, wondered how he became the monster that he was. All those years of torturing people for the British Army must have sent his mind haywire.

"You want the photos of Angus?"

Margo picked up Wee Duggie, came over and looked over McCoy's shoulder. "Only if he's young. Before . . . you know."

McCoy nodded. Put the photo in the keep pile.

"I'll take him through to the kitchen," said Margo. "Give him something to eat."

She walked away, making goo-goo noises into Wee Duggie's ear.

He kept going with the photos. About twenty of some banquet in the castle, men in dinner suits, women all in fancy dresses and jewellery. He flicked through, put them in the no pile. Picked up the next one. Margo's brother with some of his private army, lonely young lads he picked up from the Territorials, taught fieldcraft and who knew what else.

More private army ones. Looked like they'd been taken a while ago; he must have been at it for years. Then a colour one, much newer. Margo's brother as McCoy had known him, older, thinner. He was sitting on a fallen tree, two lads beside him. McCoy looked closer. Recognised one of the lads, Crawford. Angus Lindsay's second-in-command, called himself his son they were that tight. Threw himself in front of a train when it all went wrong and the police were after him.

Put them in the no pile. Got up to go and see how Margo was getting on with the wee man. Stopped. Picked up the tree photo again. Looked closer. Couldn't be.

But Crawford's dead.

His stomach dropped.

Now you know how it feels.

Recruitment poster, my arse. He grabbed his jacket, shouted through to Margo that he'd be back later and hurried out the door.

SEVENTY-FIVE

The Salvation Army building was all closed up. No lights. McCoy went round the back, knocked on the door. Wasn't long until it was answered, and Kenny Lowell was standing there. No uniform this time. Jeans and a camouflage T-shirt, black boots. He grinned. Held the door open.

"Come on in, McCoy," he said. "I've been expecting you."

He turned and walked down the corridor towards the main hall, all the while like someone answering the door to a friend he'd invited over for dinner. He opened the door at the end of the corridor, pulled down some switches, the overhead neon flashed and fizzed, and the hall was suddenly full of light. It was the usual thing, varnished wooden floor, low stage at the other end, markings for various sports painted on the floor. There was an army rucksack and a holdall sitting in the middle, coat folded on top.

Lowell stopped, turned to McCoy. "You're just in time. I'm off soon."

"You're Crawford," said McCoy.

"Yep," said Crawford. "Thought you'd rumbled me the first time we met, despite all my efforts to look different. That beard took months to grow, you know."

"A recruiting poster," said McCoy. "You said you were on a recruiting poster."

Crawford grinned. "Yes, I was quite pleased with that, had to think on the hoof." He looked as if it had suddenly dawned on him. "Here's me forgetting my manners. Come on."

McCoy followed him as he walked to the other end of the hall and through another set of doors, opened a door in the corridor, and they were in a bedroom: single bed, linen folded on top, drawing pins in the wall where posters had been, a small sink.

Crawford opened a cupboard, took out a half empty bottle of whisky and two glasses, poured them each a measure, and handed one to McCoy.

McCoy looked at it, looked at Crawford.

"What? Ah, don't worry. Look." Downed half of his, sat on the bed, pointed at the chair.

McCoy sat down, took a sip. "How?"

"How come I'm here? Not six feet under? Easy. You plant your ID on someone who looks like you, then you shove them in front of a train. Train was going at sixty miles an hour, so the body pretty much vaporised. Only thing left to tell anybody who it was? Their army ID."

"Did you kill my dad?" asked McCoy, trying not to let his voice shake.

"Me? No idea. Didn't his pal do that? Hood was supposed to do it, but he chickened out. That's why it was all a bit of a mess." He grinned. "I did, however, facilitate it somewhat. Handed him the bottle."

"What did Hood do?"

"Ah, Hood was a lost soul. Came to the big city to be a policeman, found out big cities aren't like back home, that they can be very lonely places. He was in the right place at the right time. I made friends, took him out to dinner one night, told him how similar we were, beliefs we shared. We took some wine back to his, and I fucked him."

"Hood's . . ."

Crawford shook his head. "I don't think he knows what he is. He was just so desperately lonely that it was some form of human contact at least. And before you ask, it's not my usual predilection either, but needs must."

McCoy thought back. Two bottles on Hood's windowsill, a memento.

"And after that he was putty in my hands. Gave him an Ayn Rand book, whispered sweet nothings in his ear. Told him people like us were better than anyone else and the streets were full of useless people who would be better off dead. Didn't take much to persuade him. Seemed to have a thing about down-and-outs already. I just fanned the flames."

He took a sip of his whisky.

"I really thought he would go through with it. Still, can't be right all the time . . ." He looked at McCoy. "So, tell me. How did it feel when you knew your father was dead? Were you heartbroken? Did you cry your eyes out?"

McCoy nodded.

"Good. I hope you felt as bad as I did when Corporal Lindsay died. When you killed him. You did kill him, didn't you?"

McCoy was going to lie. Didn't. A flashback of making Lindsay drink all his morphine in one go. "Yes. He was going to die anyway. The cancer was terminal."

"Just like your dear old dad. Some might say we're even now, eh?"

"What about the others?"

Crawford shrugged. "Collateral damage. You'd be amazed how many male down-and-outs that look like your father there are in this city. We were close a couple of times—your dad's pals rather than him. And how is Hood anyway?"

"He's back at work."

"Really?" said Crawford, sounding surprised. "I thought he'd have done himself in by now. Must be coming soon. Me cutting him off, knowing about the murders and doing nothing, guilt about who he might really be. It's inevitable, I'd say."

"You did all this to get back at me? Joined the Salvation Army, everything?"

Crawford nodded. "Lindsay was the father I never had. He meant everything to me. He loved me. He deserved revenge—and now he's got it." He smiled. "And do you know what the best bit is? I'm going to walk away scot-free."

"No, you're not."

Crawford took another sip of his drink. "Really? What exactly are you going to charge me with, Detective Inspector McCoy? I haven't done a thing."

McCoy didn't say anything. He couldn't believe it, but Crawford was right. He had nothing.

"Thought not," said Crawford. "Or maybe you're thinking you can take me on, get some physical revenge? That it? In that case you're even stupider than I thought. You're getting on, half my weight, six inches shorter. I'm trained in hand-to-hand com-bat—I'd knock you through that wall before you even knew what happened."

McCoy didn't know what to say. Seemed like Crawford was holding all the cards.

"Must be a bit frustrating, I imagine. Sitting there. Impotent. Unable to protect the honour of your dear old dad. Must be making you feel like a failure. Like a waste of space. Like a fucking nobody." Crawford finished his whisky, put the glass down and stood up. "Now, if you'll excuse me, I have a train to catch." He leant down into McCoy's face. "By the way, just in case you thought this was it—the end of it, that we're even now—you're dead wrong. There's a reason I got Hood to do it all, a reason why I'm totally innocent."

"What do you mean?"

"Because this is only the beginning. You might not see me for a couple of months, a couple of years even, but I'll be watch-ing, and I'll be back to make your life as hellish as I possibly can. Keep looking over your shoulder, McCoy, because one day I'll be there."

He stood up. "And here's a little reminder."

He punched McCoy hard in the face.

McCoy banged back against the bedroom wall. Pain was incredible. He put his hand up to his face and it came away covered in blood. Felt like one of his teeth was loose, that his nose was broken. He opened his eyes, but Crawford was gone. All that was left was his glass sitting on the windowsill.

McCoy sat for an hour or so, staring at the wall, working his way through the rest of the whisky. Crawford was right: he did feel like a waste of space, a nothing. Hadn't been able to save his dad, hadn't seen what was really going on, hadn't been able to stop Crawford from going. All he could do was drink and feel sorry for himself. Just like his dad.

He stood up, wiped as much of the blood off his face as he could with the bed sheet, walked back through to the main hall. Rucksack and holdall gone. He left the building, walked down towards the Clyde where they had found Munroe. Could hear laughing from the bushes on the bank, see the light from a wee fire, three figures seated round it passing a bottle. He climbed over the fence and walked towards them.

A Week Later

S pringburn Cemetery stood in the north of the city. It was on a hill, could see most of Glasgow spread out below from there. The rain had started, seemed appropriate for some reason. Funerals never felt right on sunny days.

McCoy looked down the hill. Margo, Murray and Phyllis were standing by the cars, Wattie trying to put an umbrella up.

"You okay?" asked Cooper.

McCoy looked into the grave, rain battering off the polished wood of the coffin. "No," he said. "I'm not."

Cooper had found him, sitting outside the Squirrel with Frank and the boy. He hadn't been home since the night with Crawford. He'd been drinking in empty buildings, she-beens, sort of remembered a house in Carntyne, some old guy with bottles of port. Spent his time passing bottles, back of the St. Enoch Hotel, sitting round a fire on waste ground in Dalmarnock. Remembered coughing up thick black blood in the street. A fight with a guy that ended with McCoy hitting him with an empty wine bottle. Hadn't stopped drinking for three days and nights.

He'd been drinking from a bottle of tonic wine when he saw Jumbo and Cooper walking towards him. Was going to run but knew he wouldn't get away. Anyway, he was so pissed he could hardly stand. He handed the bottle to Frank.

"Keep it," he said. "Looks like I'm going home."

He'd spent the next couple of days at Cooper's. Sleeping mostly, refusing to see anyone. Today was the first day he had been out. Knew he should walk down the hill, say hello, say sorry, but he couldn't bring himself to. He felt too ashamed.

"So what now?" said Cooper.

McCoy shrugged. "I've got a psycho waiting to kill me, a partner who's started to realise I'm a bit of a dick and he can do the job without me, a girlfriend who's richer than God and a pal who, at this rate, will be running the entire Glasgow underworld in about five years. And me? I'm just a drunk." He stared down into the grave. "Like father, like son."

"Speaking of sons, I didn't tell Archie Andrews about Jamieson's son, you know," said Cooper. "But I told Jamieson that I knew. Told him he was working for me now and to get rid of Andrews, or I would let Andrews know what him and his son were up to and he could deal with it himself."

"Did it work?"

"Andrews went missing yesterday. He won't be coming back."

McCoy tried to light up, wasn't easy in the rain. Two gravediggers were standing nearby, leaning on their spades. Waiting.

"You need to pull yourself together, Harry," said Cooper. "There's people worried about you."

"Me? Why would they be worried about me? I'm fine and dandy. A cop with a career that's going nowhere, an ulcer I've probably fucked again, and like someone once said, a hole in the middle of me so big even all the drink I can get down me won't fill it up." He turned to Cooper, tried to smile. "What would you do if you were me?"

"I'd stop moaning for a start," said Cooper. "I'd get off my arse and make something of myself. Come and work with me."

McCoy looked at him. "You serious?"

"Things are changing. I'm expanding. Accountant says I need to go legit like Duncan Kent. I need someone to help me do it. Someone bright, not someone whose main qualification is being able to knife someone and get away with it."

McCoy finally managed to get his cigarette lit. Stood there smoking, listening to the traffic on the Cumbernauld road, watched a plane rise into the sky from the direction of the airport. Like Cooper, Glasgow was getting bigger, changing with the times. Maybe he needed to as well.

"C'mon," he said to Cooper and started walking down the hill. Put the collar of his coat up. Tried to avoid the puddles on the path to the cars. Started thinking.

ACKNOWLEDGEMENTS

Thanks to Francis Bickmore and all at Canongate and to Isobel Dixon and all at Blake Friedmann. For their help and knowledge thanks to Brian Murphy, Stephen Fox, Peter Simpson, Alison Rae and Sam Matthews. And thanks to the good people of Possil for putting up with my stupid questions.

Alan Parks's debut novel, *Bloody January*, propelled him onto the international literary crime fiction circuit and won him praise, prizes, and success with readers. In 2022 the third book in the Harry McCoy series, *Bobby March Will Live Forever*, won the MWA Edgar Award for Best Paperback Original. Parks was born in Scotland, earned an M.A. in Moral Philosophy from the University of Glasgow, and still lives and works in the city he so vividly depicts in his Harry McCoy thrillers.